The Comeback Kids

By H.J. Luke

First Edition

Copyright © 2012 by H. J. Luke

ISBN:0997350105
ISBN-13: 978-0-9973501-0-4

DEDICATION

To my friends and family, and always to my mother Nancy,
whose unwavering support to me made it all possible.

CONTENTS

ACKNOWLEDGMENTS

You could never thank people enough, those who have helped you along the way. There's always so many people to give thanks to for a project that took this long and this much work. Allow me to apologize first if I left some people out.

I would first like to thank my friend Arthur Chou, who has read re-write after re-write from me and have assumed the role of my quasi-editor during this time. Thank you for sticking with me and without you this book would probably just stay on my shelf forever.

I would like to thank Jack Chen and Michael Chen, two friends who have worked with me through this time and helped out a lot on getting this book out there.

I would like to thank many of my friends who have shown their support along the way, either truly moved by my words or were just humoring me so I would stop talking about this and get it done. My friends such as Mike Kang, Jen Jen, Amy and Emily, Ian, Jann, David Chen, Mandy, Natalie Pickles, Michelle, Azusa Nose, San Lee, Jason Roberts, Naohiro Machiya, Kevin Kuo, Subhodeep Banerjee and many, many more. I won't forget.

Most of all I would like to thank my parents, Nancy and Tony Chen, who have given me all the love parents could give a child, who have lived with the fact that their only son is the weirdest person they've ever met on this planet, and who have given me the example of their own love of what a family is truly about.

And to E., with all my love, the one person I knew I could count on in this whole world the whole time I was working on this book. Thank you for everything!

THE ALPHA TO MY BETA

This is a story about a family.

Just like any other social groups, we ABCs always end up hanging out with other people that are just like us. It's not like we made the choice consciously, like we wanted to be different. We just find ourselves always going to the same kind of places, liking the same kind of drinks, and being enthusiastic over the same kind of sport.

I am the case example ABC, almost boringly so: strict,

conservative upbringing from a Taiwanese family, grew up in the American School, got my grades and did my tests well, and then got accepted into an Ivy League School. As Marian would say, I have always been a good boy: one of those "lawyer, doctor, engineer, party animal" crowd that we as a group never seem to run out of.

My life is such a bore that if we tell it as a story it would be a poor one. And ironically storytelling is my profession for I am a writer. An ok one, one that is actually living off his writing somewhat comfortably. But boy is my life a living bore: good education, good family, good income, no struggles.

Nothing like my friend's, the one that I'm about to introduce you, the guy that's making me meet him now at 11PM at the W Hotel.

He's the Alpha to my Beta.

His name is Flynn. That's not actually his real name. His real Spanish name is far too long and difficult to pronounce for the average English-speaking person.

That's how we came to know each other. When I met Flynn we were still kids, when he was the biggest and also scariest person at school. Everybody knew him, and they all knew not to mess with him; everyone except me. Then on the off-chance when we met, I was able to pronounce his name fully and correctly, and on top of that re-told his family history based on knowledge on his last name that I have learnt from my readings on Spanish history, (His family is very old and famous, really) it so impressed him that I wasn't one of those "stupid Americans or American wannabes" at our school, which turned out to be why he was scary to everyone, he pretty much forced me to be his friend ever since.

And some friendship that is. We have been stuck together for more than twenty years now. He's the closest thing I have to a brother.

The W Hotel is one of Flynn's favorite place to go. Quite the hot new attraction here in Taipei, The W is known for its roof side pool, its high rise bar and the best cocktails that the French had to offer. It is located in Xinyi District, the New-

Rich Neighborhood of Taipei City. It is at the heart of it, being on the same building as the Taipei Hankyu Mall, within walking distance from the MRT, the Shinkong shopping compound, the 101 building, the financial district and the city hall.

The lobby bar, named The Woo Bar (They really like their W's I guess) was where we agreed to meet. The cocktails there are pretty much all Flynn ever drinks when he's not hitting the bottles (his choice for that is usually a bottle of Remy Martin XO). He only hits the bottles when he was really depressed. When that happens, you should be alarmed.

When I got there it was quite already packed that night, same as every night. I checked at the direction of the bar table first, since I knew that's where he would most likely be at. Then I saw him, standing there with an opened bottle of brandy on the table, and I knew it was trouble.

"Hey you've made it my Boy!" That's what he always called me. It's his way of showing his affection. Although tonight it seemed awfully appropriate as he was obviously already drunk when I got there.

"I see you already got the bottle of XO opened there." I said.

The thing about Flynn is that he's nothing that meets the eye. To most he's just the primitive, domineering and childish playboy type; someone who's reached his peak back in high school and went only downhill from there. Sure, he didn't finish uni, spends a lot of time doing non-important stuff like giving parties, playing basketball and working on his music. He comes from a well-to-do family, which might explain his lack of motivation for a career. The only time he seems motivated is when he meets someone he likes, usually a girl that got him crazy.

But if you think that's all you need to know about Flynn, then you're wrong.

"Something happened today." He said calmly.

"Something big? Or something terrible?" I asked.

"The bottom line of the shit is," he says that every time

when he doesn't want to go into details, "Amy and I, we're through."

"I thought her name was Angel?" I asked.

Angel is the name of Flynn's long-term girlfriend based in Beijing.

"Whatever, the point is we're done. It's over. El finito. Nothing is left for me to go back to that city no more. I am tired of those Beijing nights. I am tired of that fucking city." He said it as a declaration of sorts.

"Ok." I said while nodding.

"I'm not done!" He said, "I say let's go there, pack a couple of boxes, spend the nights partying so the town will know what they're missing when we're gone forever!"

"Sounds like a plan." I said, "We need a toast for this."

"Who said anything about a toast to you, bitch?" He jabbed with a smile. "This doesn't call for a toast!"

"We always toast before we go out to parties." I said, quoting one of the many traditions he forced us to follow, adding for point of emphasis, "It's your rule."

There was a pause. I suppose he thought about it for a minute, his rule and everything, and eventually decided to have the bartender bring another oval-shaped brandy glass to us, as he poured me a glassful himself from the bottle and put the glass in my hand. We've known each other for too long now that a lot of our communication did not require actual words. I had a sip, it was a good bottle. After all, this was a five-star hotel's lobby bar.

"So when are we supposed to be going on this trip to that dusty, foggy city of Beijing?" I asked.

"Tomorrow." He replied, "Well more like today if you wanna be a fucking smart ass."

"WHAT!?" I exclaimed, luckily the music and all the ambient noises blocked out my voice or I would have made quite the scene.

"Yeah it's in a couple of hours." He said, looking at his watch.

I took a second just to catch my breath. Even with Flynn

this seemed a bit drastic. So I had to ask him:

"Ok fine, I'll go if you just tell me this."

"Shoot man." He said using his catchphrase, to which I aptly replied my half of the dialogue,

"I'll shoot no man."

We both laughed at that same jab we'd been doing since we were in the first grade, before I launched into my long and convoluted question,

"Back when Beijing hosted the Olympics, I suggest that you can just rent that place out, you said no. And then half of our friends moved out of Beijing when the whole smog thing came to public, and you said no real pollution could stop you from all your cocktails and Zhajiangmian. So I guess what I'm asking now is this: what makes the situation this time so special that you have to move out of Beijing now?"

There was flash of those killer eyes from Flynn as he listened to me, but once I finished, he quickly shrugged those eyes away, replied me casually but with authority,

"Nothing. Not a goddamn thing."

I stared back into his eyes, trying to see if there was something else behind the bravado, life's-a-party act he was putting onto me now. I was the kind of guy who didn't like to go into something without the full disclosure, as I resent getting caught with my pants down. It's the Ivy League in me, one that had to know what the question was for before giving my answer.

He was looking at me too, with those same serious eyes he's been trying to hide since the beginning of this conversation. The silence was quickly broken:

"To not a goddamn thing." I then finished the glassful of brandy in one drop into my mouth.

"Alright!" Flynn smiled at me for being onboard to his plan, and quickly chucked his brandy as an honor to my toast. This was not gonna be the last drink we have tonight.

TO BEIJING

I am the perfect liar. Maybe because I am an ABC, I am just naturally a little two-faced. I am used to behaving one way to my strict Asian parents, and then another when I am out with my non-Asian friends. It's really just as simple as flipping a switch, like use the chopsticks at home, and the fork when you're out. Once you get used to it, you get the hang of it quite easily.

So when my Spanish friend wanted me to accompany him on a trip to the Capital of China for his personal memento, but was too proud to ask me, I flipped the switch and lied to his face, toasting to his "nothing at all" speech. Lying and brandy, that got us through the night.

But come to think of it, did I agree to go to Beijing with Flynn when I was basically, drunk?

All I knew from this morning was that I was put in a car, drove to the airport and thrown onto the morning flight to Beijing. I mean it could be either that or Gitmo, I was not hundred percent sure. Thanks Homeland! Thanks for making us the average Americans still imagine things the good way.

By the time I began to sober up once I had my first class

breakfast. The actual flight was only about three hours from Taipei to Beijing, and as you have seen, barely the time to get through one hangover.

And then we landed, got picked up by Flynn's driver at the airport, and were on our way to his Beijing apartment, which sat right next to the Beijing Shinkong Mall. Yes, one of the same from the Taiwanese Mall that was next to the W Hotel we drank at last night.

Talk about deja vu, living in Asia could really screw with your senses.

After about 40 minutes driving on the crowded freeway (world famous now, I should say, with Chinese car manufacturing surpassing Europe as recent as 2013), we arrived at Flynn's apartment inside this steel post-modernist constructed complex known as Huamao Apartments.

Like many other complexes such as it that typifies modern Beijing, Huamao is almost a city of its own, with its own shopping mall (the Shinkong Mall), gym (Used to be operated by a Taiwanese company, now taken over by a local company possibly with Singapore money), office buildings and corporate headquarters (Deutsche Bank's being one) towering over others that looked into the Dawan Bridge that connects your car onto the Beijing Ring Highway. Traffic wise it's very convenient, with a subway station nearby (Dawan Bridge Station) in the same area, which isn't this closely available to many high class apartments in the city as this one.

This neighborhood housed the media companies, as it is but half an hour away by foot to the CCTV building, the government owned, rectangular building that is home to the Chinese national media corporation. Its surrounding office buildings housed mostly media companies in satellite relations to the CCTV, a snapshot of the workings of the Great Chinese Economy.

Flynn has chosen his particular apartment unit wisely. On the first floor of his building is Flynn's favorite breakfast place, "Le Croissant", where they serve a full 200RMB Continental Breakfast (cafe au lait excluded) every day. And as Flynn had explained many times before, "Nothing is more important than breakfast". Of course as a side note, he had also said the same thing about dinner, nightcaps and clubbing.

Inside his apartment are the double-reinforced windows it has throughout its entire East wall, from where you could see a fair part of the city and even glimpse of Chaoyang Park, the Central Park of this part of Beijing.

This part of the city is not the "traditional part" of Beijing, of course, as almost ninety percent of what is Beijing City now was never part of the Old Imperial Capital. Like any modern city, Beijing grew in size by consuming all the nearby towns, as New York and London had with their six boroughs and their Greater Authority. What is different with the Beijing's experience, is what have taken New York and London centuries took Beijing only about a decade- from the 90's to the early 2000's.

The city changes so quickly, with every change so drastic, it drives us to come back here year after year to see what is new. Perhaps that's the charm of the Beijing life, every visit you see a different Beijing. Well that's what it is for me, for Flynn it was something else. And now he was here to get rid of that something else.

Ever since we arrived, Flynn simply sat there in the living room, silently without saying a word. His eyes fixed towards the world outside of those large, lofty windows of his.

Since he didn't seem like he was in any rush to get anywhere, I decided to give him sometime while I went into my room and see how much stuff that was needed to be packed on my side.

It was a good thing that we had this little break, however short it might be. Even a whisper now could throw me into nauseating pain, as already on our way over I suffered the great Chinese brand of traffic that was filled with sudden stops and screaming horns. I have learnt my limits.

In spite of spending our post-high school years between New York (where I was) and L.A. (where unfortunately my brother chose to be his US destination), Beijing was our party town. All of our best party memories were here. A lot of great moments of our lives happening here. And now we were moving out, forever as Flynn had unilaterally declared.

No matter, I'll just do my part for my brother now.

I was listing my belonging inside this apartment when I heard that familiar fast-paced footsteps coming in from the hallway. Before I could turn myself around Flynn's words, which were always so forceful were already blowing into my ears like bullets,

"What you doing man?"

"Not much. Trying to see how much stuff we actually need to take with us on this flight back." I replied.

Those killer eyes that never seemed to disappear on him since last night were looking away from me as he spoke, looking through the windows behind me,

"This is it, isn't it? The end of an era?" Now he was calm, suddenly.

"Yeah. No more parties in Beijing." I replied.

"Fuck you." He suddenly cracked a smile as if energized by some challenge. "we are going to party like there's no tomorrow! That's why we're here! A Big Fuck You Tour to Beijing! Tonight, we will show them how it's done! And they will regret when we are not around anymore."

He then quickly went out to the hallway laughing the whole way. I was alone in my room again. But before I followed him out on our last party in Beijing, I looked out of my window, wondered what could have gotten him to say that "end of an era" comment.

And then I saw it, a Malabar Chestnut Tree in a bonsai, or I should say what used to be a bonsai, known as "money trees" in Chinese culture, which sat at the deep corner of my balcony, right outside of my window. It was all dried and shrilled in black as the whole plant, including its bansai seat, was covered with the natural dust of the Beijing sky.

And Suddenly I had this rush to say, mutter really, only to myself,

"Yeah, the end of an era."

That night we went out as planned.

Trying to keep up with Flynn on a night out was like trying to win a race against time. Like all the great clubbing stars before him, Flynn's club scene was simple: all out or nothing.

And this night proved that it was no different.

We went through the giant, mega sized city like the northern wind, where we started things off with an early supper in this small restaurant (by Beijing standard) on the second ring road that was complete with Flynn's favorite Beijing flavors: spicy cucumber, Zhajiangmian, and layers after layers of thinly-sliced Beijing Roast Beef.

We were like bandits on the run, quickly finishing our food, paid and ran out as if the cops were gonna come knocking any time soon, asking the clerks have they seen two fugitives, one Asian, the other a tall Spaniard with blonde hair wondering around here. We did make one suspicious duo in an East Asian City, certainly a conspicuous pair with one being foreign and the other... kind of foreign.

We got into the car and headed to Sunlitun, on the whole way Flynn's driver ran through the city as if we were in some race car instead of just a normal, silver Audi Q7. Flynn constantly yelled the whole trip "Step on it! Step on it!" which added to the fugitive mood.

Sunlitun started as the first and only bar street of Beijing City that came about due to its proximity to all foreign embassies. As any good Chinese person would tell you, the reason why these bars are here is because them foreign people (or white people. Depending on the speaker's mood, he could also call them "Big Noses" as white people are colloquially known here in Beijing) need to get a drink every once in awhile. Good Chinese people? We never drink.

How they say that with a straight face while they serve me a glassful of baijiu is beyond me. I guess that's their style of humor, it's the Chinese way.

The first time I was in Beijing, Sunlitun was literally just a street with only five or maybe six bar/restaurants standing there. They used to only get crowded when one of those live-band that all seemed to learnt their works from Bruce Springsteen with a Tibetan or Mongolian vocal was on that night. Then just like everything else in this city, in but a couple of years what used to be a dusty street, full of bars with dimly-lit neon signs that barely seemed opened when you come at night, has now turned into an area packed with fancy restaurants, drink joints, boutique hotels and a whole American style luxury shopping village.

That started when the Nelly was first opened. This white, small shopping building (by Chinese standard) that was built in the Spanish style with a beautiful patio in them middle of its first floor. It quickly became the new place for the now traditional nightly-concerts that was Sunlitun.

Then they built the giant, luxurious, American-sized shopping complex known as the Sunlitun Village. Finished around the time of the Beijing Olympics, the place was packed with the latest fashion brands, restaurants and lounge bars from around the world and of course, an Apple store.

Since then the Sunlitun Street was always swimming with cars, day or night, trying to crawl through it for a parking space, or somehow get lucky enough to find one on the street and would probably never move until the next day.

There were just so many things to do at this place, so we did all of them.

We went from Chardonnay at the Modo, to Cocktails at the

Blue Frog. With the grey Beijing night illuminated by the endless street lamps and neon lights under our eyes that seemed to be cheering us on to next place like we were baseball players playing a game under the blinding night lights of the Yankee stadium, we hopped from joint to joint as we had Rioja wine and imported cheese, soft crab sushi rolls with sake, before settling for a longer stop at The Cantina on the first floor of the Nelly, where the concert was about to start.

By this hour I was already pretty exhausted and full, but my friend Flynn only seemed to grow more energetic as the night went. The live-band performance quickly shaken away whatever focus I had left, with what I could only describe as a mariachi rock and roll band, playing the Latino variation of Gloria Gaynor's "I Will Survive".

A crowd began to form at the center of the patio, and before you knew it, the seven storeys building was packed with people out having a good time. That's what's curious about Beijing and the people here, in spite of its harsh climate, always skin-crackling dry throughout the year, with a devastating, snowless winter at about -15 degree C, and the problems with the smog, people love anything outdoors here.

It could get so cold, and yet the people here were so warm with their passion it was hard not to get affected by theirs. Perhaps that's why all of our best parties happened here, I thought to myself as Flynn and I were sitting there anxiously, waiting for something to happen. I saw that he seemed to quietly observe the people around us, dancing and clapping, like he was looking for that specific partner to dance with.

"Come on!' Suddenly Flynn shouted to me over the music, "Let's go upstairs!"

I guess he did not find what he wanted, as I quickly got up and followed him before his quick feet leave me behind as he vanished into the night.

As we went upstairs, I took a snapshot of the night with my phone, knowing this might be a night to remember. We went past the crowd and into this bar on the third floor for their delicious cocktails which, as it was the case with most bars in most cities, were christened with names that mingled local place names with sexual undertone.

Though some weren't so subtle, such as "Beijing Bang", which was what Flynn chose for us to drink tonight. I guess he thought it was a funny name, as the bartender who had studied bartending in Japan and was learning Spanish now conversed with Flynn and got him laughing so hard with this suggestion. Perhaps because of that, we drank two straight and was gonna get a third one when we went back to our usual shots and martini.

For some reason the last song of the night turn out to be Nelly Furtado's rendition of "Maneater". And when that was done, Flynn and I finished the last drop of our cocktails as we went out with the now subsiding crowd, towards our next destination.

"Let's go!" Flynn yelled to the driver as we got in his car, and his driver raced us through the street again before it get congested one last time tonight.

Now we were heading towards the club district, the area around the Worker's Stadium, the oldest large stadium inside Beijing City, where Angel Club, BabyFace and all the other alluring named clubs would have the latest techno music show ready, with the best DJs in town for the people who were coming for the last show before sunlight.

Under the laser lights, banners with sponsors like Heineken or Carlsberg filling the walls, it was times like this when I felt as if I had never left this town. Under the beams and the bombastic music, the club scene was just so repetitive everywhere you went. If you never leave the clubs, no city in this world would be different from the next.

Is that where the Expat/ABC reputation for clubbing craze come from? We stay in the club scene, hope to find some continuity in our lives where location and culture constantly change, as these nights out became our only stability. All I knew was I was out of it, as I should be.

I have not been in the club scenes for a while. Don't get me wrong, as my brother Flynn could attest, I had my clubbing days, but all that seem so far in the past now. I went through the motion tonight, fighting the urge to faint or vomit, the mixed taste of soy sauce and red wine constantly regurgitating in my mouth as I did my best to keep my brother company.

I can't even remember how many girls Flynn and I danced with that night. There are always so many girls at the clubs, and they are always so friendly, especially when you are foreign. It must be that same charm sailors and cowboys have to offer in our history: something different, something exotic, something with an expiration date. And if anything was expiring at this point, it would be me.

The funny thing about getting drunk is that, contrary to logic, your brain always seems to become more focused after it is drunk, and reaches its highest point of lucidity just before you're out of it. Though usually, that focus would come with the wrong topic. Taking tonight as an example, I was all of the sudden really curious about Flynn's driver. The question is quite straightforward; just how does he manage to keep up with Flynn's crazy schedule all the time?

Flynn's driver is third-generation Beijinger, a rarity since the real "Old-Beijinger" as they are know, don't work for what they consider wage jobs, such as waiting tables and delivering packages or chauffeuring. Even if the money is good, the job is beneath them. It is the proud tradition of being men only under the foot of the godly emperor.

The man is referred to by Flynn, erroneously but with affection, as Fernando; a name which Flynn made up from the man's last name, Fei. Fei was a very quiet man. In fact he never spoke as far as I could remember. And that was not simple considering how convoluted Flynn's direction could get ("You know the place, right? Go there!")

I was really curious tonight just how he could keep up with us. Picking us up in the morning at the airport. Then came back to pick us up on this crazy night of traditional Beijing dinner, wine and cocktail over sushi and music at Sunlitun, then now all the way to Worker's Stadium for more clubbing, and presumably to stay there 'til the morning, when he would drive us home. How did he do it?

Now that I thought about it though, he must takes naps or something. But when?

And that was when I passed out.

The next thing I remember after that was waking up this morning in my room, walked around the apartment with a hangover and found Flynn missing.

As I was now with a second killer hangover in consecutive nights, I really needed my smokes. So I went out onto the balcony, sat myself down next to that dusty dead tree, still sitting there by the corner, ignoring all the dust around me and under my pants, and lit up a cigarette.

He'll be back, I thought, a man's gotta eat.

As I sat there and hit myself with the first smoke, as it gently left my body through my lips, suddenly my mind cleared, and just like last night before I passed out, a series of image came to life and I was reminded of a night in this apartment years ago.

We were having dinner, Flynn and I, some Chinese take outs, probably Zhajiangmian, Beijing Roast Beef and spicy cucumber, those kind of things that Flynn always ate when it was just the two of us; when Flynn's driver carried in the Malabar Chestnut Tree bonsai for the first time. The tree's stem was thick and strong, and the leaves upon it were plenty and bushy and almost covered the entire plant.

Flynn's driver was going to put it in the living room, but I guess Flynn did his changing-his-mind-at-the-last-second thing and had it moved to the balcony in my room, "It will get more suns there." He said.

"Where you'd get the money tree?" I asked him.

"What money tree?" He was confused.

"That bonsai. It's Malabar Chestnut Tree, or in my culture known as the Money Tree." I explained, "Where'd you get it?"

"Angel gave it to me." He said with a subtle smile, very rare to see that very expressive face of his, "She said it was an anniversary gift for me and my family."

"She did? Do I hear wedding bells?" Knowing my brother I teased him right the way.

"Go fuck yourself." He said, yet still with a smile and now a laugh. "What does that little peanut Ivy League brain of yours knows about wedding bells? You piece of shit!"

"That's quite the choice of words from the soon-to-be Mr. … Hey has Angel learnt how to pronounce your full family name yet?"

"Fuck you man!" That came with a punch to my right arm, and just to be clear, with many more to come for that night.

By the time I finished my cigarette, there was still no sight of Flynn. So I left the apartment and went out for a walk, down to the garden in the courtyard on the first floor of Flynn's apartment complex.

Flynn's apartment complex had one of the best gardens of all the luxury apartments in this country.

Built as a sunken Japanese Garden, walled by flowers and a long pool of a flowing water structure, its zen concept was so strong it calmed you down almost as soon as you entered it, as you suddenly become one with the garden.

Just the kind of thing you need within reach near where you live in this city that never seemed to get tired of itself.

I sure was no stranger to this city; and neither was Flynn, and a lot of that had to do with the girl that got us here this time in the first place.

When you know that part of you is not coming back anymore, the part of you that you must say goodbye to now, it's hard to say goodbye to that. Like going through an amputation.

So I understand why Flynn was so much more unpredictable on this trip than he usually was. Everyone's kind of weird when they go through these things, dealing with the death of a part of yourself:

Flynn first met Angel five years ago: it was during those years of his failed California adventure. From the first day they met it was a match made in heaven. It was like Angel was sent by God to perfectly compliment Flynn: she was diplomatic, thoughtful and reserved, polar opposite to the domineering, vocal Spaniard that Flynn was.

But it really was no surprise coming from where I stood and watching them go through it: after all, coming from an old Beijing Family, there were a lot of values important to Angel shared by the equally powerful and oppressive background of Flynn's Catholic, Spanish upper-class family. Values such as duty, faith, and family first.

It was love at first sight for the two of them. The relationship was perfect from the start: Angel was Flynn's first girlfriend that he actually couldn't wait to introduce to his father. She soon became a regular guest to their family dinner, something that Flynn was not even a regular at times. She was the one girl that Flynn was willing to try this whole long-distance thing.

Flynn never believed in long distance relationship, but for her, Flynn was scrambling flights across the Pacific, between Beijing and L.A. He worked hard balancing his life, between his girlfriend, his studies, his music career (both of which he really only tried hard during this period) and his family. He was burning his candle on both ends, to use a very Chinglish analogy. And most importantly, he was actually happy doing it.

("Burning the candle on both ends" is a Chinese saying that meant pretty much the same as "spreading yourself thin"; this just goes to show you the kind of weird references we ABCs use on a daily basis that make no sense to anyone other than other ABCs)

This was when Flynn was at his happiest that I can remember. As he began to go to Beijing more and more often, with each stay longer than the ones before. He would never admit to this, but in part what failed his California run in the end had a lot to do with those long absence he was spending in Beijing. Although to be fair, it all nearly worked out at the end.

But that's just how relationships are sometimes. The closer you get to getting it working, the more clearly it becomes that it is never meant to work out. Even the ones started with the most perfect "A long, long time ago" is no guarantee to have a "happily ever after".

That was when the fighting began. A lot of the detail was not known until later, both Angel and Flynn were from conservative families that believed in keeping all the ugliness inside. Not to mention Flynn's pride was enough of a wall to keep all this out. But the fact that we could now find bits and pieces about what really happened proves how explosive the situation was at the time.

It all surfaced once Flynn began to stay in Beijing longer and longer, as Flynn's dream of becoming a musician was something that Angel was never willing to fully support, Angel's close tie to her family made it difficult for them to live anywhere but Beijing. Her kindness soon turned into indecisiveness, and there was never a better fuel to Flynn's anger than that of indecisiveness. The once perfect match made in heaven was starting to find its way to earth.

I'm a firm believer that there are only so many fights a person could take in life. And by the end of that drawn out fight that probably took out half of what was meant for Flynn's lifetime, he was back in Taiwan. That was the last time when Flynn ever spoke about a long term goal, or a long term relationship, for that matter.

He still talks about music over drinks sometimes, but it just isn't the same. He just doesn't have that fire anymore, that rapture of excitement, those killer eyes constantly brimming with anticipation. My guess was that the experience had created an undying bond between his failed relationship, and his failed career choice, and the failure that took away five years of his life.

That's when we all started to move back too; those of us who got tired of the Western lifestyle. Yet when we came back and found Flynn here with us, for some reason there was no awkwardness. We all just went back to like how it was in the old times, with Flynn returned to his beachside mansion he grew up in Tamsui, Taiwan, and threw parties there on a set of traditions he created that we were supposed to follow.

Nobody seemed to remember but only a short time ago, he was someone who exhaustively worked through time zones and jet lags against the sheer size of the world, chasing his dream of becoming a big-time music star in Hollywood, with a loving wife and family in China to go back to on holidays. It was as if we all have gotten used him being here, being a fixture of Taipei City and Asia.

When I say we, I mean those of us OTHER than me. Not only did I have a front row seat to most of what I just told you, I knew my brother like I knew myself. I knew what that silence about his past meant to him, as well as his bravado, his never-ending acts of childish antics and his traditions, I knew it all too well.

It's hard to say goodbye to such a big chunk of yourself, especially when you had to do it all alone. And that's perhaps why I was willing to come with him to Beijing on this trip, for I knew where all this came from. It is like dealing with your own death, where a part of yourself must now follow your memories and forever be locked in the past,

"The end of an era".

When I went back to the apartment, to pick up my wallet and go out for a bite, I heard the snoring all the way from the apartment door when I went in. I guess we had just missed each other, Flynn and I, as we had before during our college years. When in that only time we were apart, I was smooth-sailing up, and he was struggling to stay afloat and ultimately, failed; before we both returned here, leaving both of those lives behind, and picked up on our old times in a place closest to us as home.

That's what it is like for people like Flynn and I, people who are born with two or more backgrounds, our lives are spread across the globe like fragments, with change being the only constant. Saying goodbye is a constant. Always moving out of places is a constant. Becoming strangers to places familiar is a constant.

We appreciate the beauty of this sort of life of course, we all do eventually. But like everything else in life, it is hard to say goodbye when it's to something that is a part of yourself, especially when most of the time, you do that alone.

In that sense, at least Flynn and I have each other. And that's when it hit me, perhaps it was time that I start to keep track of these events -I am a writer after all- before another five years flash us by and it takes another heartbreaking event to remind us all just how long we've been here. How long we have come back and been around here and to each other, before we had to say goodbye to another big chunk of ourselves and our years.

That's a good idea, I thought. Hence I started this blog. To keep track of the ever changing lives we have as a group of people. Yes, there's more of us than just my brother and I. This time, hopefully, nothing would be forgotten.

OLD BEIJINGER

In Beijing, a cab driver could tell you the proud history of his city as long as he was an "Old Beijinger". There is a sense of pride to the city which would takes over the people as they live and breathe there.

Only they could make fun of their never ending rush hours, corruption at all power levels, the twisted mindset of their new rich and the children of their party members, but make no mistake; if you speak ill of the great people of Beijing or the city herself to any of them, get ready to get kicked off the cab and left stranded in whatever hutong (Beijing word for "small alley") you were in.

In some ways Flynn is just like an old Beijinger, loud, proud, hands on. He loves it here more than he loves Taipei, or possibly more than his home country. I know he loves it here more than LA, he has to if he has any sense.

"Let's go to the maison."

Flynn said to me as he violently woke me out of bed the next day. I almost forgot how bossy he was before this trip, but I held my peace, in anticipation of perhaps the most luxurious brunch the city of Beijing had to offer.

It was a drive of about 20 minutes from Flynn's place to the QianMen 23, the location of Maison Boulud, or just "the Maison" as Flynn would call it.

"QianMen" simply meant "Front Gate" in mandarin, as we were but a step away from one of the nine gates of the old city walls of Beijing. The very gates that used to keep the barbaric hordes of foreigners out (that would be us I suppose now, with glee) stood there now, as a relic of that glorious past of China as the "Middle Kingdom" of the world.

The QianMen 23, itself located next to the QianMen structure, was was a large garden built in Qing architecture style and home to eight of Beijing's best restaurants, each offering the finest exotic cuisine of the corner of the world it came from.

This was where the old American Embassy at Beijing was located at before. And one of these idyllic "western mansions" here, as these Gatsby Mansions, popular in the early 1900s were known here in China, housed Maison Boulud and its fine Parisian dining.

I had a lot of great memories inside the QianMen 23. Most of them centered around the fall. Beijing had its best weather in the fall, the only time when its harsh climate becomes less harsh and more liveable. It was a time of warm breeze, caressing sun with just the right amount of moisture, just like the inside of a botanical garden. Spending the fall inside these walls, it felt just like I was back in New York.

The Maison was packed today, as it usually was around this time. Hungry expats from across Beijing, perhaps all over China, would always gathered in here for its full Parisian Brunch, featuring all the Great Epoch grandeur it could possibly offered. The cost might be as steep at about 3,000RMB per person, but no one would ever give up the opportunity to be pampered with pastry, freshly-made jam and with the latest of Chef Boulud's personal recipe shipped directly from Paris in town.

There was always this overwhelming sense of charming nostalgia about the late Nineteenth Century in this restaurant, which could easily pull in the usual history buffs that Beijing always managed to attract from around the world. It may not be easy to score a table, but that never seemed to be an issue with Flynn. With most of these joints that we frequented with him, regardless of whichever city they might be in, be it Los Angeles, Barcelona, Hong Kong or here in Beijing, there always seems to be this standing reservation exclusive for him.

All we ever saw was him walking in there, giving the maitre d' a little wave and voila, there was the table by the French Window that was just sitting there waiting for our arrival. For years we have tried and failed to figure it out. It was just one of those things you accept because it was Flynn.

Once we sat down, Flynn literally went on a croissant killing spree. He had them filled that basket twice along with the butter, and that was while he was finishing their five course brunch menu, with just about the same ferocity.

As I was still working on my omelette, he finally stopped his all-out killing spree and took the time to say,

"I still think your brunch beats this crap."

"It's not even on the same level." I said, I meant to disagree with him subtly so not to spoil the morning, which he caught quickly,

"You mean yours is five star and this isn't?" He said with a smirk.

"Actually I believe these days five star is the new three star, and the seven star is the new five star." I replied, catching onto his good mood. "Remember the Tower of Babel? And now they have one in Dubai. And that's seven star."

"Those stuff from the Bible gotta catch up with the fucking world." He said while eating yet another croissant, "The world is moving on without them."

I could tell he was slightly impetuous, as his feet have not stopped fidgeting about. He also needed to make an effort to concentrate just to stare at me.

"I'm not backing down from my point, but this is good." He said, as he slob yet another huge chunk of butter on another piece of croissant he had just freshly ripped open,

"Don't forget that we are doing brunch once we go back."

"I won't, not with you reminding me." I replied.

"Ok, so remind me to remind you alright?" He said.

"Fine, sure." I just wanted him to stop choking on those croissants.

"It's almost summer so we have to start planning our Party of the Year too." He said.

"Yes."

"You guys gotta get top of these things so that it's not down to me doing everything this year again."

That alarmed me and took my attention. Flynn had always complained about us not paying attention, but he never put the idea of "us" (excluding him) doing something without him. He was always the center of attention at every one of these events, in spite of how he might suggest he was throwing them at other's honor.

After the brunch, we went to the QianMen market. It was but ten minutes' walk away from the Maison, the old marketplace that has been in Beijing since the time the Forbidden City was built.

We walked around the market street a little bit, drinking Starbucks coffee in coffeehouses built inside three hundred years old structures and eating glazed-hawthorns walking on stone steps that were probably older than that. And all this time what he said about "us" getting on top of things so he won't have to never escaped me.

The fact that he was having these thoughts meant that I had do something a little more drastic. I knew then it was time to call in for some help.

"Just cancel everything and fly over." I said over the phone as I sat on my balcony, away from Flynn, who went into his room for a nap after we got back.

"Now why should I do that?" The slightly feminine guy's voice over the phone as always, was fishing for favors with that question.

"Because Dorian, this is Flynn we're talking about. Think about the amount of favors he's done you over the years. And then think about how close I am to his ears, and how many of those 'favors' he's done for you in the past that I have knowledge of that he has none, and how I can remind him of those at any time." I dealt him my loaded reply.

"You know, for a guy that's given up on politics, you're a really good blackmailer." That's a yes.

"Glad we understand each other."

Then, as Flynn returned from yet another disappearance of his the next day, I, sitting in the living room eating some noodle, informed him passingly that we should go out to have some fun.

"What do you have in mind?" He asked slightly dismissively.

"I heard Dorian is in town." I said.

"What's that bitch ass doing in..." I knew he was about to say "my town", but stopped short of the "my", and instead he finished it with the rather weak "...here?"

"I dunno. You ask him. I bet he has tickets to some fashion show in town."

Now here's the trick dealing with Flynn or any such people really. Anytime you have an idea for what the two of you could do together, make sure it comes out as his idea. That way there is always less friction for something that you both would enjoy anyhow.

As I expected, he stopped arguing and picked up his phone almost right the way and called Dorian up. I didn't hear most of it as he was in his room but from the chuckles and laughs here and there I knew it went well. And a few minutes later he came out of the room and declared,

"Suit up, my boy, we are going to a party."

Works like a charm.

The place we were going to was in Solana, which was an outdoor mall built like a riverside resort inside the Chaoyang Park. The restaurant's name was Rive Gauche, which came from the famous South Bank of the Seine in Paris. It was a haute couture French restaurant that performed live jazz at night by their tables overlooking the riverwalk that surrounded the entire Solana Mall.

His directness and lack of shame often made people underestimate how tightly a control he had on himself; when it wasn't just the two of us, no matter how depressed Flynn was before, he would always quickly snap out of the whole thing and assume the role of Flynn, the flamboyant, unpredictable, domineering Spaniard.

While he always felt obliged to play this role, I always felt it was borderline childish in his almost obsessive compulsive need in keeping up with this appearance. His life would be so much easier if he just let these things go.

But that's just how he was. He liked that role, to put up a fighting face, so the people around may be affected by his energy and drive and do things beyond their imagination. It's an important role to his life, if you could stomach such a chauvinistic idea to be true on an alcoholic, womanizing Spaniard.

We were immediately brought to our table without a question once we entered the restaurant- it seemed everyone in this town knew who Flynn was and where his table would be. The table we were brought to was at the corner next to the patio. Behind it, the large windows through which we could see the riverwalk and a sizeable amount of the seemingly endless Chaoyang Park, which seemed like a jungle at these hours of the night.

Already sitting at the table was a group of one guy and four girls. The guy was in a white suit, wearing a pair of suede loafers. He had a neatly cut hair with a cleanly shaven face. That was Dorian. And the girls? They were clearly models, you could tell just from the tan of their skin and their high cheekbones.

"Ladies, let me introduce you to Flynn, he's the guy I told you about. And this is our friend A-Zed." Dorian quickly introduced when he saw us by the table next to him.

Now just who is Dorian?

If there's a word that could summarize Dorian's world and the lifestyle he led, it had to be the word "glamour". He certainly deserved it being the most sought after contract photographer for all the fashion magazines and big local name brands.

But, if you ask me what's the one physical feature which stood out about Dorian when you see him, I would say none of it. When you look at him from a purely physical point, there was little on his body that made him stood out from other Taiwanese guys. Even his voice, which was somewhat medium in volume and tone, was quite unmemorable when he spoke to you on the phone.

I guess that's what made him special though, the fact that he really wasn't. And he did have a good fashion sense, white in the Spring? Good choice.

"So this is THE Flynn you told us about." One of the girl said, quite blatantly suggestive.

It worked, because she got Flynn to talk to her first.

As usual, when you are introduced together with Flynn, only Flynn would receive the greetings. It's hard to notice the slender-built, slightly out-of-shape Asian guy, when the tall strapping blonde Spaniard taking up most of the view anyhow.

Whenever Flynn chatted with new people he had just met for the first time, he always sticks to one specific person there and pretty much chat only with her. With the others he would show interest, but he would make sure it was the one he wanted to talk to the most that had his eyes. He had quite the specific type, tall, of course; slightly muscular to show a level of interest in sports; high cheekbones, and a pair of great looking legs.

His move in this department is a perfect match with Dorian's, who liked to multitask and split his many interest around the table. Dorian is a bit of a flirt, and he usually hides that quite well by controlling the tone of his voice. He always speaks in such a manner as if he has the same amount of interest at what you are talking about with that of the person next to you: he never shows if the "How nice!" he commented on your portfolio was any different from the "How nice!" he just gave to the girl sitting across from you about her shoes.

And perhaps that's why they always hang out together. That must be what got us to form our hunting party. So what are my moves you say? Well you're gonna find out soon enough.

It was perhaps three bottles of wine and many, many glasses of martini and brandy later, when one of the girls suggested we all go to this house party that some Ukrainian guy, whose brother was a DJ that worked at one of the clubs Flynn and I been to, would be playing there.

Flynn embraced the idea with opened arms, with one of his hand on the thigh of the girl he's been talking to the whole night. So a bunch of us, all a bit tipsy from the drinking and the laughing, were relocating to the next place under his leadership, for more drinking and laughing.

But that's how funny Life is sometimes. Who knew that at a random house party that I didn't even feel like going would be the place where I met the girl with whom I just fell madly in love with? Who knew in a city of 30 Million people that I barely visit, I would have met someone like that?

Since I was already madly in love with this girl, let's call her Maddy.

When we walked into the place and I first saw her, she wore a white shirt and a light blue-colored cardigan, a pair of blue jeans and a pair of brown leather boots, standing tall above the crowd. And while I was cooking up a ploy, trying to strike a conversation, as luck would have it, one of the people in Maddy's group, this guy who was almost just as tall as her, who had a skinny chin, and wearing a suit and tie was waving at me just as I laid eyes on her.

Or I should say, so I thought he was waving at me, because then I got the slap in the back from Flynn from behind, as he suddenly yelled as completely unnecessary as it was always, "Hey what do you know!? I know those guys!" Before he went over to talk to Maddy's friends.

This was followed by Dorian's quiet commentary to me, saying: "What are the chances that we would go to a random guy's house party and Flynn would know someone here?"

"Pretty damn high, apparently." I replied casually. As we followed our leader Flynn to mingle with Maddy's group.

"Guido! How funny that we meet you here!" Flynn

exclaimed to the tall guy as we caught them. "Are these your friends?"

"I'm here with my colleagues." The guy named Guido replied. "This is Maddy, and..." It turns out, including Maddy, they were all German expats working at the Beijing office of a German company that specialized in international expos in Frankfurt.

I love it when the Germans use the word "colleague". Their "g" in there is always so hard and pronounced it is a trademark tell of their nationality. A little trick I picked up over the years travelling and listening to the speech of different people around this world.

"Excellent, let me introduce you some people." Flynn said to Guido as he began to move his eyes and his big left hand towards me.

Whenever Flynn gives you an introduction it's always the best one. It was his way of showing friendship in his attention to the details of your life. These introductions are always formal, concise and up to the point. He never made you feel as if you were being set up as a joke or simply being euphemistic about it. Never the kind of guy who would say "I don't know what you do actually. Why don't you introduce yourself?"

"This here is A-Zed," He said to them, "the best writer this side of the Pacific. He's a political analyst who used to work on campaign strategies and served on a number of think tanks. He has since turned himself into a novelist, and an absolute magician with the words."

Maddy was already smiling at me, while she stood behind Guido listening to Flynn's more than flattering introduction of me.

After that night, the Germans blended with us so well that we'd been hanging out all the time since. friendships are relatively quick to strike in these groups, as soon as we prove we're both strangers to the city we are in, suddenly we could skip a couple of steps in becoming friendly with each other.

But almost every time in these nights we hung out, while Flynn took his new girl out into the garden, or when Dorian showed others how to take a certain shot from a certain angle at a showroom, Maddy and I would be left alone. And instead of talking about jobs tediously, we talked just about everything else.

Maddy is what Marian would call a smart girl, the kind of girl that she thinks is perfect for the good boy like me. She's quite bookish, that part is obvious from the start. She's quite the linguist, having already learnt five languages and is moving onto a sixth one, including that devil of a language known as mandarin that really to anyone in the know, is way too complicated to be considered as "one language". she is fluent at it, having heard her sang myself just this other day when we went to karaoke, something I would never do if I wasn't humoring a 6 feet tall, blonde German who seemed to have a crush on me as I had on her.

Then there was the travel.

It was inevitable, between an American and a German in the Chinese City of Beijing, the subject of our travels had to be brought up. She wasn't the first girl that I have met who's traveled as extensively as I have, but she certainly was one of the few. It was like the two of us had met somewhere in time long, long ago, and decided that one of us was going on one direction and the other another way. Now that we have finally met again, halfway across the globe, we share the stories of our travel with each other, those exotic adventures that were so different, and yet the same in the excitements that they always bring.

When we share our stories with each other, even the tiniest, most trivial of details became important. And pretty soon, you found yourself in a deep bond with a woman you've only just met, quite frankly, only a few days ago.

We do get to skip a few steps in these these relationships.

I sure hope it wasn't her brain that attracted me the most. I've been down that road before and it wasn't pretty. Girls always say that we only look at their looks. To be honest of course Maddy was pretty and that's how I was attracted to her. To say that we men don't get attracted to pretty girls would be a big lie; even ABCs like us, we're just the same. But that's not how we stay attracted. That's not why "I" stay attracted to her.

She is exceptionally intelligent, and the more I knew her, the more I wanted to know about her. I found myself, mighty curious about that insatiable curiosity that so defined her to me. How could anyone be that curious? It seemed like she wanted to learn about everything, and certainly more about Taipei: where she would be transferring to real soon.

I did what I always do: I told her all the great things about our tropical, Southeast Asian City, while neglecting a few details here and there about what might become insufferable, and welcomed her to join us there. Since we already exchanged contacts, and really we were messaging each other non-stop since we've met, I was certain staying in touch was not the problem here.

I already found out her love for singing back at the night we spent at the karaoke and so it was no surprise to me that she grew up in one of those ski towns up in the Alps. Since the first day we met, I had pictured her growing up with braided hair, singing mountain songs and dance in the snow. I didn't know where that picture come from, but according to her (I did not ask her point blank, of course) my mind picture was pretty accurate. Perhaps I was just that good at noticing these details about people as I write them down.

I also asked her why she was here in China. And while her love for Asian pop music was clearly a big part of why she was here (She knows way more KPop groups and artist than I do), but that wasn't all of it. She also studied Chinese Culture in uni, and have been to China once or twice before this on study tours. She clearly took a liking to the whole package of Chinese culture, which may come as a shocker even to most ABCs who had a hard time fitting in here.

My feelings for her was more confirmed last night, when I found myself wanting to stay in Beijing more, the city that I was meant to move out of, with my brother who wanted to say goodbye to it forever.

Life is funny sometimes, in the all ironies it never seem to run out of. Marian would be laughing at me now for acting like the virgin that I was when I met her. For suddenly having the difficulty of being true to myself. I can't help it, that's a part of me I never said goodbye to, in spite of all the goodbyes I have said now in my late twenty's.

I didn't know how much more time I would have in Beijing. I felt like saying something. In fact I almost did say something. I came here to help my brother to say goodbye to the city, instead I found myself in trouble saying it.

BEST SANGRIA IN TOWN

I've always been a guy with great hygiene when I am out staying at other people's places. It is something that my mother taught me, "Leave all your filth at home! When you stay out make sure you leave it exactly the way you found it."

Even though Flynn is generous to a fault when it comes to friends, never keeping count of who paid for the five thousand NT per person steak dinner, (that's 200 bucks per head!), and despite how he kept telling me to make this place home, this was still his place. That's why I kept the place clean and tidy whenever I was here.

I've always been the good boy. It's like I was programmed this way.

Perhaps that's one of the many little things that made our friendship last over the years. Once I had my room cleaned up, my things packed in bags and luggages, leaving only the ones I would be using today out, I began cleaning the apartment, starting with mopping every surface area such as the dining table.

The one advantage about Beijing, over the streets of Taipei is that the basic everyday cleaning is just so much easier here, mainly because of how dry this town is. By the time you finish one corner of the living room, half of it would be dried and ready for your feet. So you'd never have to plan your maneuvers as you'd do with a ten square feet apartment in Taipei. That's a gratifying feeling to have when you had to deal with house works often. And being a bachelor living by myself, I knew what I was talking about.

I had everything done before 11. There was still no sign of Flynn being up as I heard him snort through his room this whole time, so I used the time to get started on some work. You know what they say about idle hands. And I really should start working on my next work. Although there was one thing I knew for sure that I was going to do no matter what: a blog or something, as I am already writing it now, to keep track of our days so there is something to be kept as we moved on from Beijing, even from Asia.

That is the looming question with Flynn that I still had no idea what to do. With Flynn you just couldn't be head on about anything. Being head on with him meant him taking you on as an enemy rather than a friend, and that's not an approach that would go anywhere. I wasn't sure what to do, since unless he brings it up first, we won't even be able to start a dialogue.

But then, as I was writing down some ideas, while my mind was occupied with this issue, the snoring had stopped. Judging from the noise coming out of Flynn's room I'd say that the man in there was stumbling to do everything quickly. And then, he barged into my room, all dressed and shaved, though his eyes remained sleepy in classic Flynn fashion, as he said to me,

"Hey, did you clean up the place up or something?"

"Yeah."

"You didn't have to do that. Thanks anyways." He said somewhat rhetorically.

"Don't mention it." I replied the same way.

"You hungry?"

"I could use some distractions."

"Great. Let's go get something." He said.

When we got into the car I had absolutely no idea where we

were going. I doubt that Flynn knew either. But of course, there are only so many places that Flynn is willing to go in a heartbeat here in Beijing. And they were all quite concentrated in one area.

Once we were out of the garage, and the car was pulling onto the road, he asked me,

"You wanna go to Niajo?"

"Why not?"

"Cool."

Niajo was a small Spanish restaurant on the fifth or sixth floor of the Nelly. When we were here in the day, Niajo would be our place to go for their "very authentic" Sangria and flan. I had a serious weakness for their flan. And why do I call it a flan now? Try calling it a pudding in Flynn's face, you are not gonna like it when he's angry.

Flynn was very quiet in the car. Usually when we're in the car, he'd get all excited like that child in him and talk about everything he sees that was passing by the car, sometimes to the annoyance of others. Though most of the time, he would just infect you with his excitement and you started to see things his way. Of only people he knew well get to see this side of him, others, well, not gonna get a ride from him.

We were quiet all the way all the until we were in the restaurant, where he still barely spoke after we had ordered. With him not speaking I began to observe the traffic down on the street through the window by the side of our table, which by the way was terrible.

It wasn't until when we had finished the paella (actually more like he ate the whole thing) and he was on his third Sangria (that's him keeping it sober, meaning no "HARD" liquor) that he suddenly decided to start a conversation:

"You know bro, I thought about it." He was looking out the window as he spoke, "I really don't think I wanna move out of here anymore."

"Ok." I said, I was just happy he came to this conclusion himself.

"You don't seem surprised? Why the fuck not?" He seemed

more confused than angry.

"Just say what you came here to say." I replied firmly, didn't want him to change the subject and lose track of his thought.

"Yeah I thought about it." He went on, as the traffic on the narrow Sunlitun Street become so miserable a lot of people started to jump off their Audis or Land Rovers and began to walk to their destination instead. "I like this city too much to give it all up just for..." He paused.

"...Just for one girl." And I finished it for him.

"Fuck you man." He exclaimed with a smile.

"What? I knew what you were going to say."

"You know what man," That's the beginning of sentence he uses when he's pissed off. "I don't like that smart ass look on your face. I don't like how you always clean my place like I'm not doing my part maintaining my own apartment, like the good host I am, and make you forget all that dumb everyday shit. I especially don't like it..."

"...When I finish your sentences and make them sound better than when they were in your head?"

"Oh fuck you!" He said, "seriously? This is how you're gonna talk to me about this? When I'm here talking to you about some of my thoughts and... all that girlie crap, this is how you're gonna respond? What you think you're better than me or something?"

"You're not moving out for one girl." I said, standing my ground. Again, feigning agreement to get him back on track. "This is not about one girl; this is about Angel."

"What the fuck is the difference?" He was clearly still angry.

"It's simple. I get it." I said, "Come on Flynn, half the reason you loved coming to this city was her. And that other half would just be the time you get when you're staying here with her."

"That doesn't prove shit." Flynn was pissed. He looked he wanted to storm out right then and there, but couldn't find the strength to do so, and stayed against his own will.

"Flynn, you really need to let me be understanding for you. Because you know I do understand you. And because we're brothers." I said, "I know you growing up. I know what ticks you off and what makes you feel special. How many people can you name right now that knows you the way I know you? And Angel was very special."

"Hey drop this bullshit, that bitch…" He couldn't control himself, he was on edge.

"Don't say it Flynn." I was rarely this assertive dealing with Flynn, but I knew I had to do it, just to bail him out. "Don't call her that. Don't call her something you will regret forever." I was not done, "You know in spite of everything she has done to you she does not deserve you calling her that."

I knew my words were taking an effect. Flynn still looked agitated, but now with more restrain about it, as his posture was no longer that position where he could jump up and either quickly attack the person in front of him or leave.

"You couldn't let the girl go. You couldn't even thrown away that bonsai she gave you, even as it is now just collecting dust on my balcony." I continued.

"The what?"

"The Money Tree, remember? The one she gave you as a gift to your family?" I drew the picture closer to his memory so he may remember.

"Yeah what about it?"

"What about it? Flynn, why do you think you'd always get a little depressed when you see that tree? Don't say you don't know what I'm talking about because I know that look. I'd seen that look. You also said it was an end of an era, like Beijing wasn't the only place you were moving out this time. Like you were moving on from your life in Asia completely. I knew that look, I've seen it.

"I saw it when you first broke up with her. When you first came back to Taipei and brought all of us together. When you told us you weren't leaving Taiwan anytime soon. We drank and partied like it was just like old times, and nobody asked you any questions about Beijing, about California, about your big record company deal that you knew was not happening anymore.

"And that's the first time when I saw that look on you. Then you had the same look when you saw that tree this time we came back. If you still can't throw that away, like you can't throw this relationship away, memories of it anyways, my advice would be just keep it all together. There's no point throwing away that's yours anyhow."

Remember when I said going head on with Flynn is a bad idea? Well scrap that, because that's exactly what I was going to do now.

"You know I'm right," I said, "and that's eating you up now, isn't it?"

"Yes." Flynn said agreeingly as he drank his sangria, "Yes it is. Fuck."

"Glad I could help." I said with gloating smile.

"But yeah I wanna move on." He said, "What I had with her is over now. This time finally. Now I just wanna go back having fun. It is time to drink the best sangria in the world, instead of just in Beijing, don't you think?"

"Wait what?" I realized what he was suggesting. "You wanna go back already?"

"Yeah, call Dorian and tell him we're heading back tomorrow." He said, "I know you have his number. I might be slow but I figured it out. What you don't want to go now you met your new girlfriend?"

"Stop it." I said.

"I tell you what. You just come back and visit her any time you want. Use my apartment. It's practically yours anyhow, the way you clean it all the time. But tomorrow you go back with me, because you have to make the brunch. The first brunch of the year. And then we have to decide how we're going to do our Party of the Year. And then you could do whatever you want until Flynn Day, you got that?"

I know a lot of that is confusing to you as you read them right now. But I am a little busy trying to come up with what I have to do with Maddy. So don't worry, you're gonna find out soon enough. I promise you.

THE BRUNCH

We were back to Taipei the next day, catching the afternoon direct flight. that's the beauty about Taipei, the proximity of it all.

One and half hour of flight away you have Hong Kong, Macau and Shanghai. Three hours away you have Tokyo, Beijing and Seoul. Add another hour of flying you could be in Singapore and Kuala Lumpur. All the best cities in Asia easily accessible from this city, our city, Taipei City.

It is not like in America, where everywhere else always seemed so far away. Here, when you feel like it, you can go for cocktails in Hong Kong and Tempura in Tokyo on a heartbeat. Shopping? Too many to choose from. The best and latest luxury hotels, there's Shanghai and Beijing.

It is so simple to keep in touch with all the friends you made in these various part of the world because it is only another short flight away. And the diversity here is just as amazing as in Europe.

With that being said, I hated how I left Maddy just like that, but we had a long talk the night before and she seemed quite ok with it. We promised each other we were going to stay in contact and so the next day we began to text each other. So started my long term relationship. Let's just hope this one turns out well.

Being back to Taipei means resuming our business, and the sunday brunch is the first of many things on our to-do list.

The sunday brunch is one of our rituals. It usually takes place once every month. It takes a bit of luck, as finding a Sunday with just the right weather for brunch could be tricky in Taiwan, with all the typhoons and storms and sweaty sun that seem to find this island as welcoming as we do, although so far nothing seems to be able to end this little tradition of ours.

At this event I am almost always the "court appointed" chef, with the standing location always at Flynn's mansion in Tamsui. Flynn is a big fan of my cooking, and with home court advantage, he ensures every time of my role as the chef de jour.

My Spanish tortilla always makes the menu, this traditionally-made (Flynn's words, you should be able to trust a Spaniard on his home-cooking) thick omelette that had cooked and fried potatoes in it. These traditions that Flynn would insist on that we must oblige if we value his friendship.

In spite of all his rebellious acts and bravados, Flynn is a very serious man when it comes to setting and following traditions. With our sunday brunch, for example, he would insist that we did them in the tradition of La Comida, that of the full luncheon in the Spanish Tradition. He claimed that is the real root of brunches. Therefore, it is often up to me to prepare five to six courses at the minimum at these events. Tradition dictate that there always be one cold appetizer, one hot appetizer, a soup, two main courses, the tortilla. And if I have the time, dessert.

Dessert is sort of my only weak spot when it comes to cooking. I was never any good at making desserts. So what I sometimes do is that I would make my sweet potato salad, which could double as a dessert for the sweet tooths like Pete, who's a regular at our sunday brunch.

My sweet potato salad is famously salt-less, which made it exceptionally well-suited for the humid weather in Taiwan. What's the trick you ask? The trick to making a good salt-less sweet potato salad is that you gotta have good vinegar. Good vinegar would ensure that your sweet potato give out its natural scent to the maximum. Beside that, the rest is just about good working habits.

One good working habits will be to always do your grocery a day early. Meat takes time to marinate, as do many sauce such as freshly made mayonnaise and hollandaise, who will not form together into paste without a little time in advance.

Keeping the good habit of writing down your menu will ensure you have everything you need to make the dishes and never be forced to improvise, which, as you do the grocery early would ensure you have enough time to react to certain uncertainties which you can't predict: such as the produce you'd like to use were not yet in season, or certain spice or condiment you thought you had, had actually run out.

Flynn always accompanied me on these trips to the groceries. And a brunch of this magnitude, where we had a hungry Canadian, a hungry Spaniard, and an accountant (admittedly, they are notoriously big-bellied too) and a photographer who was never on diets, (seriously, Dorian never was. You'll hate him when you see how slim he is) and the occasional guest stars, there was only one place we could realistically go for this: Costco.

Costcos in Taiwan are not so different front Costcos in the US: distant, always in a warehouse, and packed with minorities (only in Asia minority meant a slightly different group). Thus when Flynn and I got to the Costco on a Saturday afternoon, it was predictably swarmed with people. And what happened next was perhaps why, though almost always a pesky and arrogant presence, most people still liked hanging out with Flynn: when you need him the most, he would take charge of the situation without a word needed.

With him there we just cut through the crowd of people like butter. He would spot up anytime something you wanted was too heavy or too high for you to reach. And when we shop for the brunch, he always takes the bill with no question asked. Very quickly we filled out car up with sirloin steak, eggs, asparagus and okra, which were in season, and apples, arugula, fresh lemons, mushrooms, sweet potatoes and potatoes, feta cheese, butter, milk and some dory fillets.

We even stocked up on some of those Gordon Biersch beer that he loved so much, plus some red Napa wine. Then we drove through the ridiculous two lane highway that was the only way from the city to Tamsui before all the traffic could catch up with us, with Dizzie Gillespie playing in the background from his in-car surround sound system, under the remains of daylight.

Flynn's Tamsui mansion has the best view of the whole town. Through the small country alley that came up from the shoreside highway, the mansion overlooked the Tamsui River as it runs into the ocean. Great place to be in when it is a sunny day.

Tamsui is truly a beautiful part of town that reminisces the many beach towns you would see on the Coast of Spain, South of France, Bora Bora and both the East and West Coastline of the US. Tamsui in Chinese literally means "fresh water". The town is located at the mouth of the Tamsui River, is the largest river in Taiwan, that runs from the ocean straight into the heart of Taipei City.

In the old days this was where the merchant ships would unload their cargo onto smaller river boats, and from here they would be transporting those goods to Dadaochen, the oldest commercial district in Taipei City, which still functioned today as an area for buying dried goods, Herbal Medicine and fabric, products of the old trade of the world.

After we unloaded everything into the kitchen, which just the kitchen alone is literally the size of my whole apartment, I began on the prep work. I went through all the mundane work of washing and chopping the salad to be chilled in the refrigerator, carving and marinating the steaks, and salting the fish.

As I did this, I could see Flynn was out smoking cigar over a glass of drink, possibly brandy or an aperitif such as Cointreau. After He had finished one drink, and come back in, glanced at my progress quickly, and maybe to see if I needed his help, which never happened today, he would then go to the wine cellar next to the kitchen, which is temperature controlled. He would refill his glass, then go back out again, have a drink and smoke his cigar.

By the time I got everything in the fridge it was already pretty late. So we decided to spend the night here. As I went to sleep in the guest bedroom I heard sound coming up from the basement, which was Flynn's music studio that he had converted since when we were in high school. It had this home theatre set from Bosch, next to a recording room he had constructed to rival most professional recording studios in Europe and the States.

Most of the time when Flynn is down there he would be there for hours. When he is there, absolutely no one could disturb him, unless that someone was looking for a punch out. In some ways this was one of those things that made us connect, I suppose, the same kind of insane obsession when it comes to the process of creating something, that level of determination that only be understood by someone else with the same fire and desire for win.

I've heard a couple of Flynn's own songs before. They were always of a Neo-Soul nature, sometimes mixed with a few segments of classical here and there. Lyrics were always a mix of Spanish and English, and maybe a little Chinese sometimes. The stories told in those rhymes were always quite heroic; songs of conflicts and battles, honor and triumph, always with a sad overtone.

For a man who claims to knew very little history, with the grades to show for it (I believe he actually got an F from history one year), a lot of his songs vividly described the struggles and lives of a warrior. Whether it was one on horseback or flying a fighter jet, whether wielding a sword in hand or manning a gun turret, his songs had a way of bringing you to that specific period of time, as you breathed as quickly as the heroes did, and felt the bombs and life and death as closely as if you were there.

I can still remember this one time when I related to him the story of Hannibal's march to Italy, and within a day he wrote a 7 minutes long song in the style of an epic poem that described that very struggle through the eyes of an Iberian soldier. And after he performed it to me, he literally forgot what Hannibal's march was all about. But the song he wrote was still there, as evidence of the level of talent he has.

I still remember when he used to take me to jam sessions, and I would watch him just smooth into any new songs the others were performing. He could also play a tune by hearing someone simply humming the melody to him.

We used to enjoy these sessions very much, meeting new people and sharing the dream of making it one day, then over the years, those people became scarce and after Flynn's California and China ventures, you don't see them no more. I knew he would still come here from time to time, down to his studio and toil away sheets after sheets of new songs. But even I have not heard him play anything, not as often as I used to.

I slept through the night, and even when I was half asleep I could still hear whispers of music coming up from the basement. It was darkness, then it was the morning.

And it was brunch time.

As I laid everything on the kitchen table in the order of service, people began to arrive. Rach got here first, which was my cue to get started, but not before answering the question she pulled me aside by the door and whispered to me,

"Is he ok?" She meant Flynn.

"Didn't sleep that much, but looks alright this morning."

"Great. Sangria?" Relieved to hear what I said, She asked me the more important question with a big smile.

"On the table where it always is." I said before heading back to the kitchen. But not before watching her opening her arms the minute she saw the big tall Spaniard and said,

"Hi Flynn!"

Guess who she had a big crush on?

"Hi, my favorite girl."

I could see without turning around when they hugged, how small Rach looked in those big, long arms of Flynn's, and how red Rach's pearly white cheeks gets whenever you saw that little face of hers peaking atop of Flynn's shoulder. It was always such a funny sight.

Rach, which is short for Rachel, worked as a senior analyst at an international banking institution here in Taiwan. While I actually had met Rach before Flynn, Flynn was the one that Rach had always had a crush on. You'll see what I mean soon. For now, let's first talk about my Sangria.

Due to Flynn's heavy promotion, my Sangria has become something of a world famous local drink.

A lot of our visiting friends, particularly those of Flynn's, would join our brunch just to have a taste of it, and always praise Flynn for his accurate assessment of it after that first sip. I never know if they were just being polite, fearing to cross Flynn by insulting his favorite drink. I made it quite traditionally with Rioja red wine, fresh orange juice and mixed tropical fruit slices. When Rioja is not available, we would just use any red wine.

"So," enjoying the glass sangria that Flynn poured for her, (she'd looked so smitten it was ridiculous that Flynn just went out and acted like he saw nothing.) Rach asked me, "what are we making today?"

"Well," I said, pointing at each dish on the table as I mentioned them, "the Tortilla for sure. We will start first with grilled asparagus, my Waldorf Salad made with ripe apples and feta cheese, dressed in Balsamic vinaigrette instead of mayonnaise. My sweet potato salad as a side dish. For main courses we have dory fillets smothered in lemon okra, and last but not least, Steak Diane."

"Oh, I'm gonna get fat again, aren't I?" I guess she was trying to sound smart.

"Again?" I teased her.

"Shut up!" She said as she tried to slap me with her glass.

"Oh I trailed the smell and see what I've found!" Walking in from the door, the "late" Professor Pete came in with a bottle of Chardonnay. Pete was a theatre art professor from Canada who now taught at a local private university.

"Come on, man! You didn't have to bring that." I said while taking the bottle off his hands and put it in the fridge. "Have a drink. We'll be serving soon."

"Alright!" He said, "By then by, he looks ok now." He meant Flynn, who was coming in after him.

"Did he say anything about Beijing? Or what he's been doing this past week?" Rach asked me.

"No," I said, "we barely talked about it since."

"Pete, It took you long enough!" Flynn shouted from behind Pete.

"Sorry. Weekend traffic." The Professor replied.

"Yeah, that's what you fake Americans would say alright."

"I'm Canadian, Flynn."

"That's what I just said." Flynn said as if that was actually a witty remark, "So Rach, how's that Sangria treating you?"

"I could never ask you for more." Rach replied so leeringly obvious with suggestions.

And then when Flynn was not looking, Pete threw a "seriously!?" look at her; that was of course before she slapped him in the belly. While Pete was crying silently in great agony, Flynn picked up the jar of Sangria and refilled for Rach, before asking me the routine question, which he asks at every brunch,

"When are you gonna teach me the recipe for this sangria, my boy?"

"I've taught you."

"Yeah, you say you did. But then when I make it, it never tastes the same. What the fuck is up with that?"

"Maybe you just don't have the touch?" I said with a smile.

Flynn began to laugh, "Maybe." He said, "Just may-fucking-be!" This was when the doorbell rang, "That must be Dorian. Now that little bitch owes me another bottle of XO for being late."

After he came back with Dorian with undoubtedly another round of tease and berating, I was finished with the making of the dishes and presented our dining table. It was a long table right next to the wall of windows from the side of the building that looked into the ocean.

Flynn put a bottle of XO brandy on the kitchen table, undoubtedly brought in by Dorian who knew that Flynn would have demanded it from him, as we began our brunch.

The brunch went smoothly, while almost everyone made a comment about how much food was on the table, between the five of us we still managed to finished most of it, leaving behind only a small corner of the sweet potato salad and a slice of the dory fillet.

We then moved with what was left of the Sangria and the bottle of brandy to the patio, a corner we always go after brunch. As tradition would have it, Flynn took out his box of Cuban cigars and presented it to all of us. The four guys each took one, and while Rach was completely against smoking, to a biblical proportion, she'd never uttered a word of protest about it during the brunch.

"Now that," after he blew out the first smoke of that freshly lit cigar, Flynn said, "was what my grandfather would call a meal."

"I feel fat." Rach said, monotonously.

"FEEL?" I asked, and was slapped accordingly by Rach. This time it really hurts.

"Hey!" Flynn grunt to me, "Don't you pick on Rach, she's a part of this family."

"Yes Godfather." Pete jumped to answer for me.

Rach had on her face this look that mixed joy with utter-disappointment. One that we saw very often whenever Flynn said something that he thought was protective of Rach, but really only disappointed her.

"I could really miss a lot of parties for this meal." Dorian said, "Like, a lot, a lot."

"You guys ever wonder what we're doing here man?" Then suddenly Flynn interjected, interrupting that overwhelming feeling of relaxation and comfort from the fulfilling meal which we just had.

"What do you mean?" Pete asked the Godfather for

clarification, as his words were so often cryptic for their lack of refinement, and his mood always so temperamental if you got his meaning wrong you were running the risk of losing your head, sort to speak.

"Like what are we doing here in Taiwan? Ever wondered about that? I mean you," Flynn points his big finger at Pete, "you teach a bunch of classes that you don't even want to. You," now it was me he was pointing at, "you could write anywhere else. You don't even have to be here." Then he moved on to Dorian, "And Dorian, half the year you're not even here. You should have moved to Shanghai and stay the hell away from me and this town." And then, when it was Rach's turn, you could always tell if Flynn was looking at Rach. His eyes would just soften up that little bit before he opened his mouth and suddenly he was his usual rough, insulting self, "And you, well you have a good job and everything so I guess you're still getting somewhere in this town, so no complaint there."

"Hey I have problems too!" Rach protested, which was swiftly ignored as Flynn continued his point that probably had with him since Beijing.

"What are we all doing here? What's so great about this town? We can't brunch anywhere else? We can't work anywhere else? We can't be a loser anywhere else?"

"We probably can and we will get paid a lot, a lot better." Pete said, drunkenly with agreement.

"Right!?" Flynn seemed to have found a fire in him to go on with this indictment on Taiwan, perhaps East Asia in general as he continued, "There's no racetracks, no great parks or resorts, no great sports games, sports teams. And fuck, there's typhoon and earthquakes and scooters everywhere..."

"Yeah and the chicks are definitely getting worse each and every passing vintage. No offense." I was worried that Rach was gonna smack me again.

"No, I agree," She said to my surprise, "girls my age are so much hotter than those fifteen years old looking skanks that are hitting the clubs these days."

"Yeah, there must be somewhere else with a dead-end job in this world that we could be doing instead." Just when the girl subject was raging, professor Pete pulled us back into the job market hellhole again.

"Yeah sometimes when I'm in between shoots I'd think about it too." Dorian said, "I mean I make a shit ton of money doing this here, but every time I was out on assignments in Majorca, in Maldives or Tahiti, I'd ask myself that. I'd ask myself, 'why haven't I moved here?' And certainly with the market in Taiwan now you would think..."

"What the hell is wrong with you?" Flynn almost jumped up as he said. "Don't get the fuck off topic aight?"

"Didn't get any good songs last night hm?" I decided to interrupt before in my brother's drunken rage should he take out Dorian to pieces.

"I knew you were up, you bastard." Flynn laughed shortly, and then he continued, "But that's my point though."

"Which is?" I asked.

"Well, it just, I don't know," Flynn said, "I mean everybody here seems to have such a short attention span, one minute they'd be rooting for this guy, the next they jump on him for being the worst person ever. Remember that news about that YouTube video of these two white guys who sat in priority seats and didn't yield them to other elderly passengers on the MRT? I mean that news went on for what? A week? What is this? They keep blasting us about how they want more people to come here and make this island more international. How they want an open island. They always seem so friendly. And then when you're actually here, living here, working here, all of the sudden you are here stealing their jobs, stealing their girls, stealing their priority seating from the their elderly."

"To be fair, Everybody does that a little bit, everywhere else you go."

I said, finishing his point for him, or we would be here forever. As a political analyst, I was the only one with the right linguo.

"All that problem you talk about now, the short attention

span, the polarization of public opinion, the more and more extreme forms of public reactions and hostility towards specific groups of minorities or foreigners, they are problems everywhere. With borders now becoming less defined and issues such as terrorism, there's a global identity crisis in each individual country. Who we are is now a global issue, and it's not like we won't have those problems anywhere else we may choose to live in."

"So yeah, but my question is again, why the fuck here then? Why bother being here and suffer through the exact same problem with this humidity going on 365 days of the year?" Flynn continued driving his point.

"Here we go with the humidity again." Pete said, "You know, some of us actually like it a little tropical and humid..."

"Shut up, nobody's talking to you." Flynn cut him off briskly, "There's better money out there for us. Better life out there for us. Better weather out there for us..."

"So does this mean you're moving out?" I knew I had to cut him off, and help him make up his mind, "Are you done with here? Are you done with Taiwan? Are you done with Asia? Are you done with us?"

I had to provoke him to get to his point. I knew what I asked would rub him the wrong way, but you simply cannot answer Flynn's question for him, but you can direct him to answering it himself, in a way that would satisfy him.

Flynn was quiet at first, my question seemed to have put him on the spot. And after perhaps five seconds or so, with his eyes widened he answered me,

"I don't know. What I do know is that I'm thinking about it now, and I fucking hate thinking about it. I hate this feeling of having something that I'm missing. Like I'm missing my day, you know? That fucking day where you tell everybody else to fuck off, because it is your day? I don't fucking know when that day is, or when it would happen, but I feel a fucking fresh start would help, you know what I mean?"

Everyone else were sort of nodding with agreement, except me. For I have prepared my response to his point.

"That day will come," I said, "and until then, instead of using fresh start and 'missing something' as an excuse, we should stick around and most importantly, stick together as a group. Maybe by some freak accident some good could happen here. Why should you walk away now, when we have stuck around this long and saw this much?"

As usual, my answer seemed to have stopped the rage. The frustration. The anger. At least for a while. This was the only time in life when I felt useful. There was silence that no one seemed willing to break.

It was a short one. Pretty soon we all started saying stuff like,

"Yeah this was a really good brunch."

"I feel fat and full."

"You FEEL?"

"Ha you just got slapped."

"I'm gonna digest all this on my next trip to…"

I'll let you figure out who said what.

A MODERN DAY ARISTOCRAT

Since the brunch Flynn has vanished. Which was why when Mark called me up to meet him for a drink on a Friday night, a night that was usually reserved for partying and drinking with my brother Flynn, I was available to meet this friend from my New York's past.

The place we were meeting at was LMNT, this night club in the Xinyi district that was famous for its special shots. When I got there I received a text from him, saying he was going to be a little late. So I ordered a drink, and sat there at the table he reserved and waited for him.

Mark was someone I used to hangout with in New York. We used to meet up regularly every two weeks or so for lunch and catch up. He's the sole heir of a very powerful family here in Taiwan, one that controlled the oil business... or was it silicon? Anyways he's as aristocratic as our modern society allows.

About a year ago I heard he moved back, and about everything from the time I left New York until he got back was shrouded with mystery. People are just not that keen to keep in touch with you when you're so far away, as I have learnt over the years with my around the world friendship tree. There was a rumor that he had to reconcile with his family first, something that took quite a bit of time since his conservative family thought he had steered onto the wrong path during his American years.

I wasn't really looking forward to the meeting tonight. For one, Mark didn't exactly tell me why he wanted to meet me, and I was never a big fan of surprises. Two, Mark could be quite secretive at times, often act like he had a busy schedule to keep. And he has made a rude habit of leaving others early in the middle of the meal or the drinks.

Still, a man as in love with his own voice as Mark, you never know just what he might reveal to you on your chance meetings. And those are some fun gossips to write about.

When Mark finally arrived, he brought a guy with him.

The guy he brought was very muscular. He was in average Asian height, visibly shorter than Mark (Mark was quite tall, around 6"3). Wearing the Road Warrior outfit of blue jeans, vest and black T-shirt and a chain, a silver earring on his left ear, and fashioned a goatie, he was literally a movie character; no surprise there, as it turned out he worked with movies.

"Sorry we're late," Mark said in a calm, soft voice, which never really sounded sorry, instead like he was only making a statement. "This is Charlie. I'd just met him at the gym."

"Hey man!" Charlie smiled at me, a smile overflowing with friendliness.

"Which part of the Wild West are you from?" I asked, making a bold judgement based on his attire.

"How you know I'm from California?" Charlie looked surprised.

"Because we don't dress like you." I replied somewhat rudely, but I had a right to as they were late, and plus it was true. As even in these hot summer Taipei days both Mark and I had shirt and dress pants on.

"Oh, I get it, East Coast, West Coast hm?" Charlie's smile just got even bigger.

"Whatever. Just don't you mess with my Knicks." I gave my warning.

"I'm a Dodgers' fan." He said.

"Good." I said

"Good?" Charlie looked puzzled.

"I don't watch baseball." I replied.

"Yeah I thought you guys would hit it off since you both work in the same industry."

I wondered why Mark said that. Perhaps only to open the introduction he prepared for us,

"Charlie's a director, and we got to talking about making movies here in Taiwan and I thought about you. What was that thing about how the industry here works that you told me before?"

Even if that conversation he was referring to now did take place, it would have been years ago back in New York.

"Charlie, A-Zed is a very good friend of mine who's a... well a great writer, I guess that's the title."

"For real!?" Charlie asked animatedly, "You're a writer!? That's chill man."

Something told me that he says that a lot.

"What have you written before?" Charlie continued his question.

"I might have to leave soon. My dad is calling me."

Mark said, no surprise there. And then he just went out with his phone in his hand, leaving me alone with this guy that apparently he has never met before tonight.

Still, this Charlie seemed quite interesting. I told Charlie what I have written before: my book, some of my previous experience such being a ghostwriter for celebrities, writing stage plays, my work on political campaigns. After listening to me patiently as I went through those as quickly as I could, he said:

"Shit that's chill. It's so cool that we met up, man! Look I'd only just got back and it's not like I'm a big name or anything. Like you, you had published a book, you know people, you've already established yourself and everything you know? I think maybe we could work together on some projects, if you're interested, you know? I've talked with these other people who are all ABCs or foreign people like us that wanna make some movies here. They are people just as chill as we are. Maybe you wanna join us? I mean we are small people, but if we get together we just might get something done."

He said the whole thing like he had it prepared. But it wasn't about what he said, but the way he said it. His eyes sparkled when he talked about this group of people who wanted to make movies in Taiwan. A fire that could catch whoever was there, sitting by, passing by, and almost instantly made you part of the team. Something told he must had affected others like this before.

And it was in that fire that I found something intriguing about Charlie. Something that I liked to dig a little deeper. So I replied to him quickly,

"I would love to. I don't know how I could help though. I'm a writer and it sounds like you already have a story ready?"

"Yeah, yeah I got a couple." He replied readily, "But that's where we could start, you know? I'm gonna be filming this one project that I already have, but with you, I think we can talk about story ideas first. I'll give you my business card." He said, handing me this card with his cell phone number handwritten on, correcting the printed one that was clearly an old number out of use, with a logo of an astronaut monkey eating a banana, "It's an old card that my ex designed for me…"

"It's all good," I said, and then continued, "as long as the info on the card is up to date."

"Haha of course it is." He said, "You're chill, man."

No I was not.

Then Mark came back. He barely just sat down when he said, "Sorry, looks like I need to leave right now. Let's do a round of shots on me before I have to go."

The shots were gone as quickly as they came. Same with Mark, who declared his departure almost as soon as he drank, with the smell of alcohol still in the air.

"Ok I'm off! Stay in touch, guys!"

Tonight was about Charlie and me, as it turns out.

And that is fine with me.

MY REGIME

I have always wanted to make a movie of my own. That's how I started writing: I love telling my stories in a very visual way, so I first started drawing comics, and if wasn't for the sheer volume of my work (really, too many stories just come to me every day; it's not a boast, it's a symptom) I wouldn't have switched to what I do now, writing. It was simply too time consuming to draw all the stories into pictures. Of course, my main character looking the same in every comic I did probably was another factor.

So naturally I was excited at the possibility of finally working in film. And therefore beginning the next day I picked up my regime. The possibility of working in a new field, a field of my true desire, meant I needed to resume the workout, to get my body both physically and mentally ready for all challenges and possibilities to come. And I proceeded first with whipping myself to shape.

My life from the start has been a well-planned regime of routines. In high school, I made my life only about school, gym and study. And the one routine I've kept since then is working out. Work out regularly keeps the discipline alive: those regular hours of work out a day makes the other disciplines, such as meal schedule, controlled diet, the long writing hours, researches, tolerable.

I believe working out pushes your mind mentally to accept what your body is physically learning to take. To me, training my body is the same as training my mind. It gets my mind balanced, as it makes me mentally tough. I believe in that, and I have practiced it to this day.

Thinking back I was silly; I even skipped prom because I was preparing for the SATs that week, which from what I heard was great- Flynn had a great night out with his girlfriend and everything. But I was so focused, for I only cared about getting into a good school and from there, a career.

My only recreation then was writing, and it soon became part of my regime as well. By the time I moved to New York I have moved on from writing stage plays and short-stories to novels. That was where I finished my first novel.

But if I did not pick up writing I would not have learnt a lot of the things I knew today. Not just all the knowledge I picked up from all the books I read, from Homer to Pushkin to Fitzgerald, but how reading those books taught me how to have real conversation with people. I learnt to notice what makes people tick. It gave me a perspective that I found very useful in life.

My regime is why I am able to live anywhere. I built it initially to keep the outside world out of my well-planned life, but it now become the one thing that allow me to enjoy it. I became more than just a career guy, more than just another Ivy League product. And it kept going, in the face of all the changes my life has thrown at me: location, career, lifestyle, friendship and family.

With my regime I really could live anywhere I choose, so why am I still here?

Flynn's bitter words at the brunch reminded us just how vulnerable it still is for us here. His questions are our questions too. We've all thought about it at some point, usually at moments when we were reminded that "we're not from around here". Why here? When we can choose to live anywhere?

After a couple of days of thinking and working out, I called Dorian up. I told him about Charlie, how he was looking to work with me. And I guess he thought of some pointers he could give me, so he asked me to meet him at the Computex tomorrow around noon.

Computex is an annual event held here in Taipei. As Taiwan's blood runs on the IT industry, many see this as the most important business event here on this island. It is considered by many to be the true indicator of the Taiwanese economy.

Filled with events that rained you with gifts and souvenirs as you watch game and demonstration videos, It is so peaked with commercialism and eyeball-engaging attractions that you feel as laid up and dissected as the product that you are learning about at every corner. But it is a great place to learn the latest trend in the industry. Of course, most average people that are here aren't here for that. They are here to see the showgirls. And yes, they are plenty and very good looking in those hotpants and miniskirts. It makes the attraction too.

When I met up with Dorian, he was just putting down this headphone that looked a lot like the Beats by Dre.

"Let's go grab something to eat, Ivy League." He always called me that when others weren't around, "I'm in the mood for some double cheese, double pepperoni pizza."

"I fucking hate you." That was my warm greeting to him.

"Why?" He asked me.

"You weigh like a model, and you eat like a slob." I commented.

"That's right. I am like that."

"I really fucking hate you."

"Get in line."

He couldn't get the pizza stand to customize double pepperoni pizza. So instead he ordered two pepperoni pizzas, that and a large coke zero. In counterpart, I was only having a regular coke.

We stood facing each other at the table, with his two pizzas opened and giving out the smell that was mixture of marinara sauce and industrial mozzarella cheese, when Dorian began to spoke to me,

"Working in the film industry here is completely different from the States." He said, quickly eating the second slice of pizza in front of him, "The industry here is too small to even call itself an industry, and years of mismanagement, the shrinking of the market in the late 90's and early 2000's has long run it out of any kind of directions.

"Trust me, I deal with these people all the time, the TV execs here, producers, models and wannabe stars, they are all the same. They can't make any real money off their jobs, so they can only try to rip you off at any chance they get. They are basically vultures, and bad ones at that, considering how often they'd go hungry."

"What if we focus on team-building?" I asked, completely undeterred from Dorian's less-than-perfect portrayal of the state of the industry, "What if this guy Charlie can really put together a group of people that's got some great potentials? We could you know, look to the future?"

I must have been watching a lot of NBA GM interviews this week.

"Those are two very big 'if's' to have to happen for this just to have a chance of working out." He didn't even need to catch his breath, "Only two kinds of people would come back here from the States, the tried-and-failed, and dreamers. I don't know which category Charlie fits into, but clearly, this guy has some history he's not telling you. Let's just cut to the chase. I will help you as long as you wanna do this. And here's what I can offer,

"I can set you up with some contacts I have, just to get you more familiar with the game they play. I'm not in this industry professionally, which means you can actually trust me as I will be the last person to rip you off. All I ask is if this thing gets off the ground you guys give me a credit for something."

"That's all you ask?" I said.

"That's all I ask." He confirmed.

"I can't say no to that." I knew a good thing when I hear it, and I knew Dorian too well to ask for more confirmations. So instead I went on a different subject that was on my mind at the time,

"Let me ask you something else. So like you said, the business here is shrinking, and the economy hasn't been great." I took a sip of my coke, "so why do you stay here?"

"Why do I?"

"Yeah. In our group, other than Flynn, you're definitely the best-positioned to move your business and life elsewhere, so why here?" I rephrased my question.

"This is about Flynn's question, isn't it?" He asked with a smile of understanding.

"Part of it, yeah."

"Well I don't know about you, but I stay here because I have built my life here." Dorian looked somewhat wistful when he said that, a look that he did not give out often, "I have built my reputation and contracts all around this town, and most importantly I have built my studio is here. Sure I pretty much don't use it at all, since all my shoots are not here anymore; not the ones that pays, anyways. But it's nice to have a place to go back to, you know? It's cool when you get to travel the world for work, but you'll get tired at all the travelling at some point, and then it's good to have somewhere to go back to. You know what I mean?"

I took a moment to let his words set in, then I smiled, this time out of understanding as well, and said, "Dorian, you're actually a much better person than people give you credit to."

"Yeah of course. I am a good friend." He said, "So have you heard from Flynn since…"

"The brunch? No. And I'm guessing not you either."

"Of course not. The way he was, I'm the last person he'd call…"

"You're probably right." I said, "Well there's dragon boat day, he's bound to show up for that. You know how Flynn is with his traditions."

"Now we're on this subject, can I spend it with you this

year?" He asked me.

"Did you have to ask?" I said, "Sure thing. You know how I always overstock."

DRAGON BOAT DAY

Flynn and I never miss spending Dragon Boat Day together. It is a tradition of ours, to meet up at my apartment and have some zong-ji and beer for a Chinese holidays that we both don't have anybody else to celebrate it with.

I had the place cleaned up the night before, gone were the beer cans and the three days old dirty plates. The floors were mopped. The dining table was set with plates that would have otherwise stayed in the cabinet. I had to do this the night before since as I have mentioned, Taipei is quite humid and cleaning on the day would only mean trouble.

The only place I didn't have to clean was the kitchen, which was always kept restaurant clean with all the spices and knives in the right cabin space, the chop board and the stoves spotless, and a dried sink; boy you have no idea how important the last one is when you live in one of the most mold-friendly cities in the world...

Dragon Boat Day is a Chinese holiday celebrated every year in commemoration of the poet Chu Yuan and his sacrifice over an authoritarian regime that was out of touch with its own coming demise; but it is also traditionally the hottest day of summer, according to the Chinese Lunar calendar.

Traditionally it is celebrated by hosting a dragon boat race (hence its English name), which we will attend by watching it live or more commonly at home while drinking spiced rice wine, made with turmeric and other spices mixed in common yellow wine (non-distilled rice wine that is); it is supposed to ward off the summer influenza, and of course you cannot forget zong-ji.

Zong-ji are basically rice wraps, made up of sticky rice and depends on the region it comes from, can have stuffing ranging from meat (usually pork), sausages to eggs to chestnuts, the whole thing is then wrapped inside a dried lotus leaf, and tied together on strings or grass ropes, which we then boil (steam, in correct culinary terminology) to perfection.

I'm not a big zong-ji fan. It is more of a Flynn dish. And for him, every year at this time I would make this terribly oily dish from scratch, based on my dead grandmother's recipe. My recipe was very good, according to most who have had the pleasure of tasting my annual handy work.

While I was setting up the dining table so it may fit more than two people, I heard the doorbell. I went for the door and it was Rach, who I wasn't expecting, and yet I wasn't surprised to see.

"How nice of you to join us, Rach."

"Fuck off, I'm not in the mood." Was her answer.

I went into the kitchen, and ignored her as she helped herself with a beer, just to make some more zong-ji; thank God I always over-stock on groceries. But she didn't think that little "F-word" was quite enough, so she added, in high volume so everyone in that small apartment, and maybe the whole building, could hear her, "I hate my life."

"Work or love?" Something should tell you that this was not my first time handling angry Rach.

"Ok, let's see." I could visualize without actually seeing Rach, who was in the other room as she started gesturing with her small hands like the analyst that she was as she proceeded to her points, "I am still single, almost thirty…"

"Weren't you already thirty since…"

"Hey it's my story!" She exclaimed, but then quickly

corrected herself with the fact that I pointed out, "On the WRONG side of thirty, and still have to be bossed around by a supervisor half my age who doesn't know crap about what I do…"

"You have a fifteen-years-old supervisor?" I asked.

"What?" She sounded confused.

"Fifteen. You're thirty, so a supervisor half your age would be somewhere around fifteen years old." I said.

"Are you trying to piss me off!?" She exclaimed. Boy how far did her voice travel?

"Maybe? Is that why you're here?" Before she could answer my question however, someone else decided to join in on this conversation.

"You're an idiot!" Rach shouted back, I know who that was then.

Somehow Dorian entered my apartment and managed to be caught on with our conversation right the way. While I just kept on making more zong-ji without reacting, from what I could hear in the kitchen, Rach jumped off my couch and scolded Dorian,

"Where the hell did you float in from?"

"The door was open." That's all he said, before shrugging it all off, while fending off Rach's attacks of smacks and jabs, he took a can of beer out of the cooler and pointed his question at me, "What is she doing here?"

"You have to ask her." I said.

"I knew this was a mistake." He said. And when Rach succeeded at smacking him, it just so happened the doorbell rang right that moment.

"I'll get it." Yes, I would. I came out of the kitchen and went for the door. It was Pete.

"Oh it's you." I said, "Do join us." (Make it a whole family, I thought)

"Everybody's here?" He asked. "Sorry for the short notice but…"

"Dude see for yourself." I said, pointing out the fact that you could literally see my whole apartment from the door.

"And you left them there unsupervised?" He was shocked when he saw the little fight that was raging behind me, "At least you hid the booze, right?"

"They are where they always are." I replied, unconcerned as I made a gesture about going back to my kitchen.

"Oh, crap." He began to charge pass me towards the cooler, "Why didn't you save some for me!?"

At first, Dorian and Rach were still fighting each other. But the minute they saw Pete came in charging for that cooler they began to work together as they kicked the cooler to each other, whoever was the one farthest from Pete, while Pete chased that small cooler in my small living room like a blind moth.

"Dude, do something!" Pete said.

"I gotta make more zong-ji." Was my only reply.

And I did. I wrapped more zong-ji, boil them and once they were done, with the lotus wrap completely moist, and shined with the oil inside begin to soak into the leaf, I put them all into a big pot and served it on the dining table.

I then declared the completion of my work by exclaiming,

"Food's ready!!!" when I saw them still monkeying around like a bunch of juveniles and completely ignoring me, I got mad and this time went deep into my lungs and shouted,

"STOP!"

I guess Rach wasn't the only one with deep lungs. I was holding a boiling hot pot of zong-ji in my hands, like a grandmother on steroids,

"You idiots do this every year! Pop up unannounced and make a mess out of my freshly-cleaned apartment! ARE you quite DONE!? If you won't shut up for me, at least do so for your FOOD or this pot here is going out of MY FUCKING WINDOW!"

"We're sorry."

My madness left as quickly as it came. The four of us each took a side and we sat together around my tiny dining table, with the big pot of zong-ji now in the middle.

"Oh my God I forgot how good zong-ji is." Rach said after having first taste of that steaming, enthralling mixture made up of the strength of soy sauce, the inviting scent of hot lard with a hint of lotus flavor that was zong-ji.

It's always interesting to me, whether it was depression, anger or whatever emotion people were feeling at the time, all that would be passed at the sight of food. Sometimes just food, but usually good food. It is the beauty of cooking to me, which is perhaps why I have been doing this consistently since my adolescence.

Everything seemed to calm down from the boisterous riot that was raging but minutes before, right outside of my kitchen. Everyone seemed to have come with a good appetite, seeing how fast my pot full of zong-ji emptied up. Just as I was wondering if I should go back in and make some more Pete asked me a question that interrupted that thought:

"You're making a movie?"

Before I could answer it with words, my look of bewilderment had Pete making an addition to his question, "Dorian told us."

I shot Dorian a look of "Really?" Which he was working hard to avoid.

"So are you?" Rach pressed.

"Yes." I said, "What's with all this interest all of a sudden?"

"Nobody said interest. We were just looking out for you, since we're family." Rach said, and then slapped Dorian on his arm. "Isn't that right?"

"Sure." Dorian could only reply.

"Who said no interest?" Pete argued, "I'm interested. I want in."

As you could probably imagine I was quite annoyed by this point, so I said, "Doesn't this seem oddly familiar..." then I realized something, "I think we all know what time it is." I suddenly said with a vicious smile.

"Oh no! No! No!" Pete stood up, backing himself against the wall, knowing what I was talking about. "Not this year. You guys can't pull this crap every year! Draw on my face just 'cause I'm the white guy..."

"Hey!" I was so fast with the bottle of spiced wine nobody

even saw me taking it out, and now it was in my hand. "Speeches only work when I do it. Guys?"

Dorian and Rach got out of their chairs before Pete could protest again, each held him from one side, while Pete could only say,

"Oh come on guys! Not again!"

A little after that, we were all sitting around my living room now, in my tiny couch, watching TV. We've all took our turn and drank the spiced wine, so now we were all a bit red around the cheeks, warm and each holding a bottle of beer in our hands.

And then there was Pete, his whole face drawn up with the yellow color of the spiced wine, drawings of indigenous tattoo, cartoon scars and Pirates of the Caribbean symbols, depends on who did the drawing. Every time we looked at him we still couldn't help but snigger a bit, which would always trigger him saying,

"I hate you all."

And as you could imagine, that only made us turn our sniggering into laughter.

"Hey where's Flynn? Why hasn't he show up!" Rach said, looking at the two zong-ji that were still on the table, now cold and no longer steamy.

"How long did you wait to ask that?" Dorian took the first stab.

"Hey shut up!" Rach said, smacking him in the process. That would have been it, except this subject has no deterrent strong enough and scary enough for us not to take a stab at it ourselves individually every time it shores up.

"You know now that he's single, you should probably do something about it." My stab.

"Oh shut up!" She looked embarrassed and annoyed, hiding her face in her palms.

"Yeah you totally should, before somebody else snatch him up." Pete said, all serious-looking in that funny face of his, "I'm saying, Flynn is very attractive…"

"Oh I shouldn't have told any of you guys about him!" She

said with a sobbing voice.

"Is she crying?" Pete was concerned.

"How could you fall for that every time?" I said to Pete, rather cruelly. "And Rach, it's not like you had to tell us. Anybody with eyes could see that you have something warm and cuddly for Flynn…"

"What is he doing these days? I have not seen him forever." Pete said. We all decided to ignore Rach and her "sobbing" now that I have pointed out the question of its validity.

"God knows, after exploding like that at the brunch and almost moving out of Beijing, Asia really, he could be doing anything now." I said.

"He almost moved out of Asia!?" Rach, who stopped her "sobbing", popped her face out of her palms and asked me that with her eyes staring at me intently. "You mean he almost moved out of Taiwan!?"

"That would be my guess, yes." I said, "That's why I had to pull Dorian there. I knew I had to stop him somehow. You know how much of a overkill Flynn is, he could have done anything!"

"You called me there as bait?" Dorian looked mad, but not nearly as mad Rach, who interrupted him,

"Nobody's talking to you! Shut up!" She commanded, then turned to me, "You TOLD me he was fine at the brunch!"

"He was fine at the brunch." I said feebly.

"Oh I'm so gonna get you…" Rach slapped me, or she tried to as I backed away, jumped off from the back of my couch, nimbly like an athlete.

"Get him, Rach! Get him Rach!"

Dorian cheered for Rach as she jumped off the couch and approached me.

This was not going to end well.

THE LONG NIGHTS

One night next week, Pete asked me to meet him for dinner.

There was a growing wave here in Taiwan in recent years of ABCs such as myself moving back to town. A lot of it had to do with family reasons, as a lot of our parents were now getting old and wished to leave their lives overseas like the falling leaves back to their roots, their home.

These ABCs bring with them restaurants catered to a familiar appetite. It was one of those place we went to tonight.

In an alleyway next to Zhongshan North Road, a three stories high white townhouse that advertise itself as a country steakhouse, a building slightly popped out in the neighborhood when you come in from the main road.

"Nice place you found." I said to the professor as I sat down, in a wooden chair next to a table that looked like it came from the American West, with the help of a waitress dressed in a country plaid shirt and a red necktie.

"Nice place hm? I'm guessing French country cooking, looking at the menu." Pete said, all excited to me to play this little game that we played at every new restaurant.

"Japanese French." I said without even taking a breath.

"No way!" He said, "How could you tell? You haven't even look at the menu!"

"The neighborhood we're in." I replied. "This area hosts a huge number of Japanese tourists, which is why the new Okura is being built not far from here."

"I thought you said Zhongshan North Road was the American quarter."

"That's further north, across the river in Tianmu. Here in the old Taipei area it was predominantly Japanese."

My knowledgeable deliberation and my mounting number of evidence had forced him to conceit, though not without a final word, "God it's so not fun playing this game with you! You're nothing like an ABC! You know the city too well!"

"Didn't you say the same thing about me back in New York too?" I replied.

"Exactly! You're not a New Yorker! And yet you knew all the neighborhoods. If you didn't tell me you lived in the dorm back then I would never believe you came from out of town!"

"What could I say? It's my town."

"You can't have every city you go be your town, it doesn't work that way."

"It works for me." I said.

"God I so envy you ABCs sometimes." He said, "It's like the other day when we talk to the cab driver, I was giving directions and the guy was looking at you for confirmation the whole time. You guys just blend in so well, you don't have to be reminded that you're 'foreign' all the time like us."

"Well you gotta look at it this way," I said, "at least you get to be who you are."

"It's 'cause I'm white isn't it?" Pete jabbed.

"Exactly. So you never have to explain why your mandarin is so good if you're with Taiwanese people, or why you know a certain area in Greenwich Village so well when you look Asian. You actually fit in better because people know who you are just from…"

"My looks." He finished my sentence for me.

"So why here? What are we doing tonight?" I asked.

"Well first, I got one of those groupon things for this place." He said, "It gives you a deal where you only have to spend 180NT for a meal that's worth 1,800NT."

"Let me see that." I said, doing my ABC work for my expat professor friend. Something Pete and I have been doing since back in New York, when he was doing his Ph.D at NYU in performance arts.

"I know, I couldn't believe it either." Pete seemed quite proud of the whole thing. You could tell from how even that crooked red tie he was wearing was smiling too, high on coupon fever. And it flattened as he saw me taking a long time reading that small piece of paper.

"What does it say?" He asked.

"Well it only differs slightly," I attempted to soften up the blow, "it says that you get 180NT off, if you order their 1,800NT meal."

"That's nothing like what I said, crap." Now he seemed like a withering balloon as he spoke frustratingly, "Just order whatever then since this hardly seems relevant."

"Nah, let's use the coupon." I replied.

"You sure?" Pete seemed surprised that I was still interested.

"Yeah I mean it's not their fault that you're illiterate." I said with an evil smile.

"That just made your day didn't it?" He asked.

"Well there was traffic." I replied.

So we gave the coupon to the waitress. She was quite nice and asked us if we wanted what was on the set or if we wanted to substitute some of the items. I guess since we were speaking English she also tried to communicate with us in that language, and was relieved once I told her in mandarin that we were fine with what was on the coupon.

She then took Pete's order for two bottles of Taiwan Beer when Pete asked her, "hey what's your name?" She told him. "You speak with a beautiful English." She smiled quite embarrassedly and thanked him. "Where you'd learnt to speak like that?" After she giggled a bit and told him, he said, "Oh, I'm sure you're the best student there." A couple of words more and he sent her off with a happy mood with the thought that her value was appreciated by a random customer that she might never see again.

"You know when you talk to girls, you sound nothing like the guy who complains about how your school is forcing you to teach English when you're a 'theatre professor'."

"she's cute isn't she? That girl who took our order?" He was oblivious to my question.

"Yeah, sure." I replied without thinking.

"Liar."

"Oh forget about those people." He said, but he's the one that clearly needed forgetting as he now remembered my question following the one about girls. "I mean I'll just quit if they ask me to substitute for their English Conversation class one more time."

"Dude you'd been saying that since you took the job." To be fair, he really had been saying that.

"Yeah well I mean it this time." He said, "I didn't take this job to be doing all this alright? I should be teaching Aeschylus and how to position deus ex machina instead of A,B,C,D... actually that's what I want to talk to you about tonight." He said, suddenly his eyes shined as he changed the subject, "You gotta hook me up man."

"With what?" I was suddenly confused.

"Your movie. When and where? Get me in." He said.

"I have no idea if it's even happening yet." I said, "The guy was supposed to contact me after that night for a meeting and he hasn't. I have no idea who are these people he's talking about working together with, and I have no clue what sort of role that I will be playing."

"Who cares! It still sounds cool! Now hook me up!" He said, "Do you have any idea what's happening right now in my life? I was brought on this earth to teach the art of theatre, to immerse myself daily in the art. Do you know what I'm doing instead?" Pete then followed it up with a long speech that sounded prepared, but probably was on a loop of frustration played straight out of his mind,

"I am hosting teacher parent seminars to discuss very vague

directions that the school is going that is actually going nowhere. I don't get to direct my own play or have any real initiatives, because whatever I do I would have someone local who is supposed to help me actually taking charge of the whole thing. Their syllabus which comes from the mandate of the Education Department of the Government is so outdated that I've been telling them to update it for years and to no avail. Do you have any idea how frustrating that is? To have a fancy title just so you can get paid to do nothing."

"Well if you hate working here so much, why do you stay here?" I asked.

"I'm not gonna let them drive me out of this town." He said, "I have a five year contract, so I will just keep cashing my checks until they send me off with the best reference a trophy white man could find in this town. It's a win-win. I get what I want and they get what they want too."

"No wonder you jumped to agreement with him." I commented.

"With whom?" He asked me.

"At the brunch, you were the first one to agree with Flynn about moving out." I explained, "It's frustrating for you to live here, isn't it?"

"No, no, not so much living here." He quickly corrected me, "I like it here. I like having a little humidity. I like getting the sun, and my first time seeing a typhoon was amazing. You don't get to see that back in Toronto. You get something else entirely but not typhoon. I like living here, I just don't like the work; this generally fearful environment where people don't like to take charge. I don't like that."

"I guess that's why we're drinking this beer." I said, making a comment about the timely arrival of the hot waitress and our beer. "Come on, let's toast on this." I said, raising my bottle.

"So what's it gonna be?" Pete raised his bottle but stuck to his subject, "Are you gonna hook me up? At least take me to meet those people. You never know what might come around with a little extra spark. There's a lot of stuff I could help you with. Come on! You'll be doing me, your oldest New York friend a big favor."

"Fine, fine!" I said. "Yeah I'll let you meet with Charlie and his friends. Whenever I meet them next."

"Alright man!" Pete said as he broke into a new smile.

"You know, pulling New York was a cheap shot." I said.

"I know." He said while grinning as he threw in his punchline, "You're a good friend A-Zed."

The next couple of nights, I went through my old writings, trying to find something that I could discuss with Charlie about translating into a screenplay.

This research part of the job was something I termed "digging the graveyard". I named it so due to the time it usually occurred, midnight around the "graveyard shift", also because I called my pile of past notebooks filled with unfinished ideas, scribbles and notes I have compiled over the years "the graveyard of ideas". I was doing this while playing Red Hot Chili Peppers' "Otherside" on YouTube in the background.

It was my walk among tombstones, metaphorically as I remembered my past and tried to re-engage some old sparks. So many ideas and memories are left here to wither and to die, as I went through them now, I trying to find that little fight left in them, to bring them back to life.

It was fun to go through these. It was like a little piece of yourself that you have forgotten. You never know who or what you might run into, with only you and the quiet night as company. Someone long lost in the past could come to life through your own words. And that could be the beauty, or the beast.

The thing about writing stories or writing in general is that there's no such thing as a bad idea. Anything at the idea stage is always good. It's after you write it out, you can see if the story that started with this idea is actually any good, and that is usually at least after you have finished a first draft. You would never have the time to finish all of the ideas into stories. Therefore most of the time the writer's job, as any writer would tell you, is actually planning and drawing out the skeleton of the story based on the idea you have, which can best help you decide which ideas to run into a story first.

It's still a process left a lot by chance. You won't know for sure if the idea you want to run now is really that good. But then if the one you selected turn out some two months after writing it, to be a bad one, then you would be frustrated with the all the time you felt you have wasted on it. It's a process, and the process must be respected, if you ever want to find the voice.

The voice is just what I call it. Different authors refer to it as different things. Some call it inspirations, others call it by some other name. To me it's something more physical, though not visible. Something that could be heard even if you're deafened by all the noises in the word. That's why I call it a "voice".

The voice is something that you must let it speak to you. It cannot not be forced. You can only listen, and listen very carefully as it can sometimes be only a whisper. Let that whisper tell you what your story is. That's how I wrote my first book, as I search for the next one.

It's important to do other things well too. Marketing, write something relevant, keep things mainstream, how to package your story, but the most important is to find the voice first, as you cannot work without it.

It sounds like a passive thing to do; you sit and wait for it to happen, but instead it is a very pro-active thing to do, as you must go out and seek it out. It's like a relationship, you must earn its respect so it may be willing to tell you its story.

It does get easy sometimes. Sometimes when you find a character with a voice that is so strong and powerful that he/she simply forces his/her way out of the shadow corners of your mind, and make you listen to them; but those are alpha-characters, and they only come around once in awhile.

Flynn is a real life alpha. The only time when I don't hear from Flynn for this long, when I don't even think about him this much, was when I was living New York. But there was someone else like him back then too, someone with an equally powerful voice like his, who had forced her way into my life.

I thought about her as I went through these old notes from those days, old story ideas. She came to life often in my mind when I pull these graveyard shifts: about 5'5", slim figure, dyed black hair and a slightly tanned skin, always wearing a sweater of some sort that fitted her just perfect, and black flat heeled shoes with blue glitters.

My time in New York could pretty much be summed up to that girl. She was special. She was different. It almost feel like I was cheating on her sometimes when I talk about my new girlfriends, however far in the past she is now.

Her name was Marian, and she was the love of my life.

I couldn't sleep. So I watched a movie. It was a bad movie. At these hours I preferred watching a movie that I didn't like.

There is always something to learn from a story that somebody else told. A story is only as beautiful as the telling of it. And when you strip away that beauty, like watching a bad movie, it's easier to learn how they are told. Bad stories are told in ways so private and vulnerable, it's the part we rarely show others.

For example, when I watched Rocky 5, it showed so much of Stallone's nihilism you would lose your drive to even feel the frustration of life that is present in every one of his stories. And David Lynch's rendition of The Dune was so David Lynch he even tried to take his name off of it.

Of course I did not come up with this myself. It was Marian who got me into this tradition. It was her idea to go to the movies or get a DVD on the weekends. She made up the bad movie rule since it was "more fun this way".

Our days together were so full of joy and happiness that all of her bizarre traditions made as much sense to me then as they do now. I never regretted for a day that we have met, even years after we are no longer together. Her laugh was so special that I could still remember it now like I just heard it minutes ago.

I do not know her anymore, which is part of the arrangement we had when we were together. But I still remember every bit of her when we were together as clearly as yesterday. I could still hear her speak to me some nights, as I dig through the graveyard. Like I said, you have to be careful when you never know who or what you just might run into.

I carried on this routine she started, adding it to the list of strict regimen which I followed to the letter. That's how I know I'm a better storyteller, than someone whose story is told by others. My story is so boring and without interesting drama that I am truly the beta to their alpha, the person better suited to keep the record of their stories, with my Ivy League Education and my well-organized life.

That's when my phone rang, setting off a chain of events that led to me to the next chapter of this story.

MY FIRST MOVIE

My call that night got me catching the 6AM bus this morning on a raining day, towards Dorian's studio downtown to shoot a movie.

"Hey bro, do you have a friend who has a photography studio that we can use?" Charlie said over the phone to me that night after I picked it up.

"I could call someone. Why?"

"You think you can get him to let us use it tomorrow?"

"I could ask. But it's better if you can give me an alternative date in case this doesn't work."

"Ok just sometime this week. Any time would be cool." He said vaguely.

"Ok let me ask him."

"That's great man. I'm in Taichung. Man there's a lot going on in this town." He said.

"Yeah, just shoot anything." I said, a poor joke referring to a recent gang-related shooting that happened in that town that was all over the news.

"Haha you're funny bro! Alright I'll talk to you later."

"Oh wait!" I remembered something, "Shouldn't we set up a meeting with the guy or something? So you can tell my friend just what you want to shoot in his studio?"

"Sure man just set it up." Then he hung up.

I expected Dorian to still be up at this hour when I called him. After I told him what I knew, he asked me,

"So what is he shooting, Ivy League?"

"I have no clue." I could only be honest.

"You want me to lend my studio out to some complete stranger with absolutely no idea who or what they might do with it?"

It was a legitimate question, which I quickly apologized for,

"I guess that's what I'm doing. Sorry I should have thought about it more before I called you…"

"Actually, this might be good." He said over the phone, "You said he hasn't met you since the first time you guys met up right? So this might be a good set up for us to see just what this crew is all about. See what kind of smoke he's blowing."

"Smoke?" I was actually a little concerned now. "Would there be any problems?"

"Nah! I'll clear it for you this week. Just set it up and I will meet you that morning with the keys and everything." And I guess he remembered something else, "And one more thing, make sure he sends you his script before you say we can lend him the studio."

"Before?" I asked for confirmation like the order-following Ivy League kid that I was.

"Yeah. Make sure of that." He was quite adamant about it. "Otherwise we cannot give him permission. Ok?"

"Ok."

So I called Charlie back, told him the news and asked exactly what Dorian asked me to, no script no studio, to which Charlie replied me, again with the child-like naivety of his voice:

"Sure man! I thought I'd given it to you… Ok I got it on my phone… Hold on…" I could hear the sound of him typing over the phone, "ok I'd just sent it to you."

I then sent the script Charlie sent to me to Dorian, and completed my part of the bargain before the day.

The shoot was on a Wednesday morning, when Dorian's

studio would be cleared of its schedules. The plan was for Dorian, Charlie and me to have a quick meeting before hand, for Charlie to quickly explain what he would do with his short film, a slasher/horror movie titled "Model Massacre" inside Dorian's studio. He would explain everything beforehand and have the personal approval of Dorian before he could proceed with the shoot.

Dorian's studio was in an office building in downtown Taipei, right in its busy commercial district of the East District. As I got there on the date and time we have agreed on, I found Dorian there, holding two cups of Starbucks coffee in a twin-cup holder, but with no sign of Charlie.

"He's not here yet?"

"I haven't seen anybody." Dorian said quite matter-of-factly, "It's ok. Have a cup of coffee." He said while handing me a cup of Starbucks he bought that morning.

I had a sip of it without paying much attention and once that sweet, hot, overwhelming foamy taste began to take place in my mouth I almost spit it out and said, "Oh what the hell!? Is this double cream caramel macchiato again?"

"That's what I always drink." He said.

"God do I fucking hate you." I said.

Some doughnuts and half-a-cup of that disgusting coffee later, there was still no sign of Charlie. I was getting anxious, while Dorian the cool cat remained calm and unmoved by the lack of action.

"I think I should call the guy." I said.

"Go right ahead." He said, without even moving his head. "Now would be a good time."

I called Charlie, who was a little surprise to hear from me, judging from his voice. When I asked him where he was, he told me he and his "people" were just getting breakfast. They were going to be a little late

"How's he still just getting breakfast?" I said to Dorian after the phone call.

"Because he's not like you, Ivy League." Dorian said to me with a smile, "Be patient, it's gonna be a long day."

We waited for nearly an hour before Charlie even showed up with his people.

"What the hell Charlie!?" I said the minute I saw him.

"Hey bro yeah it took us awhile to get the equipments we want on our way over here." He said, though by the look of it he wasn't terribly apologetic, but more interested at knowing the person next to me. "Is this your friend? The photographer?" He said with a big smile.

"Yes." For some reason I answered him, instead of going deeper into his lateness, "This is Dorian. This is his studio."

Dorian quickly got up and shook hands with Charlie with a smile. And they got to talking. Charlie gave a quick version of the scene he wanted to shoot. He seemed pretty confident that he was able to get all of that done in one day. And Dorian asked him some questions about the kind of equipment he was using that day, they even joked a little bit about how to shoot certain expensive shot cheaply- cinematic magic, they said it was. Dorian, who seemed quite happy with guy, handed his key to Charlie and told us to "get started".

"Do you know what you're gonna be doing with them?"

Once Charlie was busy directing his people to set up inside the studio, Dorian, who was standing by the elevator beside me, asked me that.

"I am clueless." I honestly answered.

"Find out quickly." He said, "film crews are hard to hang around with when you don't have a clear role with them."

"Ok I will. Thanks man. For today and everything." I said.

"This guy," He was smiling as he thought of something else, "he's gonna need your help for sure. I'll be back around lunch and check on you guys. Don't worry if everything doesn't go as planned."

"What do you mean?"

"Just don't worry." He said cryptically as he left.

Now it was all just me and Charlie, and like, twenty other strangers.

Before today I was simply a movie watcher. I mean sure, I have taken writing jobs for directors and producers before, and not all of them professional. In fact I would argue my experience dealing with film people up to this day had been that there is a very vague definition to what a film professional is. And today's experience certainly proved it.

If everything went according to Charlie's script, Dorian's Studio was supposed to pass as a Modeling Agency. And a terrible murder spree was taking place here that threatens the very lives of everyone involved. At least that's how this whole thing written in present tense made sense to me on paper.

The cast and crew of this two minutes scene were mostly made up of Charlie's friends, some of whom were writers and directors themselves, who agreed to help out. Charlie explained to me that's just how it works most of the time: apparently in some "you scratch my back, now I scratch yours" way. Favors were the real currency of the film industry.

To give Charlie credit he did try to introduce me everyone that was there. But my poor memory aside, the sheer number alone meant I had a hard time remembering all the names. Nobody seemed to mind though. I guess that's just how it was in this business, where people were all working from project to project that they've created a method of knowing each other different from society:

Everybody seemed to know that this "bro" was different from the next "bro" and that "make up guy" was not a title but a proper name and everyone who's working on the project seem to know this from the start.

In spite of the people we had already to shoot today's scene, more people were still coming in. And people who were already there left at different time slot as well. They all had their other jobs to go to at certain hours of the day. Pretty much the only two people that were gonna be exclusively there to whole day were me and Charlie.

Make that lesson number one.

When I asked Charlie about this, he said,

"Dude that's just how it is!" He said, as were waiting for the makeup to be done for the next shot, "Everybody has their day job to go to you know!? And it depends on the directors.

"Some directors, like me, I could be very… bossy when I want something done. So they always have to come in prepared. It doesn't matter if they were doing something happy the minute before, if I want them to cry, they cry. They don't cry, they don't get it, they get out. That's why it's very important to be the director, you know? You always have to communicate and just get things done.

"Anyways, maybe you could just play producer to this one you know? You're a chill dude so who knows? Maybe you could direct something someday too? Let's talk about this!"

And he jumped back to his director's chair as the shoot was about to start.

I watched him work. In spite of the ad-hoc nature of the day, it was interesting to watch him work. I slowly understood why he was in his "Charlie" way: constantly moving, constantly jumping in and out of subjects in conversations, using certain terms on repetition as if he retained little memories of the frequencies with which he used these terms.

I understood it as I saw him work and how these qualities, whether by nature or experience worked for him, as he jumped from groups to groups to make sure of schedule in each were synched with others, as he repeat points until they were to his satisfaction, and as he stayed energetic and driven in spite of the long hours and physical nature of the job.

One line often had to be shot and shot again, and sometimes there wasn't even a line. Sometimes we would re-shoot the same scene with the light pointing this way and then that way. There usually wasn't a particular reason, as everybody just followed what the director and whatever vision he was having at the time; there was even a guy there just to take notes of the different shots Charlie shot in order to keep track, in case they forget and do something that was already done with.

And yet collectively, in spite of all the chaos, whether exhibited in Charlie individually or them as a whole group, functioned with some sort of self-propelled order.

And I realized all this repetition was a lot like writing a novel, when you go through drafts after drafts, while keeping all the copies in case they might piece together in the future into something useful. Much like what I often did in my graveyard shift. And once I realized that I realized how all these years my calling for making a film of my own was never that far-fetched, as I found this little piece of common ground between the two professions.

Make that lesson number two.

Pass 14:00, the lunch that we had ordered arrived. Charlie told me to announce it and so I did. Some People who caught a break somewhere along the line had fed themselves with whatever they could scavenge from the 7-11 down in the alley by this point. Nevertheless, pizzas and bento boxes were distributed among everyone equally, who then decide whether they wanted to trade what they got with someone else or leave it for later.

While I was enjoying my slice of pepperoni pizza I watched how everyone interacted. Charlie was going around from group to group, speaking with everyone, just for chit chat this time, by the sound of it. He took their break seriously. He told me later that it was to avoid fatigue about the job, something that he was taught back when he was working in LA. Anyways, at precisely 14:30 Charlie asked me to announce the end of lunchtime as he munched down two slices of pizza at once.

So that's my job for the day, apparently.

For the afternoon shot, there was still some missing parts or people that were supposed to show up that couldn't make it today, at least that's what Charlie told me. He was supposed to make adjustments, and indeed he tried as he worked with his crew.

But I guess there was something or someone he really needed that he just couldn't work without. How could he had possibly made me book a venue a week ago, pulling my favors and still come in not fully prepared dumbfounded me. But I held my tongue, only gotten ready if it didn't work out, to call Dorian and inform him the situation and apologize for being an idiot myself, getting involved in something I clearly had no hands over.

Luckily, this was when Dorian popped back in for his "checkup" and Charlie quickly asked him for the favor.

"Hey Dorian! Hey Bro!" Charlie said as he saw him, "Do you know…" He told him what it was that he needed and asked him if he knew someone, to which Dorian quietly replied,

"Of course. Let me make a phone call."

That's all he said. And all it took for us was just to wait. The wait was quite long, as Dorian's people could not arrive until 17:00, the time we were supposed to wrap up the shoot.

As things got started again and I realized I was not going to make the time I promised Dorian with my words, I got a bit anxious. Dorian must had seen that and told me, as we sat by the side and play audience to the last shoot,

"You really don't have to worry if it didn't go as planned, Ivy League" He said as he gave me a pat on the back, "It happens all the time in this business."

"Ok." I said, "You're really nice."

"I am a good friend aren't I?" He asked smugly.

"See, now I hate you." I said with a smile.

"And that's how it's done!" Charlie said suddenly and everybody cheered. I guess it was a wrap. Our tiny crisis was over and the job was done.

Maybe I wasn't such an idiot after all. Make that the last lesson of the day.

Something like shooting a movie for the first time, however uninvolved I might have been to the whole thing, called for a special kind of night out. We must celebrate it like it is, as a whole family. When one of us got going, all of us share the love. So I called up the rest of the family, told them about the shoot and the drinks we were to have tonight, and then it was just the matter of where to go.

Here's the thing kids. If you ever decide to take your friends out for a good time in Asia, don't go to some first time place none of you have actually gone before. Hands-on experience is very important here, as a cafe can be called a bar, a restaurant can call itself a cafe, and every damn bar here is like a club, as you really can't judge a book by its cover here in Asia.

So why did I take location advice from Charlie, a guy who technically up to this morning I only met once? A guy that's from fucking California!

We ended up at this bar, Pistol or Revolver, I can't remember its name now, on Roosevelt Road (Yes that was the actual name of a road here in Taipei- a pretty important one too).

It is a small bar, if you could call it a bar at all, a place that has no air con, completely open to the rainy moisture of a humid Taipei night, as you can imagine what that did to the T-shirt I was wearing after a long workday, and the beer is way too cheap. So cheap it should raise sanitary concerns. Another red flag would be the fact that it is the only bar within two blocks radius: the lack of competition in Taipei usually means the owner really wouldn't have any reason to care about the quality of their service.

So as I was with these "new friends" that I was just getting to know their names, post shoot, while hiding that line of sweat that was growing on the back of my T-shirt, and waited anxious for the arrival of my people, my people began to show up one by one. The very first one was Pete, who apparently was a little upset about something.

"I still can't believe you ditched me." Pete said to me as he walked in.

"What are you talking about?" I was genuinely confused.

"I thought I told you I wanted in? And now the movie is already completed?" He looked really pissed.

"Pete, I didn't even know we are shooting until last night." I said. "And besides, it was only one scene. I'm sure there would be more."

"Yeah go write that kind of crap on your blog or something." He clearly was not putting too much faith in my words this time.

"Ok, can I at least introduce you to the people that I

worked with today?" I tried to be the peacemaker.

"That's the least you can do." He said, before making an observation, "Hey are they doing shots? In this weather?"

"Yeah they are a little crazy." I said as I walked him over to Charlie and his people and began introducing them. Pretty soon, Pete started doing shots with them as I hid by the tap with a glass of slightly warm beer in my hand.

And then Rach showed up.

"Hey you couldn't find a place with air-con?" Her words spoke of anger, but her face was with a smile.

"Cheap beer?" I replied.

"You're buying." She said, "Where's Flynn?"

"Fashionably late." I said, "Let me introduce you to the guys that I worked with today."

"First introduce me to my beer." She always knew what she wanted.

As I was getting Rach's drink with the hundred NT held in my hand, I heard that familiar voice speaking from behind me,

"Hey, hey, hey! That better be my drink my boy!"

I should have seen it coming when Pete almost dropped his drink, or when Rach suddenly froze, her eyes wide as baseballs when I caught her with the glimpse of my eyes as I turned around; instead, I took no notice and just turned to the direction of the voice, who added

"Hey guys, remember Gina?"

Standing next to Flynn, in that darkness of the night, a dimly-lit face, but a face too familiar for me not to recognize: dyed amber colored hair, around 5"9 tall, looked taller wearing those boots with three-inch heels she wore tonight; who looked just like a Taiwanese Penelope Cruz wearing that skirt which was always so short, covering that beautifully tanned, smooth belly and that perky butt of hers.

That would be Gina.

Rach started to drink on her own while she stood there staring at Gina and Flynn. She didn't even remember how but minutes ago she had me agreed to buying her tonight. She practically bought the bar with the money she was spending and each drink gone in quick successions to the next. Needless to say, Rach was not Gina's biggest fan.

Pete on the other hand, was busy doing shots with his new friends, Charlie and his crew. All the while Gina was feeding Flynn every drink he was having while she… with her other hand… was feeling up his… you get the idea.

For some funny reason watching that, I was reminded of that one time she said there were too many eggs in my omelet during one of our brunches. Did I mention that it was a fucking omelet?

Well, look how she was feeling them eggs up now?

I quickly decided to make up some excuse and leave, not for me but for Rach. Keeping two combustible elements so close was never a good idea, as I thought with pride about how useful high school chemistry turned out to be for me.

But I guess Rach was not ready to leave because she wasn't gonna let Gina stop her from drinking her drinks. Eventually though, I was able to drag her out of there with me before she smash Gina's head on that bar table, or drink the bar dry. She could have done anything, really.

As we left I saw Pete was still doing shots with the others who were mostly half-his-age. Big mistake, he's gonna regret that tomorrow. We went outside and ran straight into Dorian who just got here.

"You owe me a big drink for today, Ivy League. I never been to this bar before but a free drink is always welcomed."

He asked me and a pretty passed out Rach, who was barely hanging onto my shoulder.

"I have to get Rach home, she's quite drunk already." I said, making up a lie as I was really good at always, "Here's a thousand NT. Get rich." I said as I quickly took out a thousand NT note out of my pocket.

"Nah, it's not you. Family don't owe each other. It's that Charlie guy owes me a drink now."

"Exactly!" I said while holding up Rach's soft body that was falling on whichever direction I pushed her up to. "Get it while it still counts!"

"Right!" Dorian smiled and said, "anyway you take care of her. I'm gonna go in."

We past each other as I took Rach down the MRT corridor and took her home before I went back to my own place, ignoring every call, text, line, WhatsApp and Facebook messages and went to sleep.

THE HANGOVER

Everyone had a different way of dealing with hangovers.

For me it was ice cream. Any ice cream. And it was the same for Rach too. I knew if I suggest to have ice cream together today over her lunch hour she would not say no to me, especially in the condition we both were in.

Rach is what Marian would call a "cool girl", someone that was just so cool you almost don't know what to do with her. When I first met Rach, it was at one of those nights out clubbing with Flynn, and we've been friends ever since.

Rach works as an senior analyst for one of those big international banks stationed in Taiwan. Now that is a real Asian job: any job in Asia that involves the banks, the laws or hospitals trumps any other job titles. Keep that in mind when you're thinking about asking your potential Asian in-laws' permission for marriage.

When we met on a work day such as today, we would meet at the Haagen-Dazs in the Shinkong Mitsukoshi shopping complex in Shinyi District that is within walking distance from her office in the 101 Building. We got there almost at the same time, as if we often did without planning, like there was a special connection between the two of us.

I recognized her in that white shirt and black pants that she had clearly been wearing since last night. I immediately switched off the music playing on my headphone and put away my sunglasses and waited for her to share her misery first.

"Hey Man-Whore!" She said, I guess she was trying to be cheerful. "Interested in murder? I have just the right target for you."

"In this sun?" I replied.

"Fine maybe after the ice cream." She said as she ushered me to the line.

Knowing that time not on our side, we quickly settled ourselves down in the air-conditioned booth with our choice of ice creams: I got myself a scoop of mango and another scoop of raspberry sorbet, while Rach decided on the rum raisins- her favorite.

"See? Air-con!" Rach said, teasing me about my bar of choice last night, "It's the civilized way of living in Taipei. Embrace it, don't reject it."

"Fine! Fine! I know!" I said, annoyed but smiling, "I deserve it, after the night I put you guys through."

"Having seen those friends of yours I don't blame you anymore." She said, "Not our kind of crowd hm? An open air bar in the middle of Taipei City? What were they thinking?"

"I get it. I get it. You're still grumpy from the hangover. Let's talk about the murder."

"Oh you're so getting some." She winked, ignored my attempt at changing the subject while pushing for hers, "I could tell just from the way you're eating that ice cream so slowly like you're savoring it or something. What's her name?"

"Her name is Madeline. But we call her Maddy." I answered. "Let's go back to the murder…"

"Yes. Let's." She said, "God this sun is killing me. Can we switch so I don't have to face it?"

"Sure why not." I replied and we promptly switched seats. Now I was facing the sun with my headache and hangover.

"So murder. Do you know someone who could do it?" She asked, sharply as always, "Can your girlfriend do it? I know you always go for the foreign girls so she's not from around here.

Where is she from?" She continued with her pushy line of interrogation.

"Germany. Up in the Alps." I replied. "How surprised were you?"

"What that you met someone? You're a guy, that's a given."

"No I meant… your intended murder victim?" I was trying to delicate.

That's when Rach's cell rang. "Hello?" She listened for less than a second before she cut the other person off and told that person what to do in a very orderly manner, then she said to me, "Surprise? There was no surprise. I'm never surprised." Her phone rang again, and she answered it, this time even more forcefully, "Look didn't I tell you that first part was wrong!? Well fix it!" Then she hung up and turned to me, "You! go!"

"It was your turn." I said quietly with my face down, fearing that she might unleash the anger she just shown me.

"Oh right! What was I saying? Surprise!" She said with that discovery look of hers, pointing her index finger at an invisible object in the air as she spoke authoritatively. "I'm never surprised. I knew it was coming. He needed company and she is a whore!"

"Ok!" I said, "I'm glad we have that outta the way."

"What out of the way?" She asked suspiciously.

"Your anger. You're not evading it." I said, "Let it out. Face it. It's not good to keep something bottled up."

"Oh shut up, A-Zed! You don't have to have all the answers you know!"

She suddenly exclaimed in that really, really small booth, where a mother with her two daughters, and the three people working behind the counter were all shocked and now turned their eyes to us.

"Oh calm down!" I said, "You're so fucking melodramatic!" Then I turned around to the mother and said in mandarin, "I'm sorry. She's just lost her grandmother."

We were talking like characters out of a Spanish Telemundo soap opera. I can't wait to find we were brother and sister and that she had my baby.

"God I really need a man!" She said, "It seems so impossible in Taipei now! All the guys are with their girlfriends for like 10 years since college and then get married when they can both pay the mortgage together! God how I used to make fun of those people! The mortgage gang! Now they are all laughing at me with their credit and their loans and their baby support!"

Seriously, I could hear the mariachi playing in the background

"I just need a decent guy, doesn't have to be perfect. Doesn't have to have good income or an Ivy League education or anything. Doesn't even have to be good looking. It'd be nice if he has all that, but really, he just has to be there for me so I can stick it to that short, little whore that sticks on Flynn like a gum you stepped on the street…"

"Let me ask you something," I had concerns for the PG-13 audience that we were around, so I interposed myself, "It's a question, not an answer: Why do you stay here then?"

"What you mean this ice cream booth? Because we're meeting here." She looks even cuter when she's confused.

"No I mean why Taiwan? Is it because your job pays you well? I mean you can work in some other Asian city too, where surely there's more fish in the sea and less people dating for mortgage rates?" I said.

She thought about it for a second, "I dunno, really." She paused a bit more as if to collect her thought in that always thoughtful little head of hers, "I never really thought about it. If you push my button on that now I would say I stuck around because of you guys."

"Us?" I said with bewilderment, "What the Man-Whore Quartet?"

"Yeah, the four of you!" She said smiling, "btw I want to use that the next time the four of you are together. 'Man-Whore Quartet' haha."

"Yeah we'll have concerts and everything." I said.

"Oh you're so thoughtful." She said. She could get so thick

with insults from others she really boggles me sometimes.

"So you need a man hm?" I asked the obvious question, seeing how our hangover was passing with the ice creams working, "Well I might be able to help you on this. You know I'm a wingman? One of the best in this city?"

"Do I? I've slept with the wingman." Then for some reason her smile turned into tears as she began to sob, "Always the wingman, never the guy…"

"Oh Jesus you're fucking melodramatic!" I said before I turned to the mother again and explained in mandarin, "Now she's missing her."

"Rach, forget about all that. Even wingman, you'll be with the most…" I said before I realized my mistake, "Ok I didn't mean number. I meant quality…"

"I know what you meant, man-whore!" She really needs a dictionary. But I was just happy that face of hers was cracking a smile now.

"Yeah just admit it though," I said, "this man-whore has all the answers."

THE MAN-WHORE MAN HUNT

The following week, I fulfilled my role as Rach's wingman. It meant taking over a new regime that was completely unhealthy when you compare it with the one before:

Wake up one-ish in the afternoon, zombie my way to coffee and food before I take another nap around five, then get up around seven, wait for Rach to text me to meet her at whichever club she wanted us to go.

We have become quite literally joined in the hips for the week. Well maybe not literally, but our hips did bounce off each other quite often.

The problem wasn't we were also not getting any, which by the way was absolutely nothing: it could be summed up with the first half of the shrimp fishing scene from Forrest Gump. The guys we met were always too young, too cocky, too tall, or too afraid of Rach to get anything started.

But the real problem is that it started to feel like work, as in not fun. And not just for me, but for Rach too. It seemed something that was so fun barely two, three years ago is now something that we had to humor ourselves to do, as our late-twenty-something bodies began to protest more and more each night we went out.

Of course according to Rach, it wasn't our fault. It was just a reflection of the "market":

"I did not realize this generation could be this useless." She said one night when we stepped out of the dance floor and had a little rest over cocktails. Her comments on the generational gap aside, it wasn't just her who was frustrated by the lack of result.

So when Mark called me, again out of the blue, and invited me to go karaoke with him and some of his friends, "guy friends" as I confirmed, I was ecstatic. It was an opportunity for us to change our luck, so I invited Rach to go with me. Even if it did mean going to a karaoke.

Karaoke was a Japanese word for "making the cat scream" (no it's not).

It's a common activity among twenty-somethings here in Asia where we would lock ourselves up in an air-conditioned booth, decorated to look like a really tacky 1980's disco with the lights and the smoke machines, sit around a couch and wait to take turn to pick up a mic and sing to a machine. A machine of all things.

And people here do this for fun. Though to be fair most apartments here are too small to host those wacky house parties we were used to back in the States. Maybe that's why people here just do karaoke instead.

Still, that does not explain why almost every one of my non-Asian friends, especially white people, get so inexplicably excited when they see karaoke for the first time and insist it was the coolest thing they have seen, ever. Ugh, what do they know?

"You've met Mark before right?" I asked Rach when we met in the lobby of the karaoke.

"What the super-rich homeboy you grew up with? Not a clue." She said sarcastically.

"I see you're being facetious."

"I see you're trying to get slapped."

"Ok I give up." As a writer, I sure understood timing was everything.

When we got in the booth I saw Mark was there with five

other people. I couldn't quite remember their names right the way, although as it would seem they were his friends from Princeton, at such I probably met some of them before back in New York.

Mark saw me as I walked in and immediately came to me to welcome us. But then something a little strange happened.

"Mark! Oh my God it's so good to see you!" Rach pretty much went right past me cutting with one swift stab of her heel, right between me and Mark, "How long has it been?"

"Rachel!" Mark clearly just remembered her name then and there, seeing that moment of frowning that quickly disappeared as it emerged, "Yes it had been a long time."

See how he avoided saying how long it actually was? Trademark Mark.

"How's things? Where's that girlfriend of yours?" Rach asked, and I must say being physically squeezed in the middle of this conversation was getting really awkward and warm.

"Oh we'd split up." He said it so casually, it almost escaped our notice.

"Oh I'm so sorry to hear that." She sure didn't look sorry though when she said it.

"It was time. She wanted to stay in Jersey so before we moved back we settled the whole thing." He must had answered this question before, judging from how complete and efficient as an answer it was.

"So what are you doing now back?" Rach wouldn't stop her questioning. Please do note that this whole time I was hovering there as big as a third wheel could be.

Well I'm back for my internship," He said, "I know, can't believe I'm still working entry-level jobs. I'm going to work at the Standard."

"Wow that means we're gonna be colleagues." She said. "which department?"

"Headquarter. I'll be working in the CEO office."

"Oh My God! Then we're gonna see each other every day!" She said. "That's cool."

Whenever Rach said "that's cool" she'd use this voice that

you didn't normally hear around her. It was between that of a sexy waitress and a cartoon character. I can't quite put it accurately, but suffice it to say as a person in the know I knew it meant only one thing: Smitten Rach.

"Wow, you'd been lobbying for that job haven't you?" Rach asked. "There's only five opening each year and the competition is fierce."

"Well actually, my dad and the CEO are golf buddies, which actually taught me a lesson, because I have applied for other jobs. It is actually very important that you knew someone in the company when you want to work there. It just the way they do things here in Taiwan." Mark said it quite normally, but I guess he then realize we weren't the right audience for that kind of talk, he added, "I hope this doesn't lower you guys' respect for me somewhat."

"Oh please, if everyone who got in there didn't have some kind of connection we would all be on the streets." This coming from the same woman who just recently was complaining about her "stupid as an inbred, got in on his mother's name supervisor".

I knew then I have played enough of a part to a conversation that I really was not a part of, "I'll go get something to eat." I said, pulling the lamest excuse possible, "You guys want anything?"

"No no we'll all go together." Mark said to me, "Everybody can get themselves", then he turned to Rach, "Talk to you later?"

"I'll probably sing to you too." She replied.

Oh dear God.

Rach was with me the whole time, when we were out at the buffet table.

"Hey!" She said.

"So now you're talking to me now?" I asked sarcastically.

"Very funny!" She said, "Thanks for bringing me!"

"You're welcome, for whatever it is."

"You'd got anymore cute guys up your sleeve?" She said with this playful stare.

"Cute?" I asked rhetorically. "You find Mark... cute?"

"Yeah don't you think? He's definitely been working out since I last saw him. Didn't you see all the muscles on him? He's like so different now, like... wow. And he is single too." Rach was always so unabashed at admitting her attraction to anyone it didn't shock me anymore, but it was to Mark. That surprised me a little bit. Mark was not exactly what I would call "her type".

"Ok, should I talk you up?" I asked her.

"Can you wingman?" She was quick to pick it up.

"Oh now I'm your wingman?" I teased her.

"Shut up!" She slapped my back, although not as hard as when she's mad.

"Haha," I laughed a little bit, "What do you want to eat?"

After she picked out all six of the dishes, we went back to the booth together.

There was a lack of conversation going around the booth, especially to me and Rach, being the newcomers to the party. At least she was being entertained by Mark, who undoubted was asking for some inside scoop to the company he's about to join.

Me on the other hand, hasn't got the hang of it with Mark's friends. They were almost exclusively Taiwanese, and almost exclusively rich. You could tell just by the trademark "Oh nothing" that all rich people would say,

"What do you do?" "Oh, nothing, just work for the family." "What do you drive?" "Oh nothing, just an Audi Coupe". "Oh yeah what kind?" "Oh nothing, nothing really."

It's always hard to start conversations with complete strangers, and it's even harder when they were rich people. So much of that relied on the subtlety of things, and one misstep you were out.

So much of their talks were criticisms. They criticise just about everything authoritatively with the words "I was there and it was the worst ever". I suppose that's what real money could buy, the authority to complain about everything with a been there, done that attitude.

What made it more difficult was how quickly they smelled or noticed that I was an ABC, which somehow created an immediate distance between us. Maybe Mark gave them the standard "English writer" intro of me while I was not paying attention?

Anyways the quiet attention from these people and the sugar coating of "well, maybe it was easier for you" were all ignored by me, as I was focusing on my turn of singing with the mic. My go-to song was "You've Lost that Loving Feeling" by the Righteous Brothers. And my go-to move was to actually get onstage.

You see people don't usually use the stage when they do karaoke as that would deny them the opportunity of reading the lines on screen, but not I. The best trick of making yourself sound good at karaoke is not in getting the words right, but by getting a little dance moves involved when you do it. They call it performance for a reason.

Not to mention the sunglasses I usually put on to channel Tom Cruise from Top Gun. The minute I put on those sunglasses the guys began to laugh, and then as I pulled the deep voice on the line "close your eyes" the laughters only grew. I could tell Rach was laughing, too, something that I have not seen her do the whole week, like really laughing.

I was so glad about how entertaining I was that I started to put in the full show. With the gruffing of the word "Baby" and the tapping and clapping for the chorus section, I went all in. By the time I was finished I got a huge applause which sounded even louder in that tiny booth. Suddenly I felt like a rock star on coke.

After my song Mark's friends began to talk to me. I guess they found out just how willing I was to embarrass myself, suddenly I was part of the conversation. They began to take my comments seriously. They took an interest in the film project that I was dabbling myself into, some people even began to talk about how they "heard about my book" or have read it somewhere. There was even plans made to going to Yilan together in the fall.

People here just wanted to be amused, to be amused by the equally poor singing of others, so they may get friendly about the stranger next to them. That's my take on the night.

I caught a few glimpses between Rach and Mark, as she seemed to be smiling at his every word. And he seemed to be more chatty than usual as well. You never realized how small these booths were until people started singing in there. I didn't know how many more Jay Chou and May Day song I could survive. But hey as long my friends were having a good time, I was having a good time too. And the rest of the night went as well as we could expect, to the point I actually caught a pretty decent sleep that night...

Mark took another sip of his W Ice Tea with the straw. It was just the two of us at the Woo Bar, a couple of nights after the karaoke night, when after a bit of chatter he asked me this,

"Are you guys close?"

"Who?" I wasn't sure who he meant.

"You and Rachel?"

"Sure we are." I said.

"Oh really?"

"Yeah we're club buddies."

"Oh," He seemed disappointed, "she's one of those girls. Is she from a good family."

"Her parents are pretty decent, hard-working middle class people I think." I answered, "Why?"

"No, just wondering. She's your friend."

He passed it off as unimportant. Frankly it upset me slightly just how swift to judgement he was to Rach. But then when that weeping face of Rach's at Haagen-Dazs suddenly emerged in my mind, I decided to perform my duty as a wingman first before my own swift judgment of the guy, and talk her chance up,

"No, no. Actually Rach usually doesn't go clubbing." Now there's a lie, I mean I first met Rach at a club for crying out loud. "We'd kinda have to push her to it sometimes."

"Really?" He seemed suspicious.

"Oh yeah. A real push." For some reason a slap from Rach to my face came to mind when I said that. God have I internalized her? "You know, I don't know how interested you are,"

Yes I did, why else would we be meeting for a drink on a night of the workday and he hasn't even left 20 minutes in as he usually did?

"I think she's actually on the market." I pushed. Again, remember, always make it their idea.

"Really?"

This time Mark's reply clearly came with more thoughts. So I pushed, indirectly,

"Oh I'm crazy. How would you need my help? You probably got too many girls lined up outside of your place waiting for you already. What was I thinking?"

"Well to be honest," Mark said delicately, "I was actually thinking that having someone who comes with a strong reference might be better."

I knew then he was hooked.

"Are you asking my help?" I asked for confirmation.

"Not the word I would use."

Mark's posture suggested command, as he kept his neck straight and his chin slightly upward, but his tone was without any changes and still the same slithering voice that sort of reassure you of his gentility.

"But hey, if you can hook a friend up then hook a friend up, alright?" He smiled as he said.

"Alright, I can do that." I said. And for once, our drink actually made it through to a proper conclusion of the night for the first night in years.

BEIJING IN THE RAIN

"Are you checking me out?"

She asked me point blank as my eyes wandered into the wrong places.

I certainly did not expect a question like that when I first met with Rach tonight.

This was supposed to be just another night hitting the clubs for the two of us. I wasn't expecting much. I just took my afternoon nap and energized myself adequately for the night to come as I have done for the week.

But instead of business as usual, I walked into Inhouse the lounge to find Rach... strangely alone. There was no crowd of her banking friends out with us, and it was the Saturday night of all nights, the biggest clubbing night there was in any city this side of the Pacific.

That wasn't all that was strange about it. My dear Rach was also exceptionally quiet. Fair that this has been a long week, and we have been meeting a lot, but that has never stopped her from talking before. If there was any one word that quickly defined Rach, it was energy, and there was none of that from her tonight. Not to mention that tonight was her idea, which meant that she'd usually prepare the twenty questions that she'd launched at me relentlessly and expecting each and every one of them to be answered up to her standards.

Instead we were so quiet in the window booth, with our drinks being closer to each other than ourselves that I began to actually worry about what to say. I watched her playing with that glass of Cosmo in her hand and still not a word out of her lips, nor had her lips touched the rim of her glass.

I couldn't stop thinking about what Mark and I talked about the other night. I couldn't help but think tonight would have been perfect to do that talk, since we were alone and everything. It was the perfect occasion, and yet I was unable to find the right topic to start that conversation. My thoughts were drifting away by something else.

How this would had been a great poster from the 50's, looking at us from the outside through the window. Me in my khaki shirt and a pair of dark blue jeans and she was wearing a black business suit and a black pencil skirt to match it, both looking out into the beyond as if searching for something to say...

"Are you checking me out?" That's when she broke the silence and shot me down with the question that brought all of what I'm writing now up. Her question almost didn't register at first, as my thoughts were still lingering somewhere else.

"No."

I sort of blushed and said. That seemed to have triggered something in Rach, for a second there I even wondered if she was possessed, but then her crooked smile just took all it back,

"Oh A-Zed, oh sweet, innocent A-Zed, are you not getting enough from your long distance GIRLfriend? Is that why you're checking me out?"

"Yes!" Then I realized my mistake, "No... Ok I don't know how to answer that question."

"You're avoiding the subject A-Zed." She said, "It's ok. I understand. A man gotta justify his own action, or in your case, his own inaction on certain matters."

"I was not checking you out!" I was so embarrassed I forgot to even catch on to her changing the subject,

"Don't you hate it when you see everybody else moving on

with their lives and you're still just... you?" She went on as if it was a speech she had prepared for years, "I mean honestly, as a friend, I really think you need to think about it. You're not young anymore. And you published what, just one book? I mean sure it gave you a good title and some sweet review from some fancy guys..."

"The New Yorker." I corrected her.

"Whatever." She was not impressed, "And now you moved miles away from New York to Taipei. I mean it's a beautiful city but it is certainly not the Big Apple. You're not pursuing some form of higher education. You don't have a real job. I mean you haven't even published a book since years ago...

"And now you're spending your nights out clubbing with a woman you don't even want to bang or to have anything serious... Like seriously, don't you feel stuck? Stuck in the way you are and couldn't get out?"

The way she took a breath and drink her drink made it look like she thought this was the perfect normal subject for a conversation between two people in a lounge. But was this really why she'd asked me to meet her tonight? Namely to bitch about... me? It's possible I supposed. But if it were true then it's...

"Don't you feel like a loser sometimes?" Her final word.

...such a bitchy thing to do. Ok, deep breath. It's not that big a deal. So she took a personal attack on you. There was no need to respond. No need to stoop to her level. Be the good, sensible friend you always were as the writer guy...

"That's not true."

But I just had to respond for the petulant child that I was.

"Which part? You haven't published a book since..."

"Of course I want to sleep with you."

She almost spit her drink back into its glass.

"What?" She cried in astonishment.

"Well Rach you're really hot." I could have stopped there but I shamelessly wanted to exploit the situation, "Relax, this is not a come on. But if you're not hot we wouldn't even have met, would we? Remember how we first met?"

"No, not really." She replied.

"Now who's lying through her teeth?" I asked knowingly. "You remember it like it was yesterday. I came over the bar and offered to buy you a drink…"

"Why are you bringing that up now?" She sounded so slow as if she was already drunk.

"To prove my original point?" I replied.

"Which is?" She hasn't caught on yet.

"That I always wanted to sleep with you?"

"So you'd always wanted to sleep with me?"

"That's right." I sure didn't see what was coming next.

"So why don't you, chicken? Why not tonight?"

She shot me a look that I'd seen before when I went clubbing with her as her wingman. I swallowed so loudly I could have been Donald Duck or some other Looney Tunes character. And that's when she slapped me in the arm, began to laugh uncontrollably and said,

"Like you'll get me drunk enough this time, HAHAHAHAHAHA!"

"I think you missed the point." But I laughed too. And suddenly it was back to normal.

"Seriously, what's going on with this girlfriend of yours? I have not seen her for so long I start to think she's just a character in your blog or something." She asked me.

"I'm not answering that question."

"Talk to me!" She exclaimed, her energy seemed to be back with the chance of hearing some gossip. "We're talking about you and your imaginary girlfriend! So talk to me! When was the last time you talk to her?"

"Just a couple of days ago." I replied, "Actually it was a really bizarre conversation, she told me that she would have to call me back, how she was busy planning some trip she was taking with her colleagues and Guido. And then she never really did. And I got busy with the shooting and everything so I kinda forgot about the whole thing."

"Guido? Who's Guido?" She pushed.

"Oh that's just her boss."

"Why would her boss go on a trip with her and her colleagues? They are Europeans, not Asians like us, they don't do boss/employee fake friendly, actually monitoring your lifestyle trips!"

"Ok that was a mouthful." I said, "I don't know, but to be fair Guido is not really her boss, he's more like her colleague. He's not that much older than her."

"Ok so a dude your age is about to go on a trip with her."

"Yes."

"I'm telling you this right now. If you don't go over and see her right now, this perfect girl of yours is gonna bang her boss over a glass of white spirit as they travel across the outskirts of China."

"That's another mouthful and again, not true." I said.

"I'm calling a meeting!"

"You're not calling a meeting!"

Quickly enough, she called the meeting. Pete and Dorian arrived shortly after being scolded by Rach on the phone and physically threatened. Yes I did mean physical. Due to our sudden increase in numbers we moved ourselves to the new whiskey bar next door. Once Rach explained the situation in an equally efficient manner, the two other male members of the family both put in their thoughts on the subject at the same time to me,

"You're an idiot."

"How could you have let this relationship go on for this long without going back to visit her? Are you trying to give her excuse to sleep with somebody else?" Pete jumped in with the first personal assault.

"Don't worry man 'cause I got the perfect solution. You see you just have to pull one of my old tricks, I would just tell her all my stories about shooting the hottest chicks in towns and oiling their legs up for a shoot; and then I would casually mention I was flying over there that night and give her my hotel room number. She'll just show up there in my room that night, all drunk and ready. Trust me, You won't even have to do the work, and it always works."

Dorian should really think about just how much harder tipsy Rach hits than regular Rach when he wanted to say something like that,

"Oh my God!" Yes, he had just got slapped.

"First thing first," And Rach took it as a cue for her turn, "how do we know if this girl is not the next Gina?"

"How's that the first thing?" I protested and I got slapped.

"We are your family so we have to look out for your safety." She replied, post-slap.

"I still don't see how this is relevant."

I protested further, this time with my arms up for surrendering.

"Didn't you know that according to the latest study, all of us single people are national security risks?" She said matter-of-factly.

"In that case you're THE real national security risk, with your history and your preference and everything..." Dorian thought he could jump in for a little retaliation, and he got slapped again.

"I move to have this item striked from this discussion." I said with my hand raised.

"Second." Pete said.

"Hey!" Rach exclaimed as she slapped Pete this time.

"Let's not get off tangent. Let's talk about the fact that the two of you," I said as I pointed at Pete and Dorian, each now sore from more than one of tipsy Rach slap, "the three of you really, did just all called me an idiot."

"And?" The minute I heard that from all three of them at the same time I knew I made a mistake, "Are you saying you're not?"

I was not ready to build a coalition here, "Moving on. What do you guys propose that I do now?"

"You know Dorian is right," Rach said, "as disgusting as it is to suggest it, but the only thing you should do is just go there and have an actual date with her for Christ's sake. Just go," and then as if I was not paying attention, she said it again, this time much more quietly, "just go."

"And you two think that too?" I asked the two other yes men that were sitting there.

They looked at each other and said to me, again at the same time,

"Yes."

And now I was here, in Beijing in the rain, one of the driest city in the world was pouring on the day that I arrived.

I flew in on the very back cabin being sandwiched by tourists as it was the only ticket that I could get on such a short notice.

For some reason, while on the flight, I thought about this week and only then realized who, not what, Rach was really talking about that night. She wasn't asking me if I was tired of being single, she was talking about herself.

That realization almost made me hijack the flight I was on and made it turn back to find her and just to tell her I understand now; I understand why she told me to just go and thank her for helping me make up my mind.

But of course I did not do it. I was not a good hijacker anyways and so it won't work. Yet the realization had kept me up the whole three hours flight there in those uncomfortable seats and the armrests that were just too close together.

As soon as I got off I called her right the way; not Maddy, Rach. I called Rach but she did not pick up. So I wanted to text her, just to tell her how sorry I was and that I was a dumbass for not realizing it, that I was a horrible friend. But then I thought about how thoughtless it would be for me to admit such a thing over the phone and not by myself.

I knew this, if I go back without sealing the deal here, Rach would just hang me on the wall and murder me. So yeah, I better get something done this time around.

A WALK ON THE GREAT WALL

I had lunch at this small Chinese diner with Maddy the next day.

There really wasn't anything that stood out about this diner; it was just like any other Chinese diner with white walls with no decoration and cheap furniture and self-serve sauce and chopsticks station.

The dishes were quickly served, no surprise there, time was money was a Chinese saying. The dishes weren't anything special either, tomato fried eggs, stir-fried mushu, and some white Chinese buns.

But the location, well,

As I looked out the small wooden window next to our table and saw there stood the Simatai section of the Great Wall, or "Tower for the Commander of Horses" a direct translation of its name, the section of the Great Wall that was bearing down on us now. It was so close to us that it made me feel really small and really contemplate our place in the world.

When you looked up you could see that it was literally shrouded in cloud and fog that from the looks of it, had been there ever since the wall was built and has now become a part of the wall, added to its charm of mystery.

The Great Wall was one of those buildings due to its sheer size and the geography it generally possessed with its location, since it was for military use the wall was usually on top of an impenetrable mountain itself, that really struck you with awe every time you see it. Not to mention it being the most recognizable building of China, a symbol of its culture which strived for security and safety above all else, meant for it to be seen close up with your own eyes.

But how did I get here? Well,

"This is such a stupid idea."

Maddy asked me to meet her at a section of the Great Wall known as JinshanLing, or the "Golden Mountain".

It was a lesser known section of the Great Wall due to its slightly inconvenient distance from the City of Beijing. Not only was it farther than the more popular Badaling section of the Wall, but the route that went to JinshanLing were mostly local roads that were harder to travel. But the picture of the Great Wall you usually see in postcards? The Prettier ones? They were taken here at JinshanLing.

Here's what I was looking at when I got there: Maddy, in her hiking outfit, wearing a pair of blue jeans, a pair of Dr.

Martens, a blue top with a white jacket, was waving me to follow her onto the wall.

Behind her was the famous JinshanLing section of the Great Wall. It was a famous tourist spot, particularly for German hikers as it was apparent to me once I saw the mostly European crowd there.

Maddy explained to me later that day they loved coming here to take a three-hours march (with their well-trained legs that were used to a weekend hiking in the German mountains), it finishes at the Simatai section, where the diner we're in is nearby.

This idea of hiking the distance of some 18 kilometer through mostly serious mountainous terrain, between 600-years-old towers and walls that had traps that might never been discovered before everywhere, Maddy seemed to expected me to say yes simply by smiling at me.

"You're crazy!" I protested.

"Come on, it would be fun!" She said, still filled with that enthusiasm.

"My dear, the people who used to do this only got paid like two dollars a month. Exactly where do you see the attractions?"

I was not hundred percent sure that the Ming Chinese soldiers who guarded this wall only got paid two dollars a month; what I was sure was that Maddy had refused to continue this subject. She simply turned around and marched toward the entrance without saying another word.

"It must be a German thing." I said quietly to myself before I began to follow her, reluctantly.

I could complain all I want, but once I was up there the humid hot summer sun suddenly became cooler, and the view, Oh dear God the view. It was beautiful, said the writer with a thousand words.

It went beyond just a simple wall. A fortification. A picture on a postcard. Even though we were followed the whole time by not the other hikers, but some local Chinese people who were eager to help take us pictures for 5RMB, there was a level of solitude around this walk that made us closer, as it would seem.

I could tell at first that Maddy was actually a bit shy that I was here. It was awkward and it took us a couple of tries before we really got started with our first conversation, with a lot of "um…" and "look at that…" and "nice day…" along the way as when I finally asked her about her travel plans, did things got on a bit right track. She revealed to me the route they would be taking: across northern China, through Inner-Mongolia, which was the part of China on the Mongolian border largely inhabited by ethnic Mongolians, before heading further North into Manchuria, the Northeast of China, the part that made up the Cock's head, if you will, of the map of China, and conclude at the City of Shenyang.

"So you're following the old Manchu trail into China in reverse." Once she laid it all out, I commented.

"Yes exactly!" She exclaimed, "That's exactly it."

Feeling pretty good about myself and the way the conversation was going, I asked, "So whose idea was it to do this trip."

"Oh it was Guido." She said,

I tried my very best to hide my disappointment at bringing up the name of what Rach said was my obvious rival,

"I wanted to have a trip before I transfer out of here, and Guido suggested this plan to me, he said he's done it before in the summer, and it was the best time. He even helped to pick which hotel to stay in and where to go horseback riding…"

"I bet he did." I thought to myself.

"So when is this transfer happening?"

"In the summer." She replied quickly.

"Sounds like a good time." I said.

"Why?" She asked.

"Because I'll be around." I replied quite simply.

I must have looked so cool there with my sleepy eyes and puffy hair style that could have only come out of a cold shower in a hotel in the morning I thought I was the most attractive man ever.

I watched the endless sky as we went passed every tower and realized, I really knew China and its history like the back of my hand. Like right now without thinking it, my mind was reciting the history of the Great Wall to me.

Great Wall was mostly remembered now either for the size of its structure, being supposedly the only man-made structure you could see in space, or the tyranny behind its building under the oppressive reign of Qin Shi Huang, the first emperor of China, who used POWs from his bloody unification campaign as slave labor to build this wall, and then disposed of them at the end of its building. The State and Dynasty of Qin under him, was now largely remembered as the Prussia Germany of China, and not in a good way.

A similar concept had been treated to the Pyramids, best remembered for the cost it took to build one man's tomb, while most of us today watched on from the viewpoint of the Israelites, awaiting for the coming of Moses.

But really, Great Wall was still great. Roman legions may have built as just many fortifications across Europe, the Middle East and North Africa at about the same time as the Great Wall, many just as impressive. But none of them would prove to be as well-preserved or as impressive as the Great Wall now. It's not hard to see why, one only simply need to look at the intent of these two armies: while the Roman legions were really political tools of ambitious Roman politicians in their vie for power, and therefore saw no need to keep permanent fortifications once they reached their mean of supreme power of Rome, Qin Shi Huang's Army was designed to unify China, and equally saw no reason to put down their fortifications once that purpose was complete.

The only downside with the inner-working of my brain though, was how unromantic it was when I was going through these tongue-twisters with myself, how little attention then I was paying to my companion. Realizing that, and feeling rather delighted by the weather and the cheerfulness that was fully-exhibited by Maddy in every move of her body, I decided to continue our subject of her travel plans.

She told me that we would meet up with Guido and Agneta, another colleague of hers that she didn't remember, at my questioning, if I have met before, at a small diner that was a ten minutes' walk from the entrance of the Simatai Section.

"So that would be where we conclude this hike?" I said, trying to hide the fact that after having been on it for nearly 30 minutes I was getting a bit exhausted.

"Yes!" She said, rather chipperly. I doubt there were any people in the world who could be as chipper with a word as simple as "yes" as the Germans.

Never mind, it was just another question my mind was trying to distract myself from the beauty that I was seeing now, both the view and the companionship I was with.

As soon as I realized that I wasn't as tired as I was before. And before I knew it, the three-and-a-half hour hike had come to an end.

Not bad for the first real date since meeting each other three months ago.

That's quite a wait for a first date. But,

Better late than never.

PUSHKIN AND ME

As soon as the four of us met up at the diner, we made our way from the Great Wall into Inner-Mongolia via bus, discounting the wisdom of my ancestors, who built the Wall in the first place to hide behind it from whatever was out of it since everything there was so damn scary.

And pretty soon I began to understand why Maddy seemed so uncomfortable about me joining her trip when we met up this morning.

It was like she'd changed into a different person over lunch, when she was so excited and lavish with her happiness, but as soon as Guido arrived she has seemed a bit distracted. I didn't mind, at least on the bus ride there had some great view. But the deeper we were into Inner-Mongolia the more I suspected. And naturally as every man would do, my suspicion fell on Guido.

Guido was tall, blonde, quite knowledgeable and annoyingly self-aware of that, and on top of that quite good looking as an European man can be. Basically he was like a female version of Maddy. And if that wasn't worrying enough, the fact that the two of them bear-hugged each other while laughing uncontrollably while speaking to each other in German and completely ignoring me should.

"How do you do, A-Zed?" Guido said to me in perfect British English as their little German-circle get-together-ritual was complete.

"I'm well." I said, rather self-assuredly in a jackass way.

After we shook hand where I rediscovered unpleasantly that he had quite a grip, I managed to embarrass myself further by allowing my language deficiency ran wild on Agneta, the fourth member of our Mongolia Safari; whose name for some reason with the "ne" and the "t" was impossible for me to pronounce correctly. However I tried the end result always sounded something like "Netherlands", And no matter how many times she laughed and eventually told me "it's ok" in a understanding and yet oddly annoying way.

Great, not only had I signed myself up for what looked to be a very physically-challenging trip with a bunch of hiking enthusiasts, I was doing it while perpetuating my own national stereotype of Americans and foreign names. Excellent. And this was the group of people I was supposed to travel with for at least another four days or so.

That won't be too big of a problem, certainly when there were other bigger problems that could distract me from. For apparently the item we would be doing next was horseback riding the next day at some random horse ranch that Guido had visited before more than once.

The ranch we were heading to was located inside this great forest park known to the locals as the "Red Mountain"; which in spite of the conservation implications of its name, also served as a hub for the local timber industry. Exactly how that works and how it was called "Red Mountain" when I saw no Red Mountain there was oblivious to me.

The relation between these three "expats", seemed to went beyond just the professional; as every time he smiled or the two girls giggled to what he was saying I wished there was a mountain lion somewhere that would jump out and maul him. Not to mention how annoying it was that all I ever heard from him in English was how important it was not to drink the local water.

Yeah I got it, I was American so I didn't travel much and didn't understand the crucial problems unsanitary water sources in certain remote areas of the world. It's not like I have travelled some thirty plus places in the world myself, some places more dangerous than Inner-Mongolia for sure. No I am not jealous.

I am just a New Yorker.

And this view had captivated every inch of my cosmopolitan, "been there, done that" attention.

When it comes to Mongolia, the word that came to mind was the word "steppe", a word to me that was filled with romantic connotations in either half of my cultural heritage; that of the Chinese and that of the American. In my bilingual mind, the word "steppe" was almost synonymous with the word "West", as in from the "The American West".

While the thing about living on the American West involved revolvers and cowboy hats, cactus and water, The thing to know about living on the Chinese steppe as it would seem, was its windiness, which might explain for the volatile nature for the weather there. En route to the ranch there has been at least two drizzles that came as quickly as they went. And then when we arrived it was so sunny it actually felt warmer by the minute. It was no help that Guido explained all this weather phenomenon to his two volunteer listeners and one prisoner who was forced to follow along in meticulous fashion while making all the jokes that only Europeans seemed to understand.

We met the owner, this small stature person with skin so dark it was as if he had spent his lifetime under the sun. Efficient like any good small business owner, he took us to the horses and assigned us each one trainer.

I was luckily assigned someone who was a Han Chinese, an elderly gentleman who could not hear well by the name of Zhang; whom I trusted if I cried "help!" He would save me from the off chance and being run down by evil animals.

And then there were the horses.

Although affectionately called "ponies" by Westerners, (Honestly I'd never understood that considering how the Mongols used to ride on these things and ravaged half of Europe) these animals were still huge when you came face-to-face with one of them. The horse that I was selected to ride was, however, by comparison, smaller in stature than the others in its herd and yet was ironically named the "the Big White". I guess ironic humor was universal for I didn't understand the white part either, since the horse to me looked a bit more grey than white.

"Come on, get on it!" Zhang said to me. His tone was this mixture of "impatient rudeness" and "kind thoughtfulness", something that I'd given up long ago to describe completely rather than simply labeling it "perfectly Chinese". I nodded in agreement while trying as uncouthly as possibly to get on this animal who may or may not drop me just 'cause it felt like it.

"No! No! The other foot!" Zhang said to me. "Oi!" He said, this time apparently something that I should know without him actually uttering it. But after that bit I'd miraculously understood and up I went on a horse's back. I guess it's just like riding a bike.

"You did this before, right?" Maddy asked me.

"Sure. Haven't you?" God the things men would say to

impress a woman.

"A couple of times." She said, somewhat worriedly. I guess she saw how I'd gotten up the horse earlier. "Guido was saying that we'd head down to this part of the ranch where they'd let us ride a bit ourselves. You don't have to come if you don't want to."

I knew she meant nice, but if the alternative was to shiver around some porta john without even a cup of coffee then I wasn't going to get off this horse; which I couldn't really, anyways.

"I'll be fine." I said as I gave her a "cowboy" salute; as if that would have made me looking any manlier than my weird of trying to keep balance while failing miserably on the back of a small horse would.

At first I tried to keep up with the trio, as I was trotting behind them after a long gap. They were all obviously more experienced than myself, as they seemed to understood how to control their horses better, while I was barely able to keep myself upright on the back of mine with it pounding against my butt and more importantly, my boys; just a couple of feet down the road I already wanted to scream and watching them chatting endlessly at a distance and laughing so loudly I could hear perfectly behind them sure fueled my inclination.

So I decided to distract myself by starting a conversation of my own.

I had few choices, with only Zhang and the horse to choose from for conversation, so I picked normal one. I spoke with Zhang, who warmed up quickly and began to tell me how rare it was to see a fellow Han Chinese at this part of China.

"The Mongols!" He said, "They're all animals! Always pretending they speak no Mandarin until they want something from you!"

I asked him how long he's been in Inner Mongolia.

"Long!" He said, "Since the service!"

And when I asked him what service, he didn't really answer. I guess at this part of China people all had something they didn't talk about.

But nature had its way with people, as I began to immerse myself into the surroundings. It was truly a beauty being around here, flowers of different origin, endless fields of grass and cattles and sheeps size of Volkswagens that numbered to the same the number of taxis in China roaming free in it, yet it was so spacious it was as if you could see the end of the world over the horizon.

I cannot describe my feelings at the moment. Except perhaps that I began to relate to how Mongols could have produced someone like Genghis Khan and his genocidal horde of an army in an environment like this. This was truly where the tough gets going. This was where you would lie down in the grassfields and felt as if you could reach the sky as you looked up into it. It was a feeling as if you were your own limit, and anything was possible with a horse, a scimitar and a bow and arrow. It didn't justify anything; rather that it made me understand; creating something common between me a City Boy and the Mongols of Ancient Central Asia.

My horse trotted on, as the gap between me and the party in front grew further, Agneta, whose smaller stature seemed further minimized next to the towering Guido and Maddy, turned around and shouted to me, "Come on!"

I'd waved my hand and signaled them to move on with a smile. This time a genuine one. I saw that she turned and told the others something in German, and then this time it was Maddy who turned around and, seeing that I was ok, smiled at me, before turning around as they began to gallop ahead.

"You want follow?" Zhang asked me in mandarin.

"Not a problem, 'old sir'," I said, using the traditional Beijing title translated as "lord" or literally "old sir" literally in English affectionately.

"Aye." He said. I guess he understood. "You see them small yellow flowers?"

"Yeah?" I guess he felt obliged to have some small talks with me now that I had addresses him with respect.

"They are poppy flower. Those Mongols use them in their tea to get high." He said.

"Maybe that's what makes the magic?" I thought to myself with a smile, delighted by my little jab that entertained myself. At that precise moment I felt the wind blowing and little drops of water fell, little by little, and while I would not say anything got soaked, I still said to Zhang,

"It seems like a rain."

"Hum?" He groaned. I guess the wind made it a little harder to hear.

"I said it looks like a rain." I said it again, this time louder.

"Rain? That happens all the time! All the time!" He shouted back.

"Oh, ok." I agreed simply.

I thought about asking him if we should head back. But seeing how he's not stopping, and that Maddy and the others were so far ahead and didn't seem to have any intention of stopping, I wasn't gonna be the first one call it quit.

God the things we men do to impress a woman.

By this point I began to feel a bit more comfortable with this horse. For a horse with an ironic name, Big White was a very nice horse. For one it didn't try to throw me off. And it's got good temperament. If you ask me how I know that well, let me just point out, it did not throw me off its back. And just like every man, when things get comfortable, I wanted to try and mess it up. So just as I was about to give it a little kick like in those western movies, suddenly Big White "preemptively" groaned.

"What's the matter?" For some reason I was actually saying that to the horse. But of course Zhang turned around and said,

"Wha?" and he saw the horse and somehow immediately understood it without speaking. "You wait." He said to me and proceed to unbuckle the saddle, with me still on it.

That's when I thought if any time it was perfect for Big White to throw me to the ground and break my neck, this would be it. I began to remember all the stories I have read about 18th century cavalryman and the sad tale of their life expectancies in combat and how often they broke their necks. Just when I have gotten myself so worked up I thought I was gonna wet myself, I heard a strong psss noise coming from under me, and all I thought was, "Surely that could not be me."

I looked down and realized that, well, the horse, instead of me, was taking a leak.

"Good boy." Zhang said to the horse as he buckled the saddle back upright when it was done. And off we went.

The climate here was indeed volatile, quite harsh for the average person unused to this kind of plain weathers. And yet it crossed my mind that this would be perfect to set as the backdrop of Shakespeare's "Tempest". You would just have to change the ship into a caravan and made it all about the Silk Road. Make it a mix between "Tempest" and the Chinese classic of "Journey to the West". That makes sense.

I'll talk to Charlie about that idea when I get back, or when my internet connection liberates itself from the Great Wall of China.

Mongols weren't the first of China's great power that arose from the status of horse breeders. Qins, arguably the first who unified China into a nation state, were Imperial Horse Breeders for the Zhou Kings. The Qins as a people claims their origin from the legendary Yi, the almost king of China who was forced out when Yu, the king at the time, who was known as the legendary engineer who cleared up the Yellow River, defied the meritocratic tradition of the time, passed over his trusted lieutenant and instead passed his crown to his son.

The Chinese liked to claim invention on many things, but I suppose a legend this old may not entirely be fabrication. I suppose there was an off-chance that China began with a system of meritocracy and professionalism much earlier than the West. Perhaps they were right to arrogant about their history.

Contrary to popular thoughts, before the modern US driven globalized economy existed, China had long advocated a system of global trade and cultural exchange, with the Dragon Emperor and his advanced and yet kind subjects leading the world much like the American Hegemon. The Chinese created the first system which emphasized the rule of law, true equality of rights, and first understood the industrial power of communes and villages.

In these commune and villages, clever merchants made fortune by branding and selling silks produced from organized village labor of one region to nationwide, and then to the world. In those days China was the envy of the world, and the market the world sought after to enter. And all this, perhaps, because of that endless horizon that they could look over when they were here, and dreamt of the limitless.

There was indeed something poetic about the steppe, as Pushkin summed it up so well in his Eugene Onegin. Rus had no monopoly of that pride, however; only the Chinese, whose power created many things, including the Mongolian Empire that Stretches from one end of the world to another, can.

When Big White, Zhang and me finally caught up with the others to the free ride zone, it began to rain so heavily, as if the mythical flood was about to arrive.

"Oh dear we'd better get going!" Guido shouted, to the benefit of all of us.

While I watched them scramble, with Guido having a hard time controlling his ride, who was possibly frightened by the sudden downpour I saluted to them in the style of Chiang Kai Sheik, the pathetic Prussian Fool who made the West dreamt about the contemporary Lost Christian King, knowing full-well that this might be the last time that I was this comfortable with an animal, as I said to Zhang and the horse, lightly,

"Let's get outta here."

At my command we swiftly turned around, our trio, and head back to where this all started.

The next day we headed towards the Gobi Desert. Gobi Desert is massive, and the specific part of it we were heading today was an oasis national park, which is in the middle of a mountain system that used to mark the ancient border between civilized China from the lands of the Barbarians.

You see, I knew what I was talking about. I didn't need a

tall, blond German man basically repeating these facts that I already knew to me on our whole bus ride there; a bus filled with tourists that Guido had set up for us to tag along with. This travel agency he knew well agreed to take us on for this part of their tour which saved us a little money in the process.

This bus ride would take us some 120 km away from the hotel we were staying near the ranch to the oasis park. You have gotta give in to the Guido's ingenuity. Even I began to like him if my penis wasn't constantly telling me to kill him.

But I promise I won't complain so much today, not after I have become the center of attention ever since I showed up this morning for the hotel breakfast with a flask in my hand.

"What's that?" Maddy asked me while using her chopsticks like a real Chinese person.

"It's a flask." I said. Turns out my dry humor or no humor was perfect for the Germans as she laughed and said back to me,

"I know. I meant what's in it."

"Just you know... good stuff." I replied secretively.

Then when we got on our bus ride to the desert, both Guido and Agneta got curious about my flask the same way Maddy had. So I told them it was just something to drink since we would be heading to a desert today.

"Good idea, you could dehydrate there awfully fast." His "awfully" very British for some reason, which did not sit well with the American in me.

"Can I have some later?" Agneta asked me with a smile.

"Sure." I replied.

The content of my flask was actually coffee. Not just any coffee, it was Yirgacheffe, a type of specialty coffee bean produced in Ethiopia. I brought it with me from Taipei. It was given to me by Flynn, when I went to visit him in his Tamsui Mansion, shortly before I left.

"It's the perfect aphrodisiac!" That was what he said to me as he handed me this little bag of coffee beans. Of course, that was before he spent about fifteen minutes trying to pronounce the word Yirgacheffe and telling me all the great sex he's been having with Gina, all the while I was trying very hard not to listen to him and stared at just how the dining room needed cleaning as it had become quite dirty. "I would not have my brunch here," I thought.

I sure hope he was taking care of himself. But Flynn would not be Flynn if he was not a passionate man, so there really wasn't a point worrying for him unless he was worried himself.

When I got off my flight I took a ride around Beijing and bought what I still think was the most expensive cheap coffee grinder ever, along with a travel coffee maker, which was this plastic funnel along with some coffee filter paper; all of which I had to carry around my long and arduous travel across these lands, a road so far of perhaps 300 km, before I used the apparatus this morning to make my coffee in my room.

Though I must say, having spent three days of travelling rather difficult terrain with these German people who were all in such good physique, as we hike along the Great Wall, or horseback riding across the steppes of Inner-Mongolia, I did feel rather good about myself.

All the working out paid off and I was becoming more aware of the weather conditions around, the often changing sky of the steppes. I found the perfect attire for it, consisted of a light waterproof sport jacket, T-shirt with jeans, and I would never leave my scarf now hanging around somewhere that wasn't my own body, the same with my hat. Finally a haughty New Yorker such as myself was made aware why those Southwest Americans, Texans especially, wore those hideous cowboy hats. Their terrain must be just as windy and changeable as the steppes of Northern China.

It was quite a bit of walk from where we got off the bus to we were going, the hilltop that had the best vantage point to look over the entire oasis park. But it was nothing that I have not gotten used to by this point.

We first slowly climbed up the sand dunes, then a further climb up this small rocky slope, before we got to this metal ladder that went up a rock that was perhaps five-men high. And yet in this process I barely broke a sweat.

It would have been the perfect place for a kiss, if you have seen the view. Before today I never understood why a lot of botanologist and geologists have talked about the importance of studying the habitat system of an oasis in order to understand the complexities of desert life and politics in certain areas of the world with these geographical features, areas such as the Middle-East and Central Asia.

It was a feeling quite different from when we rode on horseback through the Mongolian steppes the day before: there it was about the limitless nature of a man's life, while here in the desert it was the opposite, the message here was the overwhelming sense of mortality, the realization that everything we did in life had its boundaries and reach, as the endless amount of wasteland composed of sand was a reminder to us all the limits of human ambitions.

Oasis, because of its role as an important source of water supply, were to desert warfare as instrumental to victory as the high grounds and the major cities; any long existing oasis system, you could put your bet on it being once a slaughter ground between different factions vying for power.

Watch your westerns, remind yourself how many of those long chases on horsebacks ended with an ambush next to an oasis?

Yet as I sat on top of the hill, looked over the desert that probably at one point of history lied thousands of my ancestors here dead, rotting under the sun and were made food to the vultures, the only thing that concerned me seemed to be Maddy, and how I couldn't kiss her right there and now.

You may find me heartless. But history has no place when you're with a girl that captured every attention of yours.

Maddy was genuinely happy. She seemed to be able to find the freshness in things, wherever we went. I watched as she played with the sand, as she got fascinated by the different kind of local vegetation that grew in conjunction with one another which would be difficult to find in a warmer climate.

The four of us were the first to get on top of the rocky hill, and looked down at perhaps the most beautiful sunset in this world: the remains of the day in those red ray of the sun washed down through the sands, the water pawn, the small pocket of grass and then, us.

We sat down and formed a circle in awe of the view. As we sat there, with my jeans filled up with sand, I opened my flask and poured some of that coffee out. the smell was amazing, it came out of the container like perfume out of a spray bottle. I had a sip, before I tagged Maddy, who was staring straight into the sun with her left hand covering up half of her face, and passed to her the now-opened flask,

"What? Oh, you brought coffee?" She asked.

"That's what was in the flask." I said teasingly, "Want some?"

"Yes please." She replied.

So I passed her the flask, and watched her have a sip from it the coffee I brought from Taipei, freshly grinded and brewed this morning.

After Maddy passed me back the flask, as the man of my word that I was, I passed it around the circle to Agneta, and then Guido.

"Wow this is very good." Agneta was at first a bit shy to drink out of the same flask, but after some encouragement from all of us she did. And clearly she did not regret it.

"Ah it smells very nice. It's Ethiopian isn't it?" Guido asked me after his smell and sip.

"Yes. Yirgacheffe." I replied.

"Very good coffee. It's really nice to have some of this in the afternoon because the caffeine isn't quite… what's the word? Strong, as would with other coffee."

"Yes, and we're drinking it just as they did in the desert, sitting around a circle and passed it around as it create a bond between all of us today."

They quite agreed with my romanticism. And it was like with the nodding and the smiling, our relationship deepened. There were no words. No words were necessary. Suddenly there was no barrier of language or culture. We became four people sitting around a rock in the desert, drinking coffee together.

"So is this why you guys came to work in China? To have coffee in the middle of the Gobi Desert?" I asked, trying to make a footnote of what today's trip meant to all of us.

But I guess no answer was necessary. The view was just too beautiful for a footnote like that.

THESE HUMID NIGHTS

I woke up the next day around 5AM mostly out of necessity…
As apparently the desert sun comes out quite a bit earlier than
in the civilized world.

Waking up at those hours was no fun for any human being,
let alone me. I was just glad that some of my regime of gym
and diet were still in effect and not completely ruined by the
filmmaking and the wingmanning of the past month.

We headed for breakfast from the revolving restaurant on

the top floor. It seemed to be the most fashionable thing for Chinese hotels. Ever since the success of the Beijing International Hotel back in the early 90's, every government-funded Five Star Hotels in the second and third tier cities were all built with one of those on its top floor, until it became out of fashion even in the most remote of these hotels.

Our group have gotten closer since the coffee sharing yesterday. No longer was I the awkward fourth wheel in the group. We joked about how much faster we were ahead of the Chinese tour group on every step of the way, which as anyone in the know knew it was quite difficult to do (as most average Chinese person were too physically fit to beat on a race like that). How stupid it was for us to be drinking coffee in an environment where we were supposed to be keeping ourselves hydrated and monitored our heart rates. Of course, clumsy performances on horseback was one of the topics as well.

And before I knew it, it was time for another long bus ride.

Over the years, having travelled to many places myself, I must say if I had the choice I would travel by land over flying every time. Not so much that I was part of the fear of flying crowd that grew significantly in our Post-9/11 world, but more about what you would be missing if you went by air.

Sure travel by land usually take longer, but with planes there's always the possibility of delays, (which was as common in China as it was in the US) the hassle of security checking, that they almost cancel out the fun.

(This one time in an inland Chinese airport, a couple of years ago, this middle age gentleman who was passing the security checkpoint in front of me simply took out a short knife from his bag. When the security people told him that he couldn't bring it with him onto the flight, he replied rather sharply "How am I gonna eat my pears then?" To this day I still smile when I remember that incident)

All the things you would see on the road were different from country to country. In the US, for example, every town you come to past, even during the winter when things weren't as visible, was slightly different from the one before. You have your beach towns, your old factory towns that looked dirty from years of not operating, and regular suburbs with just houses and very little else. You knew just by looking, which towns were the suburbs and which were the city centers. Each town is different, and embraces its own diversity with its town flags and banners.

In Taiwan, for some reason, most towns were always so closely-knitted and interlocked with one another. Every town is so close to the next it is like a long stretch of a megacity as you went past them. The farms are right next to the small factories, factories next to the high rise luxury homes, as everything got mingled together into a big blur on the speed of the highway.

In China, it is about progress and history, two that are perhaps not at their finest, but certainly at their most ruthless. It is a sight filled with anachronisms: small villages completely without the use of electricity, modern piping, working with farm tools powered by animals that sits next to an automated factories and a hundred-stories high office buildings from the twenty-first century. It is like two hundred years of human progress melt together into one big neighborhood.

It is a moment where you were hit by both power and sadness at the same moment: empowered by the days to come, and sadden by the very same foretold future, as you watched in these cities hundreds of miles of wasteland raised for cities to be built, and jobs to be created. It is not the end, it is but a step to move on. But what a step that is.

And we travelled on, the four of us sitting with thirty others in a tour bus towards our destination, the city of Shenyang, as we leave all this Chinese countryside behind us.

Shenyang was, basically, a city built for war.

It started as a military fort that guards trades and intimidates the local Manchu tribes. As the Manchus became unified under the leadership of Nurhachi, the future first emperor of the Qing Dynasty, the city was quickly conquered by them. And it was from Shenyang where he and his sons began the process of conquering Ming China.

Since then, Shenyang became the political and military center of the Qing Dynasty in their dominion outside of the Great Wall, a status that remained unchanged throughout their 300 years run in spite of them moving their capital to Beijing after the conquest. Hence the city's old name, Mukden, which meant quite literally "by heaven's will".

Shenyang's connection with war did not end with the establishment of the Qing Dynasty and the prosperity of Eighteenth Century China. At every street corner here there is a monument commemorating the war, a different war that to the memory of every mainland Chinese people started with the infamous "Mukden Incident". The most standout of these monument is the giant stone plaque inside the Mukden Incident Museum in the middle of the city, upon it forever frozen in time is the date September 18th 1931

Indeed, if there are any two cities in China more embedded with its memories of WWII it would be Shenyang and Nanjing, and the Chinese are a very unforgiving people when it comes to their history. Yet whereas Nanjing is forever shrouded in the fogs of its past and completely devoid of life, Shenyang is spirited; it is moving on from the history that once occupied its entire meaning to the memories of others. Like a lot of Chinese cities, under the slogans of prosperity it marches with feverish loyalty under the banner of New Chinese Socialism towards progress.

Though if you examine the history of the city it's again hard not to see why it is Shenyang's term now for development and prosperity in the great plan of Chinese Socialism.

During the Civil War of 1945-49, old Manchuria, of which its traditional capital was the city of Shenyang, was the first major area of China to be fully "liberated" by the Communists. To many Yan'an maybe the cradle of Chinese Communism, but old Manchuria was where it reached adulthood. It was through consolidation of its control here, that the Communists were able to march into Beijing City and declared the founding of the Republic back in October 1st 1949.

This made the city holy ground to many Chinese people, even as it dramatically revamped itself. There was construction everywhere when we came in to town. The city was building two subway lines, the entire market street had been rebuilt into a pedestrian zone matched with malls and major commercial brands instead the old rickshaw stands. Someone told us that the city was also constructing the high speed rail stations and expanding its airport.

I have seen this before in other Chinese cities. In Beijing before the 2008 Olympics, in Shanghai before the 2010 Shanghai Expo, and Guangzhou before the Asian Games. Each time, there was great enthusiasm around the city in the name of progress. Although there were inescapable political connotations, it was nice to see these cities in China with your own eyes, seeing them building something from the ground up. It gives those of us from a developed-country's background a perspective of the rags-to-riches enthusiasm that has gone missing in most of our upbringing, as what were stories for made-for-TV movies in the West are often stories of a whole community of people here in China.

We needed a stay in a modern city after days spent on the outskirts of Northern China; a place where we could rejuvenate with some city nights out. So after we checked into our hotel, we agreed to grab a quick dinner on the shopping street before we decide what we were going to do later that night.

There was a small rain that night, but it ended quickly. For a city this far north and windy it was surprisingly humid here.

A number of suggestions were offered up for what we were going to do. The more traditional street side yakitori was predictably brought up, which we would either follow up with Karaoke or maybe a techno bar.

I however, had a different idea.

"Let's go to a Salsa Club." I said.

"A Salsa Club?" Maddy said with her wide-eyed curiosity as always, "What's a Salsa Club? I'd never been to one here."

"You've never been? It's one of those places where people go to dance some salsa over drinks." I said, "There's nothing more China than that, trust me. I can't believe you guys have never been to one."

"Do you know a place like that around here?" She asked me.

"No. But I'm pretty sure I could find one pretty easily."

And did I find one easily. You see all you had to do was find the bar street that is usually right next to the shopping street, and there on the corner there usually is one. It was the same in every Chinese City. It wouldn't say Salsa Club on the door. But if you go in there, there would be a dance floor filled with people of different ages and level of dance skills there just to dance over a glass of mediocre cocktails. Also the fact that I saw one on our way into the city earlier today also helped with my search.

When we got there had about eight pairs that were already on the dance floor. But really, Salsa, Samba or rumba, throw me whateva.

A dance is the perfect way to find out things about your partners that you couldn't really find out with words. It's a form of conversation, which I did not learn about until my first time dancing with a girl: I found out more about her than I ever did in the same class with her for two years: how she liked astrology, what she thought about having fun, and how she liked "taller" gentlemen; I've always wondered why Flynn had such an edge with the ladies, and I knew why then.

Agneta, the shy and not quite talky Agneta, turned out to be the best dancer out of all of us, which came as a surprise even to her colleagues. She was just one of those people that was really naturally really quick to catch the beat. In fact Agneta was so good, that even though she never danced the salsa before, she quickly got the hang of it and began to teach the others who were just picking up.

Guido clearly had some classic ballroom dancing training, but nothing quite as upbeat as this, my guess is it was probably something like the Waltz. I myself actually knew the salsa pretty well, good enough to lead and teach Maddy, who was having a hard time picking it up. It wasn't her fault really, dancing was always harder on taller people. And to be honest, I enjoyed it.

We had great fun, so much that by the time I noticed how long we've been on the floor without break I was already quite exhausted. Early hours did that to me sometimes. So after one more pairing with Agneta, who kept saying from the start that I danced very well (where did she get that idea?), I went aside, sat down at our table and used a glass of mojito as an excuse and watched them danced on.

I was sweating a bit, from the small exercise we'd just had, the poor air-conditioning of the club and the humidity of the night. I finished my mojito quite quickly and as I expected, it tasted low on the alcohol and the mint, so I quickly asked for a second one.

My mind was drifting a bit, as I was reminded of a different place from a city of a different continent all of a sudden:

It was a bar, similarly lit as this one, with sweaty air, also due to lack of proper air-conditioning, and quite noisy with all the college kids, such as I was, sitting around, taking forever to drink that one drink they only had money for that night while chatting endlessly on some subject that I was sure, wouldn't mean that much a year from that moment on.

Marian took me there. It was sort of our first date, now looking back with hindsight. Although of course being college kids with ego the size of the world, we said we were just "hanging out".

"So you wrote a books about New York, but you've never actually been here before?"

I still remember how unconvinced she looked when she asked me that question. And how I thought that look she gave me, one of disbelief mixed with tempting haughtiness, was exactly how I would have imagined a New Yorker would look like when I was writing my books.

So I signaled her a "V" with my right hand, which stood for the number two.

"Two. Two books based in New York without ever being here."

"You're such a dork." I'd say the same as her had I saw myself doing that in the mirror.

"Thank you."

"I respect that though." She said.

"Respect what?" I asked.

"You, being a writer." She said, "I mean a lot of people I know said they'd write a book or they wanna be a writer but you're the first person I met who actually wrote something and is pushing to have it published." She said while playing with her drink, a vodka tonic was it? It had a green straw, that's for sure.

"I respect that." She concluded.

"Thanks for that too."

The rest of it was a bit of a blur. All I remember was that we did some more drinking with her friends, these two girls she'd known since High School. I did some shots. We danced a little. And afterward...

It was a mid-September night in the Big Apple. The heat of the day stayed well past midnight. When we left the bar her friends said they were going clubbing. And then Marian told them she was gonna pass as she had to write a paper for tomorrow. So it was just me and her.

I remember, how it was odd for me that I didn't feel the warmth creeping up my cheeks, what we'd call blushing. I didn't have a rush of blood coming up my back and to the head. I felt no nervous energy as I listened to the clacking sound her necklace, or I should say necklaces, were making as we walked the streets of New York.

"So what's Taipei like?" She asked me.

When it came to questions like that, I always wanted my answers to be as complete as could be:

"A lot like this weather, just not as many clubs but more street food."

"Oh, is that what you guys call 'night markets'?" She clearly knew her globe.

"Yeah. That's how we tell if you're foreign or not, actually."

"Oh yeah?" She seemed intrigued.

"Foreigners always asked for direction to night markets."

"Is that right?"

"Yes." And I went on, "And actually for some reason all of my non-Taiwanese friends would get fat from eating those. Because you know, those food are usually really fattening and bad for your health. But the average Taiwanese people are quite fit, even though they ate the same food, with more frequency. Somehow they just don't get fat from it."

She chuckled, "And they say there are no differences between people in this world."

"Yeah, go figure." I replied.

"It must be genetic." She said thoughtfully, "Maybe I should major that."

"You haven't declared your major?" I asked.

"Nope." She said, "I always tell myself I have time."

"Wow things are different here." I said. "Back in Taiwan, if you went through the local system, you pretty much had to decide what you want to study in high school. And if you're from my family and you're in uni and still didn't know what your first job is gonna be? It's a problem."

"Are you sure you're not FOB?" She asked me with complete disregard of the connotation of her words, which I must say I quite liked it at the time.

"No," I said, "No way."

"Why not?"

"I DON'T want to fit in here so badly, so I can't be FOB."

My answer got her laughing a bit. We crossed the road and were now only two blocks away from the dorm building I was staying in.

"I like this neighborhood."

I said quietly almost just to myself.

"You like East Vill?" I guess she caught it.

"Yeah. Love the graffiti." I said. There were a lot of them around but really I was only picking up something so that we could have something to talk more.

"Ok," my argument galvanized her somewhat, so she asked as she pointed to one of the walls, "what does that one mean?"

She was pointing at this one Smiley Face on what I thought was a roller shutter of a Kebab Place.

"Mona Lisa?" I really thought I was being funny, though her chucking seemed to confirm it.

"How about that one?"

This time it was a cat sitting casually and smoking.

"Whistler's Mother?" I replied.

"And that one?"

This was 2, maybe 3AM in the morning. I had no idea where all her energy came from. What was more confusing was, for a guy who once past 1AM become radically tired and short-tempered, I was willing not only to indulge her with my ridiculous answers at whatever question she was throwing at me, but I was actually happy doing it so.

And before I could make another clever remark. Before I realized she wasn't pointing at anything anymore. Before I felt her lips against mine, we kissed that night.

It was as she slowly moved away I looked at her and asked, "Why?"

"No why. Just 'cause." She said to me.

It was a night as humid as tonight, years ago, when I kissed the girl I loved for the first time.

And now, back in China, back in the salsa club in Shenyang, I was finishing my second mojito. Maddy was getting out of the floor while Guido and Agneta were still down there dancing.

I ordered two more mojitos and asked Maddy if she wanted to get some fresh air outside, since it was so warm in here. She said yes and we went out together.

Just as we got out, with the door shutting the music away behind us, as she was just looking at both sides of the road to see what was around, I caught her from behind with her eyes widened, and we kissed. When it was over, as her green eyes were still wide and staring right at me, she asked me,

"But why?"

And I answered: "No why. Just 'cause."

ALWAYS STAY WANTED

"Always Stay wanted."
That is the Marian mantra for dating.

The next day, for the last tourist attraction on our list, we went to an underground river, the longest one in China, if not the world, something like 18 km long. It took us quite a while to get in and out of it on the speedboat we took.

For the most part of our trip, we were dressed up in these red winter coat at the entryway, which with their "Asian friendly" size meant that we all ended up looking like the little red riding hood wearing them. Especially the girls, with Agneta winning this contest, already the dancefloor champion of last night, who had the most likeness to the children's book character.

As we went in this long, crooked tunnel that led us to the boatyard, I tried not to think about Maddy and the kiss we had last night. So I sat next to Guido at the back, who as the European gentleman that he was urged the ladies to sit at the front "which had the better view".

I've never been to an underground river before, the strength of the current surprised me. Even though we were in motor boats I could still feel the stream pushing us back.

The current was so strong, and the place was dark, there

really wasn't much to see around, almost everything in there you had to feel their presence. All I could do was sit in there and tried not to get sick. Fortunately this being the most physical trip I have taken yet, my body was pretty well-trained to face anything.

Probably because we couldn't see much in there, but it felt like we came right back out as we got in. As we got off the boat and were ushered towards the exit, we stood next to the area where we were to return our jackets and that's when we couldn't resist the temptation and took pictures for each other in our early Halloween costumes. Agneta really looked the part, but my eyes were on Maddy the whole time.

I tried not to. It's not nice staring at the girl you kissed just last night the next day. It goes against the mantra. You need to be cool to stay wanted. But I had to; that's just what Maddy did to you. She made you forget all about the rules.

I wasn't sure how she felt about last night. Actually to be completely honest I did not know how I felt about it, even as she came completely into the camera frame on my iPhone smiling, I didn't know.

Then it was my turn. And when I saw myself in that ridiculously small jacket, with a smile almost as big and full as Maddy's in her picture, it suddenly made sense to me. I knew what I had to do next.

So over dinner I declared that I would be heading back to Taiwan tomorrow.

They were surprised, of course. Maybe it was my imagination but I thought Maddy was the most surprised. They asked me to stay, but I said I had to take care of some things back home, so they didn't insist. I invited them to come to Taiwan for a visit, out of courtesy of course. But I was honest.

After we got back to the hotel, I went back to my room and began to pack. I travelled light and I didn't buy much, so I had it done awfully fast. I was then about to draw myself a bath and unwind one last time before tomorrow, as I thought about whether this mantra I questioned every time I used it would work this time, when someone knocked on my door.

I thought maybe it was one of those escort pusher leaving behind a business card or something. So imagine my shock when I opened the door and about to look down when I saw Maddy standing there instead.

"Hey." She said, cheerfully.

"Hi." I replied.

"So we were just gonna get some drinks and play cards at my room. You wanna join?"

Her "you wanna" and "my room" being in the same sentence almost gave me a heart attack, but I quickly composed myself. "Maddy, did you really come just to ask me to play cards with you guys?"

"Yes," She answer me like the honest German she was.

"Ok." I said, "let's play some cards."

When my train arrived in Beijing South Station the next day it was already late in the afternoon. It was raining out there, but I had to be quick if I wanted to make my flight back to Taipei. I rushed out and took my quickest turn to take the airport subway line.

I barely made it with enough time to check in. After I passed customs it was already time to board.

My seat was in coach, behind this Chinese mother and son travelling together. The son, who was around fifty years old, was clearly someone who has flown frequently; while it was the first ride on an airplane for his 70 years old mother. Evidence mounted as she almost had a manic episode when we took off. As she needed to be reminded FIVE times that there was a reading light she could switch on and off when she complained that it was "getting too dark in there". And the fact that she whispered loudly to her son that she wanted to turn down the inflight dinner because she didn't want to spend extra money; and when she found out it didn't, she tried to ask for two, and was very please to find out there was refill to her drinks.

I was glad that some people still find flying in a jet plane exciting.

Not me though. I have flown so many miles in my life I

should have lifetime membership for all the frequent flyer miles I accumulated.

There I was, being thrown around as the wind made special by Northern China and sat there calmly like a man who's been there and done that. But if it threw anything, it did not throw my mind away. I began to thought about what Flynn said at the brunch, about why here? And I thought the best way to boil down his long, profanity-laced speech was this one question:

"Are we really so different?"

That's a very politically loaded question, as we lived in a campfire society now that was all about holding hands around the fire singing kumbaya, a society all for assimilation of our interests rather than recognizing the differences. The no-scoreboard world: where we were supposed to enjoy just the game and not keeping scores. where we discount personal efforts in the name of team spirit. We believed in keeping to ourselves the differences we might have with one another in the quest of creating a single, harmonious world.

But we could not truly embrace each other by suppressing our differences; for that would be the same as pushing down our identities, the things that made us us. We must learn to understand each other, and for that we must learn where our differences are.

I am an ABC, being "different" is the one thing I have to embrace growing up as part of myself. For my parents, I am the "American kid". For my classmates, I am the "Asian kid". For the local Taiwanese, I am the "foreigner".

ABC is already by far the more generalized and blunt term of endearment I grew up with. And I embraced it. It took a while, but once I realized that I would stand out no matter what and where, I took it upon myself to never try to be otherwise. The equality of my heritage had ensured of that.

And look at my life, look at the places I have been, the things I have seen and the friends I have made. I have a Spanish brother. I went out drinking frequently with a Canadian College Professor obsessed with everything theater. I hit the clubs with two people, one guy and the other girl, that would never get along without me being around. I wouldn't have all this if I did not embrace all the differences we have with one another.

People said friendship is about being able to see things eye to eye. I disagree. I find it more important to have that difference. For when you and friends could stand on two sides of the seesaw, it was much easier to reach a balance, and keep the relationship going.

That may not answer Flynn completely to his satisfactory, but at least it's a start.

The service light from the seat in front of me was on again. I supposed it was the mother who needed another blanket. But this time it was actually her son, who wanted to order some Duty Free,

"I'll be right with you oh!" the flight attendant said in perfect Taiwanese accent as she went back for the merchandises. Taiwanese people love to end their sentences with an 'oh'.

"Did you hear that? She's really Taiwanese! 'I'll be right with you 'or'!" Said the son, excitedly to his mother, imitating that "oh" the stewardess said with his strongly Northern accent that had turned it into an "or".

That little act of jest seemed to have attracted some attentions, as all the neighboring passengers began to laugh at his mimic act. Suddenly it felt like the whole cabin was around some campfire, holding their hands and laughing together.

I guess we were not so different after all.

PARTY SEASON

It did not take long for me to integrate back into my life in Taipei after such a long trip away in the countryside of Northern China. I was not so seasoned that I needed time to get back into the city life, as I was born to adapt to changes quickly.

When I came back and checked my Facebook for the first time in weeks this side of the Great Wall and found out I was invited to attend "the premiere"; not just any premiere, but one that involved the one picture I had a hand in making.

That's right, Charlie's movie is gonna hit the big screen.

It is the summer in Taipei, and summer is party season here in this city.

Let this be that first big splash of the summer.

Here's how I found out about it. The first morning after I got back, I had a forceful visit from Rach, who couldn't wait to hear me confirm that she was right about me going on this trip.

"Wasn't I right?"

"Don't gloat." I knew just what to say, "It makes you look fat."

That's when she punched me in the arm. "The next one

won't be so nice." She said.

"I realized that." I said as I nursed my wounded arm, "But yes, you were right. We kissed."

"No way!" She exclaimed with excitement, quite loudly as it echoed around my small apartment.

And that's when Charlie sent me a text and asked me to attend a premiere where he and a number of other directors' work would be shown together in front of a group of people.

I hate to correct him on the difference between a premiere and a showcase, especially since I took part at his work. And the opportunity of seeing it on the big screen, with a real audience was just too tempting to be questioned.

That's the charm of film-making, no matter how the artform faded, everyone had a story somewhere in their heart that they wanted to see on the big, silver screen.

"So do you wanna go?" Since she was right there, I asked Rach.

"Who's going to be there?"

"Well Dorian definitely would want to go to these things. And Pete would kill me if I don't invite him again." I explained, "He's still sore from not being part of the production. Mark is probably gonna be there. And of course Flynn…"

I could barely say the words "the usual crowd" before I realized how inappropriate my guest list was. Rach was an explicit person, both in words and with her face. She couldn't hide how upset she was when she heard Flynn's name. But she quickly hid her momentary displeasure away and said,

"So Mark is coming hm?"

"He should be." I replied cautiously.

"That's interesting."

"Why's that interesting?"

"No reason." She wasn't telling me something.

"Do you guys hang out more now that you're in the same company?"

"Not really. It's a big company and we're not exactly in the same department." She replied quite quickly, "So there's gonna be other guys around?"

"Yes. It's a premiere." I answered.

"Alright, then I'm definitely going."

When you attended something called a "premiere" it's all about the glamour. It's all about showing up at the right time, with the right clothes, the right car, and most importantly, the right date.

And that's why I came by the bus, without a date and appeared in nothing better than blue jeans and a shirt from Shimending.

(That's like an area for indie shops here in Taipei, guys)

The premiere was hosted at this small studio on the third floor of a five-story building. On its first floor was a seafood restaurants, by this hour was already filled with people drunk on beer, kaoliang and drunken shrimps.

At first I thought I was in the wrong place. But then I remembered how those art lofts looked back in New York, always located in buildings stuck in another time zone, and so it made sense to me that this 40 years old building with falling white paint, with the only way up a skinny staircase that had wires and flyers hanging everywhere was the place to be.

Then there was the piece of A4 paper on the first floor wall that had the words "Premiere Here" written on it, taped next to the entrance to the bottom step of the staircase.

So I went up, found the steel anti-theft door and entered into a place that I could only call was an amazing, Bohemian wonderland:

The studio, in an area no bigger than 700 square feet, had a full home theater set on one end, a bar at the other, with a smoker's lounge behind it that was actually the balcony behind closed door with a sign that said "smoke out here", a small chandelier hung on its ceiling, and a wall filled with pop arts, with a small study complemented with books and art magazines on modern arts at the corner.

"Dude you here!"

Just as I was admiring the place, I didn't even notice Charlie when he came running behind me. I turned around and there he was, wearing a red suit jacket and a black T-shirt, and as his usual-self proceeded to introduce me to everyone that was already there, even though I have met most of them before, if not during the shoot then it was later that night when we went drinking.

It worked well for me though; at least I did not feel underdressed no more, seeing so many pairs of jeans and T-shirts showed up for tonight.

The only person there that I have never met before was Wayne. Wayne was the guy who owned this studio where the premiere was. He's a pretty cool guy, very friendly from the first moment, perhaps a little too friendly. He had on this white suit that had an Armani cutting, and a cologne that was very strong.

"Wayne wants to get into films," Charlie said to me as the three of us stood around the only table while Wayne poured us each a glass of whiskey, "he owns this studio and he wants to build a bigger one."

"That sounds interesting," I said, "What kind of work do you produce now?"

That question was meant for Wayne, who replied,

"I'm a photographer myself."

"Oh, then you must know Dorian." I said.

"Who?" He asked.

I told him Dorian's full name.

"Yes I know of him." Wayne replied smoothly, "In our business he's really big. All the big contracts are attached to him."

"Oh he's a big shot? Really?" Charlie said as he faced Wayne, "I met him with A-Zed at his studio. That's where we shot Model Massacre. He's a hella chill guy man! His studio was huge!"

Sensing there was an awkward silence brewing with

Charlie's comment on the size of Dorian's studio, I changed the subject and said to Charlie, "Are you presenting later? Ready with everything?"

"Yeah man, I got it all in here." Charlie said, pointing his finger like pointing a gun to his head. "You're gonna hear from all of us soon."

"How many shorts are going on tonight?" I asked.

"I don't know, Wayne," Charlie said as he scratched his head, "It's gonna be me, Aaron, Byron, Camille and… is Nick doing his?"

"Nick's not here." Wayne replied, "He had to leave this week because of visa."

"Oh ok I think Byron is presenting his." Charlie said thoughtfully, "So Byron is gonna present two right?"

"Yes I think so." Wayne didn't sound as sure.

"Ok, so like five?" Charlie said.

"My you guys sure sound organized." I couldn't help but quip in, "I can't wait to see what's next."

Charlie started to laugh as I said that. And as soon as he did so did Wayne. Then people began to show up, those who were actually attending. And Charlie moved to greet them, I guess a lot of them were his friends.

I continued my chat with Wayne, who was telling me why he wanted to get into film,

"It's really an economic consideration." He said, "The way the industry works here in Taiwan, you have to do a little bit of everything. That's why I felt very fortunate to have met Charlie, Byron and the guys. They want to do something here and I think this is a good cause for me to help out too."

"I see," I said, "so are you part of their group too? Are you involved with the production of any of the shorts we are presenting tonight?"

"We all help out." He gave a rather generic answer, "That's what I think is great about this group. Everybody helps out, nobody is only doing their own thing."

As Wayne went to help Charlie to get the speakers organized, I found myself moving from conversation to conversation.

I was only expecting family and friends, but to my surprise by the end of the night near one hundred people, at least, made it to the premiere in this seemingly small studio.

I did a silent count while I was there on the nationality of people attending. There were French, Hungarians, Chileans, Koreans, Japanese, Vietnamese, Americans and Canadians, Indonesians, Poles, Russians, Ukrainians, Taiwanese, which was a guarantee but the minority for the rare occasion in Taipei, and of course Australians, who were almost always there when you had an expat party in Taiwan.

This was a very SOHO group of people. Their Bohemian aura of life almost got me to start singing show tunes out of the musical Rent. Actually meeting them, as it turned out, was as good as it gets.

I was talking with a white guy in glasses next to me, who came to Taiwan on a path more typical of foreigners: teaching English.

"But I don't wanna teach English forever man." He said, "I'm really a screenwriter. I mean, do you know what a script doctor is?"

"Yes." I replied, "Someone who helps develop scripts."

"Yeah man. That's what I wanna do." He seemed very happy to have met someone that he didn't need explaining everything he was talking about. "I am right now help developing a script about Koxinga."

"Really? In English?"

"Yeah I work with this guy that has done many years of research on the subject and wanna make it bigger, you know? More international."

He then proceeded to introduce me to his partner, who was like someone that walked out of a 1960's caricature: with long wavy grey hair and on top of it a green US army cap, he mumbled everything he said that I could barely make out.

Some pro-independence movement sentiments, about the importance of restoring the truth of history, that was about all I got.

I found myself moved again, this time talking to these two girls, one Vietnamese and the other from Australia, who were students studying mandarin here in Taichung. That's when Dorian showed up and found me,

"Hey hey!" I was already a bit tipsy then, I admit. "Did you come by yourself?"

"No I took a ride with Flynn." He said. And then being his typical self, made a comment about my company: "But I see you're doing pretty well yourself."

"Join us!" I said. Not only that, I turned to the girls and introduced Dorian: "Ladies my friend Dorian here is a famous photographer. You ask around and you will know."

"Really?" The girls were very smitten the minute they heard the magic words "photographer" and "famous".

"Of course." I slapped Dorian on the back before I left them for some fresh air. I went out the door behind the bar to the smoker's lounge.

I smoked quite quickly while I was out. The space was very small and was packed with people. And somehow I began chatting with the guy next to me: Byron. The same Byron that Charlie and Wayne were talking about.

We started speaking quite easily in part because we had mutual acquaintance, but also because Byron was a very personable and chatty guy. I quickly had a picture of his background, an Irish-American with Elvis Presley sideburns from Oklahoma, Byron lived in a cattle farm until he became a published writer, writing poems. He had by this year lived in Taiwan for five years. The reason, as it seemed, was his fascination with Taiwanese folklore.

He was also a chain smoker, had been smoking non-stop the whole time we were out there. While we were there he finished three cigarettes as I barely finished my first. And would have lit up another one had Wayne not come out and told us the screening was about to start.

Time was the one thing I completely lost track of the whole time we were out there. Byron had a feminine, almost quiet voice, but he was a great storyteller. By the time Wayne showed up, I already promised Byron that I was going to take him to the most authentic Mexican restaurant in town.

"It's a deal." I said, "I'll facebook you."

My 2004 self was laughing at the me now as I laughed with Byron and Wayne walking back into the room. They were already dimming the lights to signal the beginning of the screening.

Most attention was paid to the five men and women standing there with the blue light of the empty screen on their faces on the opposite end of the room. But not mine, because the minute I came in from the smoker's lounge, a tall, strapping blond who, in his arm, a tanned, half her face covered with her long hair girl in boots, shouted at me,

"My Boy!"

God no matter how many times Flynn did that to me in a room full of people, I still got embarrassed. Thank God Gina was there with him, or else in an artsy studio filled with filmmakers and wannabes it might give out the wrong message.

Gina smiled almost like she rehearsed it when she saw me. Not just that, she actually gave me a big hug, and said to me half-threatening and half-with-jest, that she was "going to kill me if I ever make her climb up the stairs like that in her boots again." She said it while laughing the whole time.

What could I say? She was crazy.

While I was smiling and not sure how to react, Flynn came to my rescue by also giving me a bear hug and said, as if to everyone since he shouted, "All your drinks are on me, my Boy! All your drinks tonight. My boy's gonna be working in films soon!"

And that actually got us a little applause here and there sporadically and a few cheers. It was like in a baseball game, when an unknown batter hit a homerun, and people cheered for him while unsure if he was on their team. That's Flynn. His gestures while always loud but were always meaningful as well.

We were then ushered towards the screen, as we all got down to business and began the screening portion of the premiere.

" Ok guys! Thanks for coming!" Charlie said very animatedly in front of the hundred people that were forming an uneven semi-circle around the screen.

"We are really happy to have you guys come and see our collective work. We have five shorts to present tonight, with their directors here on stage ready to share their thought process and work to you. After each screening, we will allow a short Q&A before we move onto the next one."

You could tell he's done this before: the improvised-style speech that was catered for a live audience, the way his arms flung out every time he was making a point, or the precision when he was pointing at someone or something he was talking about at the time. You can't do that without a bit practice.

Once Charlie was done telling us who each of the presenters were, and a round of applause was given to each and every one of them, they began to play the shorts.

In spite of my drummed-up expectations, they weren't particularly all that interesting, I have to say.

There was, of course, the one short with the white character speaking mandarin the whole time in voiceover about what he thought about Taiwan. Anytime you attend a screening catered for foreigners here in Taiwan you would see at least one of these films, and this one wasn't even the best-made one out of them.

Sure, the subject matter was cute and heart-warming, so it more than made up for its wandering direction and poor camera work. In spite of my best effort to critique while I was watching, I couldn't help but think, how many times have we watched a movie about a simple immigrant in New York and got a kick out of it? How many times, as we listen to their accented English, speaking about the difference between the Big Apple and Warsaw, Moscow, the Indian countryside, or even Taipei, wherever they were from, and we just found ourselves smiling at their youthful enthusiasm, regardless of their age? How many times have we found ourselves in tears when we hear of their struggles for the simple goal of fitting in? And so we forgive them for the poor directing and overly-simplified plot, and simply applauded their courage to speak up?

Just how many times have we done that? I leave that question to you.

We then moved onto the next film. It was a black-and-white film. Again not surprising when you attend these screenings to find one.

It was done more in a silent-film style, by someone who clearly was a cinematographer, who was more comfortable staying in his specialization of the camera rather than the storytelling. The picture was beautiful, with just the right lighting. From his angle the small party in the film was mesmerizing, the men and women attending were beautiful, and the mansion that the party was hosted in was simply historic. Every frame was pretty, but there was no story that would create a memorable moment for you to remember these pretty pictures afterwards.

Then the next one was from Byron, a story about river ghosts and the tradition of replacement deaths. It's a story you would find in many East-Asian cultures, such as Taiwan and Japan. About at places where people have died of drowning, those who have drowned would wait there so they may claim someone else's life when they pass by, as that then allows them to stop wandering aimlessly in the afterlife.

To be honest this was perhaps the most disappointing one for me to watch. Byron, while a great storyteller in person, was not a great storyteller on the big silver screen. The film, which went on for about fifteen minutes, was meant to be a peek piece for the feature film he clearly hasn't made. It showed no great scope or grip on the material. with choppy shots here and there, with dialogues that did not inspire interest for others to follow the story further.

What's worse, it was followed by Charlie's Model Massacre.

You could tell from the beginning of his film that Charlie was the only professional that night, with every one of his shot and line at the right places. An classic slasher horror film, it was shot in a very British Punk style made popular by Guy Ritchie.

It was a short cut to resemble a professional trailer, and the whole thing clicked. It was the most fitting choice to conclude the screening of the night. Waves of applause came, and as it would seem, were all aimed at the last picture showed.

In the midst of it Flynn was shouting and jumping from where he stood, his right arm punching into the air,

"That's my boy's shit! My boy made that last one!"

I was literally right next to him, with Gina standing in between us. He went around her and swiftly gave me another big hug, and that's when I saw it.

Behind Flynn, at the corner behind the bookshelf in the study, Mark had somehow come in slipped by our notice. And next to him was Rach.

I thought I saw it wrong, or perhaps it was just a coincidence that the two stood so close together, but it quickly confirmed my suspicion when the lights came up that Rach and Mark began to distance from each other, as if they saw me seeing them and wanted to hide something.

Now that's the story of the night.

We ended up hang out at the studio until 4AM the next morning. If I did not jetlag before that night, I definitely had it after the premiere.

I introduced Flynn to Charlie again, who were even more buddy-buddy than the night when we all went out drinking at Revolvers. As I watched them high-five and laughed like catching up on old times, Mark came over to say hi and asked me,

"So what did you think about Charlie's film? I thought it was pretty good."

Rach was a few steps behind him.

" I thought it was great." I said, "very well-knitted

together."

I did not want to go into the details. So I stopped there.

"Yes. He's the professional." Mark commented, "I want to hear what he thinks too."

I could tell there was a slight bit of awkwardness there. This was the first time the three of us were there together in a very long time, Flynn, Mark and I. That and Charlie there, and what I just saw between Mark and Rach… It was too much to process at once.

So I decided to excuse myself, ignoring Byron who had clamored up to our group and probably wanted to ask us what we thought about his picture, as I went to grab some cocktails at the back and took Rach with me.

Rach didn't know what was going on. She actually wanted to talk to me about something else, when I interrupted her and asked,

"What was that?"

"What was what?" She was confused.

"What I saw with you and Mark, next to the bookshelf?"

"Nothing!" She said that, but that ghost of a frown she had just seconds before told me otherwise.

"It wasn't nothing. It was something. I thought you said you guys weren't hanging out often?"

Seeing that it was too late to cover this up from me, Rach proceeded to explain how during the time I was away, Mark began to hang out a lot with her during lunch hours, and later would offer her rides home in his Mercedes.

"He's a real gentleman." She said, "Not like the kind of man I was used to, Mark's very… refined. That's the word. He even told me he's not interested at pursuing a relationship right now. Look there really isn't anything… we're just friends now, ok?"

Rach just looked at me as I stood in silence. The only thing in my mind then were the eight glasses of cocktails, as I waited for them to be made so I could drink all of them.

"We're still friends, right?" She asked.

And that's when I relented. I softened up my face and replied,

"Yeah, we're friends."

She always knew which button to press on me.

"And you will keep this secret for a friend?" She pressed on.

"Why are you guys keeping this a secret?" I asked.

"Mark asked me to. He didn't want people to think we had something going on." She said simply.

It probably was nothing, but nevertheless Mark's desire of keeping this a secret even from me made me wonder his intentions. Still, I had a more pressing concern in the form of an almost-thirty senior banking analyst who had been struck out lately and who just watched her secret crush going back to the worst woman on earth, so I replied her the only way I could,

"I will keep this a secret." I said. "But only because you and I are family."

Relaxed somewhat, as she knew that family included her, Rach went back to her most recent favorite topic, "Can you believe how Gina is clinging onto Flynn right now? Giggling at everything he says. God it's so disgusting."

I turned around and saw exactly what she just described.

"Yeah I thought I would have gotten used to it this time around." I said, "I guess I was wrong."

We went back and joined them, each with four glasses of God knows what cocktails in our hands. Each with questions and answers that we were keeping from each other.

PARTY OF THE YEAR PART-I

The next day I called Pete after I woke up late in the afternoon.

"God I feel old man." Pete said to me feebly over the phone, "I don't think I could keep up with you guys anymore."

"Keep up with us? Were you there last night too?"

"Oh man... don't toy with me, eh?"

"Well my friend," I should say that I honestly couldn't remember if Pete was there. "that's where your thirty-something body can't keep up with us twenty-somethings."

"Damn you." Pete sounded like he was chuckling. "You just wait. You guys would catch up real soon."

"Not if you still don't work out!" I went for his Achilles' heel.

"Don't tell me you're doing that now. Not with a freaking hangover like this." Pete once again put my concerns over his.

"What did you drink last night?" I asked rather mindlessly.

"What DID I DRINK!? YOU WERE RIGHT THERE NEXT TO ME!"

He wasn't particularly happy, to say the least.

It's not good if your hangover made you forget a whole

person, which was why I ignored him completely and went to the gym for my work out. I gotta get in shape if I wanna keep my relationship with Maddy; I've noticed about how important it is to be physically fit to be going out with her, as shown from our trip together.

Since then I have fully picked up my old routine: gym, quick lunch and coffee and write. And then one afternoon, on the bus enroute to the gym, I was surfing Facebook to kill time when I discovered a status update that included two of my friends in the neighborhood. On the rush of the moment I decided to go find them.

I had no shame about crashing a party, with no intention of asking for permission, but of course, I was only a product of my generation. Stalking was now officially cool.

If Mark Zuckerberg did it and became a billionaire in the process (watch the Social Network for proof) then there couldn't be anything wrong with it, could there?

Where those two were meeting wasn't exactly my favorite coffeehouse this side of town, so I'll just say that it was in a good location but had so-so food and awful coffee.

In this case, the coffeehouse is a restaurant. As I have explained, never take places for their names in Asia.

The coffeehouse was in the middle of a busy lunch service. No one was greeting me at the door as all the waiters were expediting, which fits with me perfectly as I would like to have my presence as unannounced as possible.

Through the wave of people I saw the two men that matched the names on the update, who were still oblivious of my presence. I crept my steps as quickly and smoothly as I could with something shiny held firm in my hand and hidden from view. And then there I was, behind the slenderly-built man and with my hand raised...

"So what are you guys doing here?"

I could almost see Dorian's face melt as I poked the back of his neck with my iPhone. I bet he even wet himself a little bit, which proved to be quite amusing to Charlie, sitting across from him and was trying to control his laugh and greet me.

"A-Zed man!" Charlie shouted to me, "WAZZUP!"

"WAZZUP!" I didn't know why I said that, every time. I sat down next to Dorian, ignoring the fact that it might belong to someone else and said to him, "Oh Dorian, the troubles that you're in."

"How did you find us?" Dorian asked, unconvinced.

"Well I got skills." I said pompously. "You should be more careful when you sign yourself in on social media, you never know who might be checking these things. Hey Charlie, when are we gonna talk about your project?"

"Let me go get you a waiter." Charlie said, "They have really good coffee here. You drink coffee?"

I tried not to grin when I heard his question, "yeah sure." I replied and watched Charlie jumped off his couch and ran straight to a waiter who was actually taking order from another table, as I turned to Dorian and asked,

"What are you guys meeting up about?"

"He wants to use my studio again, so he said." Dorian said with sneering smile, "But once we met up all he's been talking about was money, and how much he heard from Wayne about how much of a big shot I am, and how he wants to learn from me. You know, blowing up smokes. You know, I didn't tag our meeting on Facebook."

"Really? So he did?" I said, "Well now that sounds annoying insincere."

"Well he is a nice guy, Ivy League." Dorian said with another smile like he was holding something back. "I'll cut him some slacks. It's always nice to hear good things about yourself. Even if it is fake."

"Is that what you really think?" I asked, knowing his tendencies of not speaking his mind at times.

"Yeah we'll see, he might prove to be very useful." He said, somewhat thoughtfully. "He's getting us a waiter now, that's useful."

"God I really hate you sometimes." I said as I went back

to checking Facebook updates on my phone, "Oh wow I missed something."

"What?" Dorian asked me.

As I flipped my phone and was about to close the Facebook app, I saw something there. Out of the string of status updates on Facebook, only one stood out and was taking up all of my attentions now as the rest, with their selfies and cute kitty pictures completely ignored.

"Maddy's here in Taipei." I said.

"Who's Maddy?" Asked Charlie.

Maddy was only staying in Taipei shortly, as it turned out. she had made some plans to meet up with some friends here over the week, take some trips to the countryside, before she officially report to her posting here in the city much later.

I thought tagging along with her on another trip the countryside, this time in Taiwan would really push it, so I watched her busy making her plans to meet up with her "other friends" without saying anything. Finally I was able to get her to have dinner with me on Thursday night.

The problem was, I was also supposed to have dinner with Rach and the guys that same night. I obviously couldn't abandon my family, when we have such a clear "bros (which included Rach) before hoes" policy. Not especially when Flynn was breaking that golden rule this time.

Yeah he did. He said that he couldn't make it because "he was doing something with Gina".

Whatever. Gina being there would only be awkward. I could only think at this moment that he did this avoid that, instead of the more obvious ditching option.

The restaurant we were meeting at was called Le Ble d'Or. It was a microbrewery restaurant that was the first built to this long established US concept here in Taiwan. In a way, it paved the way for one of the more recent culinary revolution in Taiwan, with the number of taster bars and similar restaurants growing around the island.

To be honest I quite like their brew, even though it's

exuberantly high at almost 300 NT a bottle, compare with the modestly cheap and yet delicious Taiwan Beer that only cost 45 NT. Well, if we were to live frugally we would become outcast of this, our own generation of excess and self-awareness. Let's just hope this place can survive us.

The place was a rarely-seen large location in Taipei City, with its two hundred tables and up to a thousand or guest capacity. It was therefore a popular location for after hour parties. Built to look like a German beer house, with immobile and heavy wooden furnitures and brick walls, tonight's party theme was apparently Hawaii night, as the whole place went Hawaii-themed with the fire torches, the exotic plants of flowers between tables, and the flower garlands all the service staffs were wearing.

I got there with Maddy, who followed my instruction and met with me at the nearest MRT station. It was never hard to spot her, with her height and her blonde hair. I didn't know this, but apparently Rach pulled a few strings to get us our table.

"Oh not much," she explained when we found her alone at the table, on time as usual, "I'd just casually mentioned my corporate account and they offered this table up without a fight."

"Excellent work." I said, before I proceeded to the conventional first time introduction. "Rach, this is Maddy."

Maddy, who at the moment seemed to be captivated by the environment she was in, which I guess was both strange and familiar to her, as soon as she heard her name being mentioned, she quickly turned around and said to Rach,

"Hello!" Now that was a thickly Germanic greeting.

"Oh hi!" Rach replied jovially, "I heard so much about you! A-Zed said all the nicest things!" And then they hugged.

There was something poetic about the hug, between someone of Rach's height, that of an average Taiwanese girl and Maddy, the colossal German that was probably taller than Flynn.

As I controlled my urge to laugh, I asked Rach, "Where's

Pete?"

"Men's Room." She replied.

"And Dorian is late?"

"Has he ever not?"

"Watch out," I turned to Maddy and "whispered" as loudly as I could, as if I was doing this for someone else's benefit, "she's gonna pull the twenty questions on you."

"What's the twenty questions?" Maddy asked me with a straight face.

"Why do I keep insisting on using American figure of speech on this girl that I knew is from Germany?"

"'Cause you're an American?" Rach said cleverly.

That's when Pete showed up, sat down next to Rach and said, "What did I miss?"

"Hey Pete help me out here. You're from Canada, that's practically America which means we're on the same boat. These guys are..."

"Oh whatever it is, you're on your own." He said simply.

"I see what's going on here." I protested weakly at my isolation and was awarded with a round of laughter at my expense. Luckily Dorian had joined us by this point, with a date.

"Hey!" Dorian said.

"Hey!" We replied.

"You guys remember Tanya?" Dorian said as he pulled the chair for his lady.

"Have we met, Tanya?" I asked.

"Of course not, A-Zed." Tanya replied with a smile.

Dorian quickly caught on to what we were doing, "Oh you guys are messing with me now aren't you?"

Tanya was Dorian's girlfriend, who only showed up for paired functions of the family. Dorian didn't really have a type, but Tanya seemed to be just it. Tanya runs her own art gallery up in the high-tech rich neighborhood of Neihu, and she's someone who's ok with this "are they, would they" relationship they had. If you look away from the expensive jewelry on her though, she looks so young and unworldly, you would think she was someone who was still an intern earning her masters.

"Did you know they have a dart machine?" Pete asked me.

"As a matter of fact I did not." I said.

"I have a great idea," Rach intervened, "Why don't we do it in turns? Boys versus boys and then girls versus girls. How's that?"

"No that's not gonna work. Let's do couple versus couple." Dorian said.

"Hey you're overlooking the clear team that wouldn't make this game." Pete said, pointing at himself and Rach.

"No I am not." Dorian replied.

"There might be another team here very soon. fingers crossed." Rach said, which took almost everyone at the table by surprise.

"Single Rach is getting a boyfriend?" Pete said.

"Yes. Single Rach is getting a boyfriend. Maybe." Rach was very calm tonight.

"Please reserve us a double date when you do." Tanya suggested immediately.

"Maybe a triple date?" I said.

"Who knows, maybe we could plan the weddings together too." Tanya continued.

"Oh I volunteer as your maid of honor!" Rach immediately jumped to it.

"Somebody please shoot me." Pete spoke now the only single-party at the table.

Eventually we decided we were not going to do any teams. It would just be whoever wanted to go. So as I volunteered to take Maddy with me, Pete and Dorian followed while Tanya and Rach were left to drink and chat for the first round.

Nowadays instead of the classic experience of metal darts that could easily kill a man, dart games now had these new light, soft-headed plastic darts that are actually harder to throw effectively as they are too light to create a curve projection.

I saw on the table there were only two sets of darts. So I picked one up from one of the sets, tested it in the air with my wrist to get a feel of how it might run, and said to Maddy,

"You have a lot of dart boards in Germany, right?"

"Yes." She replied crisply.

"Should we leave you two to this round?" Pete asked us.

"Don't ask the obvious question." Dorian told Pete aside. And I smiled at the opportunity.

I went first. Even with everything I said about the soft-head and the curve I still managed to make all three shots stick, with the last shot right on the triple ring.

I must confess that I'm quite good at darts. Having played against Flynn on just about every game my life, this was the only one that I could actually beat him at.

I let Maddy try to even the score herself while I was pulled away by Pete and Dorian for a conversation on the side:

"You're not letting go that title easy hm?" Dorian said, referring to my currently unbeaten scoring title (I told you guys I was good), "So who's Rach's boyfriend?"

"His name is Dick None of Your Business Harry John." I replied, which actually got Pete smirking at my response.

"Come on, remember what we always say, we're a family? No secret in the family."

Dorian looked really like a puppy begging for food,

"Say that the next time you're about to cock-block, asshole." So I replied jestingly with a jab.

"Oh that was cold." Pete said.

That's when Maddy came back. I didn't really focus on the game but judging from her hand folding on her mouth coming over I was guessing it did not go well.

"These are hard! I couldn't hit any of them." She said.

"Yeah. It's different from the metal ones we grew up with." I said, confidently selling my knowledge, "I'll show you later."

And I did. Although not after a couple of rounds of the game where I dominated everyone there. We then went back to the table, and suffice it to say, my title remained safe in spite of the international competition. America rules.

"What were you gals talking about?" I asked when I saw that Tanya and Rach were laughing as we got back.

"We were just talking about Flynn's party." Tanya said, "It looks really interesting on his Facebook page. Too bad I can't go tomorrow."

"Flynn's having a party?" Maddy asked.

And that's when the floor began to shake, when the lanterns with luau decorations began to shake, it was an earthquake.

"What's happening?" Maddy exclaimed.

"It's an earthquake." Pete said.

I looked around, except for some people saving their beers from dripping out, most people just went on with whatever they were doing before like nothing happened. It went on for several minutes. And I used the time available and did the current generation thing. I went on Facebook and checked just what this party was that Tanya was talking about. I quickly scan through the event list, the guest list of hundreds of people, the numerous shots of him and Gina and the helps doing the prep work at his Tamsui villa, and the name of the party:

"Party of the Year"

I swear I felt a chill the moment I saw that name, like a cold stab to the heart. He didn't even tell us at the premiere about this year's Party, let alone inviting us! But again, I did not have all my feelings revealed to all my friends at the table.

And then once the earthquake stopped, I said to Maddy with a cheery face,

"Welcome to Taiwan dear, now you've really got the experience! The earthquake and tomorrow, Flynn's Party of the Year!"

"Party of the Year is tomorrow?" Rach was suspicious.

"Yes," I said, "tomorrow."

PARTY OF THE YEAR PART-II

There was music from my neighbor's house through the summer nights. In his blue gardens men and girls came and went like moths among the whisperings and the champagne and the stars...

Oh sorry, wrong book. Where was I?

It was never hard to spot Flynn's Tamsui mansion from the outside. This time around though, it was impossible to miss it. It was Party of the Year after all, the once a year supersized house party that Flynn threw for the one thing or person he felt special about that year.

Even from the MRT station it seemed like every departing passenger was heading that general direction. You almost felt compelled when you came out the train to follow this crowd of people in their twenty's dressed in flip flops and holding beach balls and towels on their general direction, just to fill your natural curiosity where they were all going to.

And as we went up the crooked, narrow alley that used to only have a passing scooter here and then to avoid, it now had a full line of SUVs on it, like a weekend to the countryside. The noise of car horns, people chatters and what sounded like Fatboy Slim music was descending down to us common mortals like we were the faithful on a holy pilgrimage.

As we went up, men with trolleys filled with flattened cardboard boxes that, from the label, used to carried fruits, wine and liquor went down the slope like an army supply train.

The five of us, Rach, Pete, Dorian, Maddy and I arrived together. It was my idea that we did that; I thought I should let everybody knew Maddy better with the limited time we had at hand. She seemed very excited to go to a Flynn party, to a point I suppose she must had cancelled whatever she was supposed to do today.

"That sure seem like a huge crowd." Pete said, "You don't suppose they're all going up there, do you?"

None of us wanted to give Pete the obvious answer that he knew full well even before he asked it.

Maddy was certainly amazed by the scale of this party. Midway up the road she asked me,

"What does your friend Flynn do?"

It's never an easy question to answer, whenever people asked me that question. But it was nevertheless a question I have mastered answering,

"He's a musician," I said, "with a big house."

Not just one, I should add.

When we got in the place, there must had been 300 people there in their swim shorts and bikinis taking Bacardi and Tequila shots, cannonballing the pool, jumping to the music while the surround sound system blasted it away like a gun salute.

"Where is Flynn?" Pete shouted to me, even though I could barely make out what he's saying.

"I don't know! Let's try the inside first!" I replied.

"Oh God it's those guys." He said suddenly.

"Hey hey!" Before I could even react to what Pete was saying, "those guys" as he called them came over. I turned around it was Charlie, Byron and some other guys from the premiere. "Wassup?"

"Wassup?" (Seriously, I don't know why I do it every time)

"Hey uh… we were just gonna do some shots by the pool. You guys wanna join?" And then Charlie smiled as he looked back at Pete, "This guy! This guy is ready!"

"Yes, of course I am." Pete said. His face didn't say ready though, instead it said "help me".

"Cool, well I'm gonna find Flynn first. you guys know where he is?"

"Don't know man. We kinda just got here too."

(Just got here and already doing shots? Ok...)

We went through the crowd, passed the long white buffet table filled with burger sliders, cheesecakes from small micro bakery brand that must took days to order in advance, and a champagne fountain rivaled the villa itself in height and scale.

We went past all this and got in the living room, where it seemed there was even more people inside, yet no one saw Flynn. I cut through some chatters from people I passed by who wanted to befriend me or maybe just to ask for direction around the house and I found Gina.

She stood over the breakfast table with a glass of red wine and was chatting with this one girl who looked kinda familiar to me, and kinda didn't.

Keeping only Maddy behind me and knowing full well Gina would keep track of where her boyfriend was at any moment, I went straight to her. I knew Gina saw me too, since she was whispering something in her friend's ear and then kissed her cheek and watched her off, something she usually did when she was expecting another company to show up that she needed to entertain.

"Hey!" I greeted her once we were in audible distance.

"Hey you guys came!" Gina replied, "Like my party?"

"Yeah thanks for the invite. Great party!" I said it rather dismissively.

"Yeah I told Flynn that I thought it was time to have a pool party... I mean why waste a good summer right?" She replied like she had practiced this speech to give all the guests that were coming in, "And who is this?" She said pointing at Maddy.

There was never a new girl that Gina did not want to know first. And by first I mean before Flynn. I would hate to disappoint her to tell her about Beijing and Flynn's girl there, so instead I did the introduction,

"This is Maddy. Maddy, this is Gina."

"Hi." Maddy waved and said to Gina.

"So this is the new girl." Gina said, "Hi."

"Sure." I said while completely ignoring Gina's slightly deprecating comment, "So where's your man?"

"What man?" Gina winked at me as if she was being funny.

"Oh Gina," I said with a smile, "I'm not your type. I actually like women."

"Ha," She laughed somewhat joylessly as a comeback, "he's upstairs with some of my friends from the music industry."

"Thank you, Gina. And again, great party."

I took Maddy with me and went upstairs as quickly as I could, away from Gina. My guess was Flynn was entertaining his guests from his room's balcony which overlooked the pool and, in extension, the Tamsui Town and the River. It was where he usually took his VIPs to drink his dad's brandy and smoked the cigars that came in from Hong Kong.

My guess proved to be correct. I found Flynn out on balcony through the French window, with four other guys all facing us with their backs. He was wearing a black shirt and a white tie, and a set of white suit to match it.

He looked like he was telling a story that had the guys around, who all had a glass of amber colored drink in their hands, laughing uncontrollably, while he smoked his Montecristo No. 2 cigar. He saw me. Like a gentleman he opened the French window for us said,

"You guys made it my boy! Hi Maddy, how do you like my party?"

"It's very nice!" She replied with a smile.

"She's a closet party girl, this one." Flynn clearly was happy, a little tipsy too, seeing how he was literally smiling the whole time since I was there. "You guys care for a little Scotch?"

Care for a little Scotch? Did I just hear Flynn spoke a grammatically correct sentence without a single F-word in there? Fucking 'ell, I'm impressed.

"Yes. You like some too Maddy?" I said while looking after my girl.

"Yes please." She replied.

While Flynn was pouring us some 25 years old Laddie, I asked him,

"Who are your friends?"

"Oh let me introduce you to them, here's..." He began to introduce them to me while tightening the lapel on his suit.

These friends of his were the type that come to a pool party wearing shirts and ties and had business cards up in their shirt pocket, which they would thrust to your hand before the conversation even begins. He told me their names and made the effort of mentioning that they are Gina's friends.

"So you guys been talking sharp?" I said that in Mandarin, knowing full-well everyone there including Maddy would know what I was speaking. Somehow my American directness seemed to have spoiled their cordial mood that they began to smile while none responded directly to my question.

I gathered something was missing here, but then Flynn interrupted me as he would and said, "They are pretty interested in my stuff."

"They are? Great!" I said, "what have you shown them?"

"No man, just my vision and stuff. I'll be performing a piece later as like a showcase of sorts."

I had a funny feeling about what he said, in words such as "performing a showcase" and "Interested", but I couldn't quite put my finger on it.

"Alright I can't wait. Let's drink to that. To the showcase!" So instead I raised my glass for a toast. Lying and Scotch will get us through today, I thought.

"Yes my Boy!" Flynn said as he turned to direct his new friends, "Come on you guys drink with us! You too Maddy. To my showcase!"

I lost track of time afterwards. It was as if time itself had become irrelevant in this mansion in its walls, among the hundreds of people in attendance of this great party.

After the toast, I took Maddy back down to the first floor and left Flynn behind. For a while we lost sight of each other, as the party was just too crowded and loud to notice any single individual. But then my knowledge of the mansion kicked in and I remembered the corner where we always sat around after brunch was behind the champagne fountain and therefore could be empty. And that's where I found my people.

By the pool, where Pete was doing shot with Charlie and Byron and a girl that again I kinda knew but I kinda didn't, while Dorian and Rach were at the corner under the shade I just mentioned sitting in the beach benches and resting. I decided to join them.

So I found Maddy, pointed out where they were to her, asked her to join them first, while I grabbed the shiitake mushrooms, slices of Iberico, glasses of champagne from the fountain, still cool under the hot, humid Taiwanese summer sun, along with some crackers and cheese and ham and like a well-trained waiter carried all that with my two hands went back to my friends and our exclusive, VIP bench.

"Oh wow, see Maddy? This man is a keeper." Rach, who was talking with Maddy when I came over, made a comment about my serving touch. "Not only does he have big hands, he knows how to use them."

Maddy actually began to laugh. I don't remember she ever laughed that hard before.

"You guys know about men with big hands in Germany too?" Rach continued to sell her slightly dirty joke. "Dorian, hold all the food plates with your small hands please."

"Yes Madame." Dorian did not dare say no to that.

With an announcement from the MCs and the background music of Beethoven's Symphony No.9, Flynn went up the stage with his Les Paul guitar in hand.

While others mostly had their attention at Flynn, I looked up and saw Flynn's new friends were standing on the balcony along with their mediator, Gina, looking down on the whole party while talking among themselves.

Flynn opened his performance by announcing that he'd like

to dedicate this to "the one woman he loves", then proceeded to perform this Neo-Soul piece I guess he's been writing since the night before our last brunch, mixing English with Spanish lyrics that I hardly understood, neither did the crowd I thought. Luckily though we had Maddy the linguist who could show us some insight into the Spanish part of the lyrics.

"It is very beautiful." Maddy said to us, "He basically… sings about his love for this woman he had met by chance, and the many times they have been apart, their love only grew strong… His use of the language is very… smart? Is that the word?"

"I think you mean clever." I said.

"Yes. Clever. Yes." She confirmed.

While we were having the conversation, Rach was quiet, sitting there with the glass of champagne in her hand, probably heard everything we said about Flynn's song.

The song was long, almost ten minutes long. But somehow even with this generation of people with short attention span, Flynn sold his performance completely.

When he finished the song again with his signature minute long solo, the crowd went completely crazy. It wasn't even like your usual concert in Taiwan where one or two person from the crowd first called out "encore" before the others followed in an organized manner, but as soon as the song finished, the whole crowd cried "encore" at the same time.

Flynn was obviously very happy with himself. He waved at everyone as the sound of "encore" continued, while moving himself slowly off the stage. He then in one swift wave signaled that this was indeed the one and only performance this afternoon, and then pointed at the DJ to spice up the music. And the craze for "encore" was soon replaced with the floor music and more drinks offered by the service staff.

"I'm gonna go talk to him."

To this day I still did not know why I said that then and there. But I follow Flynn down to his studio, where I knew in protection of his instruments he would be alone as he clean and lock up his guitar, the best time to speak to him alone.

When you think back, everything in life went by so efficiently it always seemed planned; but like most great game of all-time in sports, intuition kicked in more at these moments than any man-made plans that sparked the perfect score.

I went downstairs to his studio, and like I thought he was there alone, all the noise upstairs silent by his impregnable studio walls. At first he looked up annoyedly at who dared to come down and disturb him, and softened up a smile the minute he saw me.

"Down to catch the real drink my boy?" Flynn asked as he rubbed his guitar with a cloth to remove all the sweat and prints from a live-performance like that.

"No you gave the real party upstairs, we have enough drinks as it was." I replied.

"Why do you hang out with that piece of shit Mark?" He asked me suddenly, "All he ever does is lie. Why would you associate yourself with someone like that?"

"Associate myself, you really gonna talk like that?" I was slightly provoked, but what I said next still came out of nowhere. "I could say the same about Gina."

"What did you say?" He put down the guitar as his smile disappeared and his eyes suddenly gleamed with anger.

"You heard me." I was not going to give in.

"So this is how it is hm? You guys still pulling this Gina or No Gina crap." He seemed like he had quite a lot stored up for quite some time. "I know how it is. All those little meetings and hangouts you guys been doing without me. I know all about them. I know what you guys been saying about me and Gina behind our back."

"Doing without you? Flynn,"

One thing I never understood about myself is how once I would get into an argument with someone I would talk like I was a different person, someone scary with great clarity.

"You missed Dragon Boat with me without a word. Those two zhong-ji I made for you are still in my freezer. You wanna talk about how we'd been doing things behind your back? You haven't told us shit about Gina, about her friends. You didn't even bother to invite us to this Party of the Year!"

It was like my mind become sharpened beyond my own wildest imaginations with my body filled with the fire to fight it to the bitter end.

"This is not how this family works, Flynn!"

"Don't talk to me like that. This is still about you."

"Don't talk to you like that? Don't fucking talk to me like that." I jumped on his point, "We know each other too fucking well to talk like this. Say it!"

I knew Flynn knew what I was talking about.

"Alright you fucking piece of shit!" now Flynn was finally shouting, going out of control, "You fucking assholes better start accepting the reality that Gina is fucking with me! She's my woman, and either you fucking idiots take her in or you're all out!"

"Now we're talking. Now that's the fucking Flynn I know!" I said, "Why couldn't you fucking talk like that before? What you're letting that bitch run your life? Big Shot? Is that do-no-good, not part-of-the-family bitch running your life for you now? Is that what it is?"

All we could hear in that completely sound-proof box was our shouting to each other. Even if they were burning the house down from out there, we wouldn't know.

"You fucking shit!" He shouted, his brimming voice echoed in the room like a haunting ghost, thirsty for blood of the living. "You think you can come to my fucking house, drink my fucking drink and talk to me like this?"

"You listen to me Flynn, I'm gonna say this again, in this family, you wanna do anything? Fine! You talk to us first. You have a problem with us? You still fucking talk to us first. Anything you're fucking not happy about? YOU, STILL, FUCKING, TALK, TO US, FIRST!"

Flynn's smart was always subtle, and often he was overlooked for his intelligence at times. When he was faced with an argument he can't fully win from, like the one just now, he would hold his peace and wait it out. It was a more instinctive way of containing the situation from escalating, an effective approach that was often not attempted in our "speak first, think later" liberal society.

"You know where to find me." I drew a temporary conclusion to a no-resolve meeting, "The next time you want to talk to us, you come to me first."

I then turned around and left, leaving Flynn to steam in his studio by himself. I went outside, as I went past the champagne fountain, I once again skillfully took six of them. This time though, they were all for myself.

We partied all day. It wasn't until people realized if they didn't leave they'd be missing the last MRT out of Tamsui did the party finally began to disperse. I drank the whole way through, watched as the SUVs again lined up out there, this time for picking up rather than drop offs.

I went from first the champagne and moved on to the Martinis and eventually just whatever I could get my hands on. I did not see Flynn again. Although I knew he was somewhere, watching us drinking with each other, with Charlie and Byron, with random people, playing beach balls and throwing random people into the pool. Even as others came up and told me about seeing him doing something, Flynn and I never met again that day.

We were there until the very end, before we all decided to leave on the MRT together.

Sitting at one corner of the MRT, with Maddy, me and Rach on one side and Pete, who was really wasted as we all could tell, sitting on the opposite side with Dorian holding him up.

"Every time I'm the guy," Dorian said, he was obviously annoyed. "Every time I'm the guy handling the drunk guy."

"How else are you useful?" Rach said sarcastically.

"So was it fun?" I asked Maddy.

"Yes." She said with a big smile.

"Ohhh…" Pete suddenly moaned, quite loudly, "Oh I can't keep up with those guys. How do they drink like that? It's like they don't even have… a brain."

"The most sensible thing you said all day." Dorian said.

We all laughed at that comment.

"Oh I'm not gonna drink with them anymore." He said, ending that sentence with a burp filled with alcohol, mint, lemon and whatever else they put in drinks these days.

"Say it again," Rach said rather viciously, "this time without burping."

That got us laughing even harder.

In the reverse order of how we got on the train, one by one we began to leave at our individual stop or transit station. First it was Dorian, then Pete shakily but much more soberly than when he got on the train next. Then it was Maddy's stop.

The train stopped, Maddy and I waved good bye to each other, I wish her a safe trip to the countryside, She was smitten shy with her silence as she waved me good bye.

Almost as soon as Maddy left the MRT, when now it was just Rach and I still in the long MRT bench, without a word of her own, Rach suddenly rested her head upon my shoulder. It was unclear at first, but soon I could hear her sobbing, quietly.

I realized at the moment that as a man you would always be a selfish prick no matter what. Whether it was the rich jackass who threw a huge house party just so he could say "I love you" to his current girlfriend in front of thousands of strangers, or if you're the slightly less well-to-do jackass who spent the whole party entertaining his current girlfriends and drink, and had the time to have a full-length argument with his rich jackass friend in a soundproof studio, while completely forgetting about the girl who obviously, with all the show of love she had to suffer through today, had had her heart broken, yet again.

I leaned my head against Rach's, my right hand held her left, as I said,

"Come on Rach, what's wrong? Don't cry."

"Nothing." She said.

"Come on, talk to me." I said.

Normally Rach never allow herself to speak her mind in moments like this, but I guess the wound was so deep this time that she couldn't hold her silence no more,

"He said 'I love you' to her. In front of everyone. He never used to say that to anyone like that."

Then sobbing just stopped.

"We're moving on." She said, "We're moving on."

And so closes the "Party of the Year" for us, as we moved on to the next chapter of our lives.

THE DEMONS

At some point in your life, you have to face those demons you left in the shadows long ago. They are like your family, something that cannot be taken away or replaced. No matter how you have changed yourself, they will find you, as they are a part of you, wherever you go.

Which is quite fitting in my case, considering that my demons are my parents, the people that raised me up that I want to have no part with.

After a completely sleepless night, I went to meet my mother at a jewelry store this morning near Zhongshan North Road.

Most traditional Taiwanese jewelry stores make lucrative business in second hand trades. A lot of people in need of cash would trade in their once prized possession for some much-needed cash, to some jewel dealer who had no regards of whatever sentimental values were with these inanimate and cold objects, which was exactly what my mother was doing here today.

I haven't seen my mother in a while and I must say she has aged quite a bit. I could hardly recognize her. She's slowly gained weight as I grew up, and ever since her retirement a couple of years ago she began to show signs of edema.

Her eyes were swollen from lack of sleep, a problem she's always had ever since I could remember. And her hearing had gone so poor that half the time in our conversations I would be repeating what I have only just told her seconds ago. I could tell from how she came off the bus that her back pain was still persistent, even though she told me that "she's fine".

My vision was quite blurry this morning. My eyes were constantly watering, too sensitive to the light when we met outside the store. When we met she, rather painfully and yet with a smile, like all mothers do when they speak to their children about something that was embarrassing to themselves, told me that I had lost yet another bit from my inheritance.

It's a good thing I did not believe in inheritance, and I almost said that to her. I almost said to her that it was more important we face the problem at hand first, as we could buy these things back later, something stupid like that. I did not even have to think to realize that it would be a cruel thing for me to say these supposed words of comfort out of impulse, about a sentimental piece of jewels from her collection that took a lifetime to accumulate.

She went into the store by herself, refusing to have me witness like always things that happened to her that she felt embarrassed about.

The piece she was selling today was her wedding medallion, a traditional piece of gift for Chinese families to give on wedding days to the bride and groom. It could be a gold bullions or medallion, to commemorate this day to the bride.

I have seen this procedure too many times before through the glass door from the outside, the dealer would test the medallion with lighter fire to authenticate its material, before weighing it like a piece of meat. If it proves satisfactory, pay my mother with some meager amount of cash off so she survive another day in our society that was all about liquidity and self-support now.

As I stood outside and waited, I thought about my mother. I thought about how I never thought for a second when I was a kid that she would be living a life like this after I grew up.

This life of poor health and means due to inability to afford them both.

My mother supported me for a long time, from when I grew up in the American School, the most expensive school in Taiwan I might add, to when I went to uni in New York City, not exactly a cheap place to live in either. In those years, every time I called her to see how she's doing, she would smile and tell me that it was "fine".

Except I knew it wasn't fine, and yet I never realized how bad things were until I sold my book, began to support myself as a writer and moved back here. When I saw how she was living, in a small rented apartment in an old, shaky building, carrying her now swelling body around those narrow and badly designed stairs and hallways, trying to survive on what's left of her savings.

She was always having troubles to makes ends meet, something that was meant for a person of a much younger age who was just getting on his/her own feet, someone of my age for example, and not the now-retired, post-middle age woman who once was the most powerful executive in the Taiwanese advertising industry.

And yet she insisted still, that her life was fine whenever we meet, something that had as much truth as those fast food ads about how healthy fast food was, something I was reminded of this morning at my breakfast at McDonald's.

I spent the night before at the ER, where I had to keep my father company, who was unconscious, ailing from some sort of kidney and prostate problem. I haven't caught a wink of sleep since. I had to sit in a fold out chair the whole night. My parents' lack of means to hire helps meant the other members of the family had to play the part: the other being me. It was either that or my mother.

She must have noticed how tired I was this morning. After she had finished her business with the store and came out to meet me, she gave me something in a white paper bag she's been carrying, something which turned out to be quite heavy: a pack of six grape juice packets that was imported from Japan.

She told me she came out from home in a hurry and had to grab something quick so that was the only thing for me, to thank me for last night. I knew it was a lie, I knew this was the only kind of luxury she could afford now: imported sugary drinks. She also said she bought them and realized they were too sweet for her diabetic body, so she decided to give them to me.

I could say nothing but thank you to her. I wanted to say that I would share her burden. I wanted to tell her it was ok, and that we as a family would work through this. I wanted to tell her dad would be fine... But I just stood there, saying thank you to her like a proper Chinese person, as I was too polite to say anything other than a promise to her that I'll come back to the hospital tomorrow and check on them.

She told me it's all fine, and dad's got a room now and out of the ER so I didn't have to worry. We were more like strangers now than family, in spite of how at one point we used to share everything and had a life together; now we were just two people who were both too polite to say anything substantial to each other.

I said goodbye, holding the bag of juice in my hand as I got on the bus and left for my apartment, hoping to find that calmness that could bring me to sleep before going to the hospital again, tomorrow.

The next day, I went to the hospital.

When I got to the hospital my mother was already up. The smile she had the minute she saw me was both warm like sunshine and dampened as the rain.

She got busy clearing up the space so I had a place to sit, even though I insisted that it wasn't necessary.

I could tell she probably had slept very little last night, and the minute she'd told me how everything went last night I had an idea why: apparently my father, even with his prostate problems, still insisted on going to the toilet by himself rather than using the plastic chamber pot provided by the hospital.

A man in his condition should really be more considerate, I

could only imagine how last night went by when my mother barely had a wink of sleep with my stubborn father constantly needing someone to assist him in and out of the toilet while failing to accomplish anything but pain for everyone involved.

My father seemed to be asleep now. I looked out the window and saw that the day was quite wet and a rain seemed possible, so I told my mother to go home and get some sleep before it starts to rain, and that I would meet her for dinner. She told me to take care of myself, and noted me as thoroughly as always about all the little details I should watch out for here in the ward. I nodded as I pretended to listen and walked her out of the ward.

"Goodbye, mom." I said to her.

"Bye, my good son." She said, "I'll see you tonight."

"Ok."

And I watched her out, onto the elevator before I went back to my father's bedside. I watched at how peaceful he seemed.

My father seemed smaller than I saw him last. Frailer, no doubt, as he could hardly sit up from his bed or share any brilliant new business plans he had. Over the years, we had grown to be so different in such separate directions, I thought, and we were now completely apart.

There was no greater difference in men, than that between sickness and health.

I apologize for my conscious plagiarism, as it seemed to suit the occasion.

I sat down next to him without uttering a word. And, like a good Chinese son that I was, I opened my book, which was an in depth analysis on the Taiwanese film industry, and read silently to myself, tried not to disturb whatever dream that engulfed him at the moment from this reality, where he had lost everything.

I could still remember when I was little that my father used to walk me to school every day. I remember then even though I was almost always one of the tallest kid in class I was a dwarf next to him when we walked together.

Those were the happiest days of our time together, if not in my life. My father seemed so knowledgeable then and patient as he answered all of those funny little questions that had sprang out of my childish mind, that those mere ten minutes of walk every morning had become my most cherished memories.

From as far back as I can remember, my father was a talky person. He's great with storytelling. There was not a person on earth I knew who wasn't charmed by my father's wit and loving spirit from the start.

Some of his favorite stories, like the namesake character of "Tom Brown's School Days" revolved around his colorful career all through elementary school of whooping the asses of every kid in the military village he grew up in, his achievement of never doing a day of homework, and how he'd managed to obtain guava and sugar cane and all sorts of exotic goods without "monetary" means.

And then there were the more romantic ones, depends on your definition of the word romance. He talked about how he had the love and affection of every girl in the village. And then he always ended those, whichever girl it might be, some even after the marriage, with the mentioning of how he won my mother, the best woman in this world by his manly charm.

He was a smart man, who understood the importance of knowing your audience when you speak, always say the things that make them click, that make them remember him in a positive way. It also helped that he possessed a wonderful set of etiquette to impress even the most conservative of families. And my father, who could recite key phrases out of the Bible at ease, often gave out the impression that his faith had made him a very spiritual and loving man, a good family man with great success in life.

Almost every story my father told, he could turn them into tales of morality. The importance of being honest to your family. The importance of being responsible. The importance of keeping your words. And Everyone loved and adored him to a point where they never forget his stories, or to remind me of what a wonderful father that I was fortunate enough to have.

I used to listened to everything he said and believed him to a fault. I never questioned him and certainly I never wondered for a day the validity of the stories I was told. To me, he was my dad. He was the reliable man on earth. He had the biggest heart. He could do anything that he set his mind to and when things go bad, it was never his fault. And they've gone bad plenty of times.

I remember that lasted for maybe a year and a half, before one day when he took me out of the house without much of a smile, and I talked to him like we always did and after maybe three blocks suddenly he shouted to me,

"Why don't you shut up? Aren't you tired of asking the same dumb questions every day?"

I remember how quickly I quieted down then. I remember how I was not terrified, but rather concerned about my father and his mood and his well-being.

It was my concern that shut myself up. My good Chinese son instinct that told me not to burden my father anymore with my childish foolishness.

We'd never spoke of that incident again. In fact we never really spoke again. He still walked me to school until maybe I was nine when we hired a full time nanny/housekeeper who took over the responsibility, until when I was eleven, maybe twelve and began to go to school by myself, but from that day on I'd kept all my questions on my way to school to myself.

But that's my father for you, someone who always pretended to be a gentleman, when he was not.

The day went past quickly, a day where I did no workout, no reading, no writing, no nothing. And then at dinner time, I met up with my mother at the hospital cafeteria and had our fast food dinner, like we were still the family when I was a little boy.

I NEVER KNEW

It's been a week since my first day to the hospital. I have not done any groceries, now my fridge was empty, and all the house work was piling up, even my always clean kitchen was starting to get dirty.

I ignored all that. I was hungry. I scavenged through my fridge, trying to find something to rid of the hunger now. All I could find were my mother's grape juice as they sat in the middle of the top shelf, all six of them together as they stared back at me and my empty shell.

So I took one, poked it open with its straw and sipped the whole can in one go, before I went into my room to change.

I had to get ready. I have a full day. After my run to the hospital this morning, I was changing myself up for going out with Dorian tonight. I should have thought about what going out all night would do to my body, but two rules I lived by forbade me to turn tonight's date down:

1). Never abandon a member of the family, and

2). Never let my parents come between me and my family.

I already let them take over my day life, it was time for me to reclaim my night outs. Hence, this night I must go out with Dorian, no matter how tired I was from the week at the hospital.

Dorian said it was a "can't miss" party. It turned out to be a house party at some fashion designer's residence near Tianmu. I suited up for it, as you know, we are talking about Dorian's friends so I couldn't look too shabby.

It's always nice to know what your role is before going to parties, and on our cab ride there Dorian informed me of that, "You're my writer friend that I'm introducing to them."

So I was the talent, got it. It's one of the many perks of going to parties with Dorian, he is always so smooth you never felt out-of-place when you go out with him.

When you go to parties filled with fashion designers, models and their agents, it's good when you bring your own in-house talent along. It's the same as bringing your own wine to a wine tasting party.

In this case I was the wine, as Dorian talk with others about my writing talent the same way you talk about fruitiness and tannins while I stood there oxidize, give out scent and grinned like an idiot.

As a perfect example of what I have just described, a modelling agency took their entire regiment of newly signed foreign talents with them to this party tonight. I watched as the agents and their assistants talk endlessly. It just goes with the lifestyle I suppose. Hey, there's a lot of beautiful girls around to talk to.

It was an interesting building we were in. The house was a gated house by itself next built on the lower half of a small mountain. Although a quite small, what was nice about the place was that the owner clearly deliberately kept some of the older trees which came with the house around, and used them to build this forest-like environment. She even built a treehouse on top of one of the trees, with its own elevator from the garden, and a bridge which connected it to the second floor of the main house.

Aside from h'orderves and champagne, the party also came with Dance Dance Revolution, the game that I shouldn't have to explain in too much detail. The game was actually played on a projector in the living room which more than made up for the boxing ring feeling the game should have with it. It got intense.

And I like intense.

It didn't feel stuffed shirt. It actually felt more like a house party. Even the h'orderves didn't look as pretentious as other parties I've been to. I actually felt like we could make some real friends that night.

Dorian did his part of course, introduced me to the hosts, this couple where the husband was in construction and the wife was the fashion designer. She was actually quite famous, her name brand was all over Taipei City.

There were so many husband-and-wife teams here in Taipei it was almost a norm that a marriage in the bedroom meant a marriage in the office. However, their story still interested since it was the less clichély Taiwanese version but the more clichély American; that the husband and wife had separate business, but then molded them together into an alliance of sort, rather than just the wife move into the husband's company to work, which was the more common one here.

"They were separated so many times I'm not even bothered to keep track of how many times anymore." After we paid our respects to the hosts, Dorian gave me this little piece of gossip. "I don't know why they keep doing it."

"The marriage or the breaks?"

"Both?" He said and we both smiled.

And then we took our time to talk to all the people around, sometimes together, most of the time separately. I guess maybe the treehouse outside reminded everyone of their more innocent, younger self from their childhood days, most people there didn't give off a feeling that they were keeping a distance from you.

I even hit it off myself with this one girl who was an agent. At first it was a little awkward since she thought I was a model myself (where the hell did she get that idea?) and so she said it quite a few times that she wasn't poaching; and the awkward part was that I did not correct her at first.

She was quite talky. I found out where she went to school,

how she got into this business, the average rate they were paying to production extras now... She was the kind of Taiwanese girl that seemed to be willing to share everything with a complete stranger; a little naive and a little too trusting, but warm you up quickly.

That was the something special that people who came to Taiwan always went back home talk about. The people part of the story.

Overall it was a very successful night, I would say. I met a lot of people, probably had one or two good story line there to write about, at least to plot about, though I didn't when I would actually write them. Writing seemed like such a distant memory now.

Of I went on the Dance Dance Revolution floor tonight, after a few drinks of some quite nice Australian Shiraz, and I kicked ass. I must have danced twenty rounds without being eliminated. I was good, even my avatar was impressed that I was so quick with the steps.

Suffice it to say that I was pretty wasted when we left the party that night. I almost had to dragged out of the game, although I went peacefully. I had quite enough fun for a night.

"So you enjoyed the party?"

Dorian asked me as we sat in the cab, my head leaned against the window while my right hand was holding my the area around my upper belly on the left near the heart.

"Yeah. Thanks for taking me man." I said, that's all the intelligent response I could think of now to say, really.

"Yeah I was not gonna introduce these guys to Charlie." Dorian said, as if he wanted to explain his actions to me. "I mean, my resources I'm best to leave them to you. You can make the decision whether to hand them over or not. But I'm not just gonna give them to Charlie."

This was perhaps why we all put up with Dorian, or why Dorian was still around with us. He was actually a very good man. Fair in his own way.

"I'd never realized you were so competitive." Dorian went on to say.

I was already asleep in the cab, so I guess he didn't say another word. I could have made fun of how having been friends all these years that this was when he found out. But if I had been awake, my response to that probably would have been this,

"I didn't know that about myself either."

THE BIG CHILL

I met up with Maddy for coffee and tiramisu the next day. She seemed to settle into Taipei quite well, as she had promised herself, she adapts quickly. And if I might add, the abundance of cake around this town also helped.

I found out she had a big craving for cakes, which was why we would usually end up in one of those 85 Degree Cafe, or the German Bakery in Tianmu that everyone at her office goes to, either for the tiramisu or the raspberry chocolate pie.

I've been having insomnia for a couple of days, and it has gotten worse recently, to a point my breakfast turned into lunches and afternoon tea. It was getting harder and harder for me to go to the gym for a workout. I was not writing anything, even my blog has become stagnant, having gone without updates for weeks now.

I have just finished telling Maddy about the party I went with Dorian last night, up to the detail of how after I got back to my apartment, I passed out and slept on my living room floor, with the door opened the whole night. She laughed a little bit, but not too much.

"Wasn't that funny?" I asked.

"Yes, yes it was funny." She said, as she finished the last sliver of that tiramisu.

I've also found out on these meetings that she belongs to that generation that's more comfortable texting than talking. When we met on these occasions she scarcely spoke, and even when she did, it was usually about her work or her plans later… with other people.

"So what are you doing tonight?" She asked me almost routinely.

"I might go out with some friends tonight."

"Is it Flynn?"

No, little girl, Flynn and I don't talk no more- "No it's some other people."

She was quiet again, texting on her phone and didn't seem like she wanted to pursue this no more, so I added myself, "Do you want to join us?"

"No I can't." She said without moving her eyes off her phone, "I have to work tomorrow."

"Ok." I said, "Do you want to go?"

"Yes!" She said, all excited like how she was in Beijing.

I walked her to the MRT station, which she was going to take to go back to her office. I could have joined her, but instead as if I have gotten tired of us trading one-sided conversations, I dropped her at the kiosk and went back out. I went to the empty park bench next to the entrance and sat down there, trying to wake myself up before the night that was coming.

I thought about how uninterested she seemed to be about me and my day, and I immediately dismissed those thoughts. Ah I was thinking too much, I thought, this insomnia was getting into my head. She was just a young girl whose life had much less melodrama than mine, less strange corners to cover up.

I mean take a good look in the mirror, man. I looked like I'd been poisoned: swellings under my chin were showing, the area around my eyes as dark as the dark side of the moon, rough hair and unevenly shaven face; I wouldn't want to talk to myself.

Maybe I should do something a little more drastic, I

thought. I should just go out and play some hoops. I should just go out and break my body as hard as I could, so it wouldn't be so out of shape and unattractive as it was now.

"You lied on the floor the whole night? With your apartment door opened? No way!" Charlie said after I told him the concluding tale of my night out with Dorian. He was laughing so hard I thought for sure he was gonna need some mouth to mouth later.

After a couple of times missing each other and lagging for a meet, Charlie invited me on the phone to take part in one of his "chill party". I took it as a positive sign that he's finally ready to talk some business.

We all agreed to meet up at Wayne's studio, where they hosted the premiere last time. I got there a bit late, in a sports jacket, a T-shirt and a pair of jeans. And when I went in what I called "wonderland" the last time, to my surprise, and the ever expanding definition of the word "chill" from Charlie, it was actually a costume party.

"Yeah you didn't know?" Charlie said as I guess he deduced from my outfit that was what I was thinking.

"Thanks for the heads up, luckily," I said, "I always dress as Marlon Brando."

I was making reference to the fact that in his early days Marlon Brando was known for his slightly more rugged and therefore less-refined sense of fashion. A reference that was clearly lost on Charlie and his group of this generation of filmmakers, judging from the way that nobody laughed at my joke. No one. It didn't matter, I didn't have Brando's muscle anyways, just his fat face.

Tonight we had one girl dressed up as zombie nurse, the other as "regular zombie", another as vampire and one more as the more regular witch. There wasn't much drinks around, neither was there any snacks, so I wasn't sure if we were just meeting here and the party was gonna be somewhere else, or if this was it.

However, we soon went to the smoker lounge, the balcony

behind a closed door, and sat in a circle, when I became pretty sure what kind of a party exactly a chill party was. As I expected, one of us took out his stash, (Not gonna say who, it's punishable by death when you do this in Taiwan; yes, it's very medieval I know. And it's medicinal, I know.) rolled it, lit it, took a hit and began to pass it around; some of us who couldn't wait had lit up cigarettes, such as Byron and Charlie, both were a bit of a chainsmoker.

I asked Charlie about it and he said,

"Yeah man. Been kinda stressed out."

"What about?"

"Nah, just stuff." He was vague about it, "I'm going to the army next month."

"Oh?" I replied.

That's something a lot of ABCs have to go through when they come back to Taiwan. Taiwan has compulsory military service for its male citizens, and those whose nationalities that weren't Taiwanese but parents were, by Taiwanese law were automatically considered citizens as well.

There are ways around it of course, as no democratic country could forcefully force foreigners to serve in its military (not yet anyways) but those who chose to come back and stay would generally just get it done and out of the way.

"What about the projects you were building? You're just gonna let them go?" I asked.

"No I still have some stuff going." He replied rather vaguely, as the "roll" was passed to him. He took a hit, then said "And I'm not posted to military position, I got like a different posting to the ministry of culture. So I thought why not? Gonna build some connections there and see what happens."

"A civil post?" I said, knowing what Charlie meant by "different".

"Yeah, yeah." He replied, then, finished with the "roll" in his hand, he passed it today.

Before I continue I should tell you guys first that I don't use any drugs. I don't even take cold medicine when I have the common flu. I don't have any moral reasoning behind it, rather just that as a smoker who drinks, I thought I had enough vices as it was, I really didn't need a new one. Nevertheless, I took a hit tonight; a big, fat hit.

"So what are we doing about Model Massacre?" I asked Charlie, I didn't feel anything right the way as I passed the roll along.

"I was thinking about starting a screening club." Charlie said as if evading my question as he turned to Byron, "Yo we could do it on the weekends you know? Kinda like the one we went to at Jean-Baptiste's place?"

"Yeah man, that would be cool." Byron said with his thick Midwest accent.

I had no idea who was the guy they were talking about, all I knew was that for some reason the name "Jean-Baptiste" made me wanna laugh, a little more than usual than any other nights.

"We're thinking about building a team together." Wayne said. I wasn't sure to whom, or if it was to anyone at all. "My investor is in place now for building the studio, if we can convince them with a good team to run it."

"Have you guys decided where you gonna build it?" Charlie asked.

"My backers and I, we are still looking." Another vague answer of the night, "They know the ways around, they will figure it out. My part of this is to form the managing team."

"Ok that's cool." Charlie said as if he was satisfied with the answer.

To be honest I would be satisfied too if I could get something to eat, I suddenly felt very hungry. My hands too, I couldn't really feel my hands. My hands and my… long fingers. That's funny, long fingers.

"Yeah that would be cool. Aaron and I have partnered up. We are thinking about forming a small studio first. Aaron has also studied a number of the local movie funds to see how we might approach those."

Byron said, pointing to that kid Aaron next to him. I call him "kid" because he didn't look older than eighteen, and was really pale with grey blue eyes and a long jaw.

And for some reason the fact that made me wanna laugh too, but not as funny as my fingers though. Seriously why are my fingers so long and… weightless? I can't even feel them. That's hilarious.

Then the doorbell rang and Wayne went out to get it. I didn't know why or how, I decided to say to everyone then,

"You know you guys should put that thing away." I said, I was talking about the stash. But I guess just like my Marlon Brando joke either I wasn't speaking human language, or everyone just didn't get what I was saying. Or maybe the fact that I said it while staring at my fingers was what caused this little miscommunication to the others.

"That was the police." When Wayne came back, he said, "I don't know why he was here for a visit. He didn't even say. At first I thought it was someone showing up in a police costume, but then I didn't know him you know? Anyway he asked if we heard something funny and when I said no, he just left."

"That was so weird." That's what the zombie nurse said.

"Taiwanese police work, that's how they do it. In the States we could file harassment lawsuits but here it was just normal. If you file a complaint then they can argue plausible cause and get a fast-tracked search warrant, so most people would just not pursue it." I said, suddenly was able to field full sentences with eye contact. Maybe I just wanted to know why she dressed up as a zombie nurse?

Suddenly we were all laughing at that rather serious piece of knowledge I just dropped. And from then on everything we talked about was funny for some reason. We talked about Lucy, the Luc Besson movie that was shot in Taipei. We talked about fake news that were used to boost PRs, conspiracy theories about every year's nominee for awards and movie funds…

And then, maybe it was lack of sleep, but honestly it could have been anything as I didn't know if I was awake or asleep when it happened, or if it happened at all, but one of us went to the bathroom. And then there was a lot of noise. And then I guess Wayne went to have a look, then all we heard was he screaming over to us,

"SHIT! He's on the floor!"

We all went over and this was what I saw: one of the guys was snoring on the bathroom floor, his cheek on the edge of the bath rug, which had a kind of heart-shaped pile of vomit on it. While everybody was just there, I started laughing again.

And then Charlie, who was also kind of laughing himself, asked me,

"What's so funny man?"

"That took skills man." I said like a stupid Californian, "He vomited on the only piece of rug in that whole bathroom, that took skills man."

And once I pointed it out, everyone there just looked back at the guy on the floor and suddenly there was an explosion of laughter. I couldn't remember much of the rest, but at least for that night, I was chill.

THE SICKNESS

Isn't it ironic how going to the hospital could get you sick?

Here's something that you people never been to Southeast Asia before you come for a visit, before you come here for the cheap beers and seafood and sunshine. The flu here is as fashionable and exotic as the Parisian runway. And the news barely broke out about the new flu going around, as expected I got hit by it first.

I needed some sleeps anyway, you all know what I have been doing to myself. Not sleeping was like the ultimate way of a slow, and agonizing suicide. I'd also killed all but one can of grape juice that my mother had given me. "Maybe I should just finish all this now. Why not?" The minute that thought sprang to my mind I just didn't want to drink that juice no more.

I was not depressed. Wistful, perhaps, but not depressed. Although I don't blame any of you becoming depressed in this generation of ours. Knowledge was a known depressant; and our generation simply knew too much to be happy.

Everything needs evidence now. We view everything with a due process mindset; we were trained to follow everything with an empirical view, and when something doesn't fit that process, we're left with a throbbing headache like we were sick.

Bad people don't always have bad intentions. In most cases

they don't have any intentions, good or bad. In our society where intention dictates everything, as they lead to motive and evidence, from prejudice to rape to homicide trials, we could no longer handle the most basic of human error, ones that were made because the people who committed it didn't know what they were doing.

That's a fact. And you don't need evidence for simple facts of life like this. You can't tell if someone's bad from whether he/she has bad intentions or not, instead the lack of it usually proves the most. When people don't think about what they are committing, they are likely to cause the most damage. It is as human as it gets.

Let me give you the full lives of my parents as I know it, since it seems that it won't escape my sugar-induced fever mind at the moment:

When they first got married, they both had jobs. My mother's career was on the fly at the time, before my father quickly point out, as it was the accepted value in Taiwanese society, that the man should be the primary breadwinner of the family, and the woman should simply stay at home.

She was already pregnant with me, so she quickly agreed. that was the first of many times where she was forced to leave work because of him. She became a stay home mom for a very short time, before the first of many times the total and complete failure of my father's impossibly bad business ventures. It put us into deep debt for the first time.

I was still a baby then, a toddling reminder of reality check; so my mother went back to work, leaving my father a bitterly disappointed stay home dad that still lied to his drinking buddies: He said to them, that even though both him and my mother had busy work schedules (when he was unemployed), that he was the one putting in time to raise me up, implying to them my mother had been negligent to her duties to me.

The truth couldn't be further from this, as I told you he barely had the patience of walking me to school. It was the first of his many lies, where he put his storytelling to good use and made himself sound like Jesus Christ while others in his family mere mortals like Saint Joseph: saints, just not quite the Christ, with their fatal flaws as traditional as they got, such as being negligent to your only child.

Then came the next instance. I was barely in second grade then, when one night, my mother finally had enough and was going for a divorce, after many instances of infidelity my father had accumulated over the years that she had to witness. Such a dirty word of the quiet Taiwanese society, divorce, where a career woman might be accepted because of Madame Chang, but a divorced one was still shamed for her not sacrificing for the family.

My father beat my mother up that night, leaving her a broken nose among other things, a trail of blood from my living room to the aisle, leading up to the elevator, as she barely made it out of the apartment alive, right in front of my barely school-age eyes. Nevertheless she made it out that night, leaving me behind frightened, not knowing what to do with my father by my side.

In the end the divorce did not happen and the separation did not last; my mother had compromised once again because she couldn't bare the days without me, she said. And over the years we acted like this never happened, even my mother had forgotten it somewhat, as she claimed, who must remember somewhere in her mind that bloody face and that broken nose; why because even I remember it just like yesterday.

We moved on. We moved on as my mother with her second run, had a successful career in the advertising world of Taiwan, one that could have been more successful had she moved her career up along with the international firms to their Hong Kong or Japanese or Chinese headquarters, the prime locations in in Asia where the real successful Taiwanese ad-executives thrived in her days, after the Taiwanese market faltered along with the poor performance of its economy in the mid-90's.

Of course she had the perfect reason not to, the well-accepted one: me. She was afraid of the separation and insist upon playing a significant role in my growing up. Giving me the right family value, of lying to yourself so others may lie to you, particularly in those vital adolescent years where so many Taiwanese teenagers went down the wrong path.

Most of her colleagues accepted it as it was, and thought it had nothing to do her actual mistrust of my father, and his possible influence on me growing up, how unsafe she felt it was to leave me to just him while she pursued her career. None of that mattered as my mother successfully finished her career and was now retiring.

Twenty years I grew up in the house where the fight never ends, and it all seemed to about to end then: I was moving out the place I grew up in, the place I once called home. And my mother was retiring, finally able to live a quiet life without stress. And my father could just be happy about that, if not for the retirement money, right?

After her retirement, my father convinced my mother to withdraw all her pensions for him to go on an investment trip to China: one that ended up being a scam that nearly put my father in a Chinese prison, if my mother had not stepped in and saved him, again.

After that little instance, the once Number One Woman Executive of Taiwanese Advertising Industry was forced to live her retirement out in a state quite similar to the state of her industry now: an even smaller place than the one I grew up in, with a man she loved so much she couldn't leave for any reason: least of all of the negative example a divorce would have set for me.

I sure learnt a lot from their example though. I learnt to never get married, to never trust my life in the hands of another person who might just hurt me the same way he hurt her. The same way he hurt me. The same way, she hurt me.

I never understood why they went through the separations and the back together, the fighting and the false peace, filled with tension. If all they wanted was to torture each other over their false feeling that they thought was love, they shouldn't have gotten married. They certainly shouldn't have children, who could only serve as witness to their miserable and unfulfilled lives.

Children? Ha! Mostly me. Only me. I was the only one who had to live with this outside of the two of them. I hated them, but not as much as I hated myself, as they were only confirmations of what I was a carrier of, the sickness of their gene of unkept promises.

I vowed to never have that happening, to form my own family and pass this sickness on, as irresponsibly as my parents have. Little did I know, I suppose, that I have already passed it on, now I realized.

Look at Flynn and me? Look how everybody have grew distant since Flynn's "Party of the Year". All this come back to the point I made earlier about how bad people don't always have bad intentions.

There was no intent from my parents, whether to each other or to me, as there was no intent from me to make "my family" miserable. Did my father intent to sabotage my mother's career? If he did, couldn't he have done it without getting himself into trouble? Did my mother intent to have me distance myself away from this chaos she had a part in creating? Of course not, my mother had nothing but love for me. Did I intent to hurt them when I only refer to them as my parents and not my family? You be the judge of that.

I do not think I hate them. I pity them, because I know there's nothing more contagious as a sickness as disappointment; and that's all they were to me now, as I'm sure I was to my family.

The train of thoughts had stopped, and suddenly I had only one thought. I needed to get out. Forget about lying in bed, trying to recover or catch up on some sleep. Forget about all that. I needed to get out of this.

45 MINUTES OR LESS

I've been out playing basketball every afternoon and nights, whenever I get out of my daily trip to the hospital or dinner with my mom.

I am not a good player. I could never run very fast, nor was I very tall, but like every kid in Taipei I knew the game a little, as it was one of the main sport available to the crowded city.

It's not something that required a lot of preparations: all you needed to play basketball in Taipei was to pick up your ball and go to the nearest court and try to join a game. There were always three on three games that were looking for players for the day.

Honestly I didn't know when was the last time I caught a wince of sleep. But I did not stop coming out. I actually did feel more alive as I came out on these nights. It didn't make sense but I continued.

I stopped writing. When I did write, I wrote sporadically, mostly just scribbling notes on my blog. I have not been eating right, and when my mother asked me about how I was doing during dinner I couldn't even make the effort to tell her I was ok, instead I just grunted most of the time.

But I did not stop basketball. I still had something to live for, without a movie project, without my best friend and the guy I grew up with, with my family falling apart and my parents trying to force me back to their lives, I still had something to work out for, the take the next breath for. I said to myself every day that as I went from every half-day I spent in the hospital to the basketball court, rain or no rain, sick or not sick.

I was still recovering from my fever when Mark called me up for lunch. I was going to turn him down as it conflicted with my hospital shift, but once he made the effort to mention that Rach was coming I agreed right the way. I have not seen them both in a while.

The lack of sleep had taken its toll. I sometime wake up in time of the day where I had no concept of time; I didn't know if it was the morning or the night, if I was going to the hospital to play my role as the good Chinese son or to meet up with my friends as the smooth talking, always smiling ABC. In spite of my best effort, my parents have affected my life the way I least wanted it to be.

This was a work lunch, which was not that much different from the ones in the States. There's really no time to pick a restaurant, you would have to meet at a previously designated location. Once you're there, just order whatever there was on the set lunch menu, so you would be served in a timely manner before you had to leave for your post lunch meeting back in the office.

Expect to talk fast, ignore the constant checking of time or texting your lunch partner would definitely be doing the whole time. They're not rude; they're just professional. There is a zero-tolerance policy on lateness in Taiwan. Pays would be duct. Bonuses would be lost; and even working in these conditions, people still needed to do overtime no matter what. Hence a lot of people here still bring their own lunch to work, something we might think is completely sad in the US while here in Taiwan it's a very common practice.

Nevertheless, the three still found a nice corner table next to a window in a pasta place (Not Italian, as it was often this case here in Taipei, this was more of a Japanese Pasta & Pizza joint). I didn't even have to raise the long looming question creatively, for the minute I saw the sitting arrangement I had my answer: I was one side and Rach and Mark were sitting together on the other.

It was nice that we could skip all the pleasantries and jumped right into our conversation; it usually take ages to get on topic that way.

"This feels just like back in New York." I said, "You, me together, update each other on the things over a quick lunch."

"Whatever happened to that girl you were dating back in New York?" After a sip of water, Mark looked at me and asked rather sharply.

"Well I am here, and she's not." I said, "That should tell you everything."

"Am I gonna be the only non-New Yorker here?" Rach jumped right in.

"You have never been to New York?" Mark seemed surprised. "I miss New York! I miss those days! I have never realized how cool college was until now. It was such a contend environment. You could just make friends and do wishful thinking about silly ambitions and no one would mind. I love to go back to school now."

"So why don't you?" She asked, seeing how Mark didn't really answer her first question.

"My parents?" When Mark answered Rach that, he actually shot me a look like saying "You know what I'm talking about. You know my parents."

"They just want me to stick to banking and build my experience so eventually I would take over the family business. That's no secret, there's no shame for me to admit that. I am the only son. If that means I have to work in banks for a couple of years, I will do just that." With that, Mark concluded his little speech.

"I thought you like banking?" I asked.

"I like investment banking and equity. But day to day banking? Even zombies have better lives." He then realized Rach was there so he added, "I don't mean you Rach. I think your job is terrific."

"No you're right," Rach said rather plainly, "my job sucks."

"Well considering how much money that genre is making I'd agree with you." I said, taking this conversation back to the zombie reference.

Mark laughed. He'd always had a sort of easy humor button. Rach laughed a little too, quite reserved and different from her usual laugh.

"Hey has Charlie talked to you about his project?" Mark asked. I guess the film reference reminded him of that.

"Yeah, he's shutting it down for now. He has to go to the army." I replied without paying enough attention, but suddenly I could see on his face we had some conflicting information. "You heard something different?"

"No, no. Oh now I just feel bad." Mark said, "He came to me and asked for money. He wanted me to invest he said. He had other investors in place and he just wanted me to do the first bit of injection. I turned him down. I might be my father's son, but I had no control over his money…"

"Yeah, and besides movie investments are risky if you don't know what you're getting into." Rach interrupted him and was finishing his answer for him.

"Yeah exactly. It would be quite thoughtless for me to just jump into that. Anyway I didn't want to say this, but I feel it was really awkward for him to be asking me for money consider how little I knew about him." He concluded.

"Yeah it would be quite strange." I said.

Seeing we weren't gonna pursue this subject and the lunch was coming to a close, I just had to ask the question. I always knew the perfect timing for questions like this was to sneak it up, you're likely to get result more.

"So when did you guys make this official?"

They were at first a little confused at my question, but not too long. Once they knew what I was asking, as if they had planned this, they both said at the same time,

"We're not together!"

Which meant that they were. Since I got what I wanted

from a 45 minutes business lunch, I decided to tone down the excitement,

"Is that right?" I said it as if it wasn't a question.

I went out that night as planned to play ball, ignoring the pain and soreness that were already building up in my body.

I became more and more aggressive with my plays with each and every game. Part of it was because when you were the new comer you had to play more aggressive so others would be more willing to add you on their teams. Part of it was I was just in that zone, I guess. For some reason once I was in that court I just became that way, like something in me was unleashed.

Tonight when we were playing, I was guarding this kid who was a couple inches taller and much more muscular than me, who was posting me up in the paint. Normally I wouldn't guard someone this hard in the post, knowing the contact would do me no good, but for some reason I went all in tonight.

My left hand was on top, in position to block shots, while my right hand was aggressively trying to steal the ball down low. And I moved my body quite well. Every time he tried to shake me off with a spin I would spin with him and we just stuck in that same position for two, or three dribbles, regardless which way to the basket we were facing.

I didn't care about the sweat or the strain on effort, all I wanted to do was to keep him from scoring. And then I guess he got tired of trying to shake me off, so the next spin he basically bulldozed me with one step and shot off a turning hook. It didn't make it in, but at the same time it knocked me to the ground. I got hit in the face, as I dropped to the ground with my mouth filled with the salty taste of blood.

The guy apologized the minute he turned around and saw I was on the floor. Most of the other guys came over to help me up too, but I don't know what came over me, I pushed the guys' hands away and got up by myself with my other hand holding up my face and my bleeding nose, as I went and picked up my towel from the bench and left.

I turned a corner so none of them could see me, and just by using the towel and some water I stopped the bleeding. I spit out most of the blood in my mouth, and whatever was left I just swallowed. Then I went right back to the game.

I raised my right hand and waved at them, indicating that I was ready to play again. Everybody who saw my broken nose before was surprised to see me back so quickly, most of all that kid who gave the elbow to me, who I could see broke into some cold sweat. He probably thought I came back to beat him up.

And was he relieved when he saw I just wanted to play like nothing had happened.

Like I said, I really needed this.

I still had something to live for, without a movie project, without my best friend and the guy I grew up with, with my family falling apart and my parents trying to force me back to their lives, without something to write for, I still had something to work out for, to take the next breath for. And hey,

It was only one elbow to the face. I must look prettier now.

THE GOOD SON

I hand pinned a pair of Jade Orchids on the lapel on my jacket on the right hand side, as I got out the next day.

Jade orchids were small white flowers that gives out a scent that street vendors often sell to drivers as air fresheners in the streets of Taipei. I did this a lot in the winter, the only when you actually needed jackets in the subtropical streets of Taipei.

It's a habit that I have picked up its inspirations from my grandfather. My grandfather was from the Chinese city of Suzhou. It was he who used to pin a pair of white jade orchids on his lapel during the winter, the season when they usually blossomed.

And that's pretty much all I remembered of him as I rarely met him, even though when I lived in New York he lived just on Long Island. It was only an hour or so of commute for me to get off Manhattan to see him.

I was meeting Maddy today. As we met up in the coffeehouse on the first floor of her office building, she immediately caught sight of the jade orchids on my lapel and perhaps the scent of it as well when she asked me,

"What's that?"

"It's just something... for the winter." I explained.

"I love it!" She said, and perhaps smiled at something I did

225

for the first time since she moved here, "It's like an edelweiss."

"What's that?" Now it was my turn to ask the same question.

"It's this flower we would wear back in my hometown. Something that we'd all wear in all the towns upon the Alps, no matter if we were Austrians, Italians, German or the Swiss. It shows the lowlanders where we were from." She explained to me, quite cheerfully I might add.

"What happened to your nose?"

"Oh I broke it slightly the other day playing basketball." I said, "Don't worry, I'm all better now."

"Ok." She was still smiling.

I didn't know if it was that explanation, or the correlation between the two cultures there I could make in my mind that intrigued me, but suddenly this girl who was a couple years younger than me from Germany who never get my jokes suddenly turned into that girl I fell in love with back in Beijing then.

"Can the broken nose buy you dinner?" I asked jokingly. And to my surprise, she got it this time, laughing and replied to me, with that strong, harsh accent of hers,

"Yes."

The next day I went to the hospital. There was a typhoon in town, and there was nothing better than going to the hospital on a typhoon day. This is the kind of day when you wish you can drive; or for that matter, that you have a car.

No matter, this was my last shift.

I got up early and ran through the rain and the wind, as my umbrella turned over god knows how many times, and waited for hours when the bus tracker told me that the damn bus was only minutes away.

My bus driver's name today was Yong Xiang, which ironically had the meaning of "forever peaceful", since he drove like a maniac. Every gear change of his I felt like I was gonna get thrown off the bus. Yet with that kind of driving it still took us 45 minutes to get there.

When I finally got to the hospital, I quickly bought a rice ball and a yogurt at the 7-11. I had to have my breakfast literally in the rain since the patio behind it, despite its cover, was susceptible to heavy rain like today's typhoon wind. As I choked down my food and chugged my drink, it was already half past 10, so I went up quickly.

I entered the ward and meet up with my parents. My father was chatty as ever. While he was chatting with the nurse, who was taking his temperature and blood pressure, my mother was busy packing and putting everything together.

It probably came from her family's training, but my mother was a natural when it comes to packing. Like every time when we take those family trips it was always up to her to pack the luggage for the three of us while the two men would be in the living room watching television and being completely useless. And today just like it had always been, the minute my mother saw me, she told me to not to worry, "just go watch some television and we would be ready in a minute."

So I went to the visitor's ward. There in a room with a view out into the back of the hospital we had a hot water machine, some magazines and a television. Someone was already in there watching the news, so I sat down in a corner. I don't really watch much television myself, even though I do have a TV and cable here, as it is incredibly cheap here compared with the states, where the bill was at least four times more there than here. In spite of having it installed at my apartment and paying its bills, I rarely watched my TV. In fact I use my laptop and DVDs much more than TV.

About fifteen minutes into the twelve o'clock news my father came around the corner and joined me. His face full of smile, as he told me he was now in his full spirit and had gotten bored sitting in the room waiting for my mother to finish packing.

"She always takes too long." He said jokingly, "So what are you watching?"

"Nothing." I replied rather matter-of-factly.

Perhaps he caught my humorless tone. Perhaps not. In any

case he simply sat down next to me as if this was our living room and watched the news with me together. I didn't know how long it lasted. Perhaps only one or two more news segments, but we did not really speak that whole time. Or maybe we did.

And just like all the conversation we'd had before he probably went all over the place with his topics of choice, from what he thought was the best investment opportunity now (Not his business since he was no hedge fund manager) or the best art works now to collect quick (which he knew nothing about), or whatever conspiracy theory he was into at the time (again, he was no spin doctor, not his business). And I probably just nodded and answered all of them as shortly as I could while I sat there, knowing without looking that with my father's obsession with his own voice he was never going to notice whether I was paying attention or not.

That probably lasted until my mother showed up, now fully packed and ready to go. She now had a large duffle bag and a carry on. "We still have to go downstairs and check out." She said as I stood up and took over all the luggage.

"Not a problem." I said, "Come on dad, let's go!"

"I'll be done in a minute." He said with his eyes still fixed on the TV.

"Just watch it at home. The same news runs the 24 hours cycle you know?" I said.

"Alright, alright." He said, "Jeez a son that won't let me watch the news. What's up with that?"

Again, nobody bothered to answer that one.

It took us an hour to finish the process downstairs, mostly because it was lunch hour and fewer counters were opened at the time. Anyways while we were waiting I ended up agreeing to have lunch with my parents later. I really didn't feel like going but what the hell, you can't turn them down in their faces. Not every time.

By the time I got home from the lunch it was already late in the afternoon. I came home with a big bag filled with food that my mother had packed for me. She said that way I was good for the week. Typical mom, still treat me like the teenager that left her to college.

And in some respect I myself was willing to stay that way for her.

When I left their small apartment, it did almost feel like when I left them that year for college. I felt powerless as I said goodbye to my mother, knowing full well what I was sending her back to: now that my father has recovered fully, there was no stopping to the abuse no more. As long as she still loved him more than she loved herself, more than she loved anyone, more than she loved me, the abuse will continue. I would not have to wait too long before it happens again.

Being an ABC is a real struggle sometimes, since you have two completely different cultural heritages on you that aren't really reconcilable. The American in me wanted to do something about it, The Chinese/Taiwanese in me knew I couldn't. So the American got upset and just wanted to move away; and then the Chinese/Taiwanese just kept looking back.

There really is no debate which half of myself was there when I was with them. I'm always Chinese when I'm with my parents. That's the culture they raised me in, and therefore is the culture that I am sticking with them. I never even spoke in English with them, it was disrespectful, I always thought.

To them I will always be the good Chinese son; one that puts the happiness of my parents before that of my wife's, my children's and my own. That's the Chinese way, and no amount of multicultural counseling is going to change that.

And then I opened my refrigerator door, still thinking about how I could fit all the food my mother gave me in the tiny space in there, when I saw that last can of grape juice that my mother gave me that was left and still standing there in the middle shelf, staring at me back as I stared at it.

Then I just broke down. I suddenly felt the tiredness, the sickness that I have stored in my body the second I saw that can and I began to cry, uncontrollably. Uncontrollably like I used when I curled up in my bed, crying silently while my parents fought outside, as powerless as a child.

BRUNCH WITH MOM

It was a couple of nights after that, during traffic hour near dinner time, I was sitting on a bus on Nanjing East Road, one of the worst road in Taipei to be on during this hour. I was listening to Adele's "Someone Like You" on my headphone.

The bus was packed and with every stop there was more people trying to get in than there were people departing. I did not pay attention to any of that commotion as I normally would. I was just not in the mood.

I was coming home from a visit to my parents. My mother almost had to beg me to come so I would leave my coffeehouse chat hours with Maddy to join them for dinner. She invited Maddy to join us, but I was not so dense that I would let her find out that circus of a secret I was keeping from her.

When I got there, I discovered it was business as usual. Even before I got into the apartment, I could hear all the yelling and screaming, and all I think was I was right not to bring Maddy.

Apparently my father was on his medication again, (an excuse my mother would use that's in the vein of "he is good to me") which would agitate his mind (again, her words) that he became paranoid at everything my mother was doing: he accused her of hiding his medications. He accused her of stealing from him (what was there to steal?) and he accused her of trying to poison him with her food.

I used to try to mediate and sort out their differences and try to talk them out of a fight. But my father would always get so offended of me stepping in he'd just accuse me of taking sides and storm out the place. Then when he was back when I'm not around I knew he'd made a living hell out of my mother's life all over again. I can't always be around, and really, he wasn't in a position to cause the damage on my mother when I was in the second grade no more.

So I did the smart thing, and left even before dinner had started. After my mother found out I had disappeared, she called me and tried to make me come back, with all her lies about how this was an "isolated incident" (No mom, I'm twenty-something, not stupid), I insisted on leaving. I just couldn't stand all the yelling no more, not now, not when I was a child hiding in my room, not ever.

It reminded too much of those familiar nights of my childhood, when my father would get worked up at nights when others who had a full day would usually go to sleep began to argue with my mother.

I was forced to participate in their fights, behind those always too thin in these Taiwanese apartment buildings: how my mother was a greedy, selfish woman who only wanted money, (usually said so when he wanted money to buy another bottle of drink); how my mother was a jealous bitch (when he came home drunk with smell of feminine perfume and a clearly made up story from a drunk), or how my mother was suffering from all these illnesses because she had sinned with her wrongdoings, (no dad, you just abused her to that).

It was getting all too familiar. Familiar to a point where I was almost reminded of the fact that I was part of that family, and forgotten that I was on the bus, by myself, sitting at a corner, listening to a song on repeat, trying to be alone, as away from those two as I possibly could.

It was always the hardest when you're trying to be alone,

because the harder you try, the more others would intrude upon your life. People are always talking, whether directly at you, or talking among themselves without paying attention to the person sitting at the corner who did not want to be part of their conversation. I wanted to be alone, I really wanted to be left alone.

Which led me to my next subject. The brunch I had with my mom that weekend. When my mother asked me to join her out for a weekend brunch, I said yes, knowing full well what it was about.

Of course I knew what this was about. The way our last meeting had ended, with me walking out of their apartment almost as soon as I got there, she would want to mend that damage as soon as possible so her only son wouldn't stop visiting her.

How many families were held together by the fear of losing one another? If you ask me there's too many. But unlike Tolstoy, I don't think it's the same kind of fear. No mom, I would always visit you. I would not visit that other person that was living with you now, but I would always visit you, and just you, no matter what.

My mother took me to Malange Cafe. Now before you make fun of that name, I'll have you know that this is Taiwan, and businesses with weird English names like that are everywhere. It all started normal enough, with us ordering the famous strawberry pancakes and coffee of the place and the conversation being relatively at ease.

"So I thought we could go visit when grandpa's in town." My mother said as we were served with the strawberry waffles that this place was known for.

"Who's he gonna stay with?" I asked.

"With your aunt Judy of course."

"Sure we'll go together."

I hated aunt Judy. She's one of those snobbish idiot who spends her day going to charities and church functions and yet never helps out with anything in her family, particularly my mother.

She knew nothing about the lives of the poor people she liked to talk about so consistently like reading off a speech. And of course because she's married to the son of grandpa's colleague in the government, who had quite a bit of money, she acted like she was better than everyone else in her family. She's the very definition of a snob.

"I'm sorry about the dinner. You know how your dad is…" She said and before she could say more I replied calmly,

"Don't mention it." He's not my dad, and that's what I really wanted to say, but I stopped myself.

Then I guess she felt the apology part of the conversation was over, so she predictably asked this next question:

"So what are you doing these days? Have you finally managed to find a job with that expensive Ivy League degree of yours?"

Here we go with that question from my mother again.

"Mom I have a job. My job even employs other people, mom. It's a good job. I just got my royalty transfer just last night. How do you think I'm paying for my apartment?" Even though I tried, I just couldn't handle this one indirectly. No matter how prepared I was for it, when it comes to my parents it's all about instincts instead of judgments. It's always too close to them to let go of my emotions and speak to one another civil.

"You call where you live an apartment? In the neighborhood you live in? I don't even know how you sleep at night." She went on, "You're smart, you should get a real job. That way you can get a real apartment that we could visit you sometimes. Writing is something that should be a… hobby you know."

My mother was not a snob, but sometimes she's infuriatingly patronizing when she talks about certain things. Maybe it ran in the family considering how her whole family was like? Whatever. Like I would want you two to visit me, I thought to myself.

"I'm really worried about you." And then those words just came right out of my mother's mouth.

"Worry" is a Chinese word for you're not good enough. It's a word of shame. The fact that you would worry your parents in Chinese culture means you are an ingrate. This brand of parenting, based around "the guilt of ingratitude" was surprisingly popular in Taiwanese families and a very useful tool to make your children's lives a living hell.

Parents who knew how to manipulate their children would know when and where to push this button and it pretty much always works. That's why we never wanted to worry our parents. That's why we study what we don't want to study, do jobs we don't want to do, marry and have children we don't want to have, so we could make our children do things we want them to do because they wouldn't want to worry us, like how we don't want our parents to worry. So the circle of life continues.

"Mom there's nothing to be worried about." I said, decided to stand my ground. "Just drop it. Let's eat this waffle..." which no one has touched since it was served.

"But I am worried!" My mother said, raising her voice slightly. "You're not building your relationship stably with anyone. You need a job for that, a real job with a regular paycheck. You need to enter the system for that. Think about your girlfriend. What's her name, Maddy? Think about when you want to settle down with her, how are you going to do that without insurance or housing or anything like that? How can you settle down with her in that tiny apartment of yours? What if you want to have children? That's what's important here, or you never get the benefits you deserve. People don't want to be with unstable people, you know? Human beings are animals that need one another. No one can survive on themselves. You need to build your own family, without it you will only drift around and end up alone..."

"I said drop it! Don't talk to me like that!"

The minute I heard she said family I just couldn't take it anymore. "Who the hell are you to talk to me about family?" I said, "Who the hell are you to talk to me about career? Your whole life is devoid of a fucking family and a fucking career!

You sacrificed your whole fucking family to have a stable relationship with a fucking loser and you wanna lecture me on that!? Who gave you the right?"

It was a small part of me that was filling the rest of me with that rage like wildfire. Fortunately I've been there before, whether it was the first time the two of them got back together and forced me to watch that freak show as I grew up, or the last time when there was nothing left.

And this was the kind of moment where you'd embarrassingly found every people in the noisy cafe was suddenly silent by your melodrama and had turned their attention to you. Before I could react, my mother blushed quickly, I guess her embarrassment at both having a bad son who wouldn't understand her worries and having this on public display, both being shame which was all that made up Chinese culture pushed her to such a level that she suddenly raised her voice at me and said,

"Look at what you did! Why can't you for once just listen to me!?"

This society is so healthy, I thought, so much of it driven on shame.

I understood her. I understood my mother. I understood from her perspective. Even though she loved me, to her I was the loser without a real job who has little future to look forward to. I just wished she could look into the mirror when she said that to me.

It was the biggest difference between being a Chinese son and an American son. When you're American, you could always try to prove your parents wrong by succeeding at what you want to do, there's no need for argument. Whereas as the Chinese son, you are already wrong for trying to prove your parents' wrong: insubordination is the ultimate sin in this culture, one that cannot be forgiven. You're the bad son when what you wanted to do something different from what your parents wanted you to do.

And that's what I was, as I was always the Chinese son to my parents, and to them I was a bad son for doing what I wanted to do, no matter how much pleasure it brings me to do what I do.

Which was why I got so mad I guess, that little part of me that was tired of the inaction from the rest of me. The part that was tired of being passive and just let them drove over me, in spite of the life I might have given up coming back just to be closer to them. The didn't want me to get closer, they wanted to be close and closed off, to be just theirs.

After that little episode my mother broke into tears, and then there was silence. Silence was the ultimate weapon in these things as it forces people to re-examine themselves and imagine up mistakes they might have caused on the others for the silence they were getting.

I knew she would never stop thinking like this, thinking that I have brought her shame, regretting at how I turned out to be. I was after all, her only son, and she could only want what she thinks was the best for me. But most importantly, if any difference this fight today had made, it's that it took away just that little bit more of the hope she had for me. And more space was there now for that silence between us.

HALLOWEEN

When everything goes well it often goes unnoticed, but when things go badly they go together, and it's always memorable.

Maddy and I been going out for a while now. When we meet up, most of the time just for coffee and desserts, I would talk about her day with her. I would ask her about what she plans to do later. The one thing we never seemed to talk about was my day and how I was doing.

Her lack of concern to me at first went unnoticed: she's younger, and had less problems in her life than the melodrama that was mine. So I was quite understanding to her lack of interest at anything I did.

But signs began to show. It seemed the more we talked, the less we found we had in common. Sometimes I felt like we weren't even a couple, as I watched her make more and more plans she had for her time off that never seemed to feature me at any point.

We became completely uninterested in what goes on with each other's life, as she paid little attention to the books and movie projects I was involved in, and I began to ask less questions about her job and her plans to go out with her friends.

I felt the romance fleeing. It was as if that kiss we had in

Shenyang never happened, like everything from the first time we met in Beijing until the trip we took together tracing the Manchu Route of conquest through Northern China never took place, and we were just regular friends hanging out over cake, from time to time.

Everything I learnt about relationship told me that this was not heading towards the right direction, and unless I took some action it might never amount to anything. And it was actually very simple, another Marian mantra: Find a mutual interest. If you didn't have any, humor her by just getting a little involved at her stuff, since you might surprise each other at what it is stuff you guys like to do together.

So we started clubbing together. Flynn was so right at the Party when he said Maddy was a closet party girl, she really was. It couldn't have come at a better time. I had all this free time now as nothing in my life was going, and the fact that so many nights I spent sleepless in my bed, staring in that blank ceiling that I was growing to hate.

But still it was exhausting for me. I nearly forgotten about that. I mean we all grow out of it at one point. You grow out of the Jell-O shots, the loud music and the repetitive yelling and dancing. You grow out of it the morning you woke up after you spent the night before feeling drunk and wasted and completely unable sleep because your body was actually acting up to all the alcohol rather than enjoying it, and you find your ears bleeding with all that Korean music still playing in them.

The funny thing is, once I attended one of these night outs with Maddy, she quickly decided that I should be included to all of them. At one point when it felt like she was trying to build a wall between us, now actually felt like we were going out again. The change came so quickly I couldn't believe it.

The time we spend together increased dramatically. Maybe this environment finally reminded her who I was when she met me at Beijing: someone different, someone exotic, someone with an expiration date; and I was expiring.

We basically go out three nights a week. And it was a lot of fun at first, as Marian always said it would, when you were just happy to be with your girl. And then, as it often would when you were pushed into something, thing began to feel stagnant again. At that point, frustration will grow and you soon find yourself a ticking time bomb waiting to explode.

Then came Halloween.

Halloween is a traditional club night every city and that includes Taipei. We went out the whole night and by 2AM, my pupils were dilated, my back pain was acting up so badly I could barely stand, and I was tired. Still, I put up my smile as if the whole night has been as enjoyable as the last.

Just when I thought the night was over, Maddy said to me that we were all heading to Nangang, which was on the other side of town, for some huge costume rave. She was as excited as a puppy, and so were her friends, mostly her colleagues who were her age or younger, basically I was the oldest in the group.

"Maddy I think I'm gonna skip this one." I said to her.

"Why?" She seemed confused.

When she asked me that I could hear Marian whispering in my ears, "you're just humoring her. Don't get serious when you're only humoring her."

You see I thought about it, but clubbing makes you do stupid things.

"Maddy, I'm an old man.

"I just need a little bit more rest than you do keeping up with a schedule like this, ok?

And I don't know about you, but if we're just hanging out, then I rather not have this relationship. I mean I went beyond the Great Wall with you. I rode horses with you, even though I hated being around strong animals that could potentially kill me. I danced the salsa with you. Hell, I kissed you when we were alone outside the club… If we're just hanging out, and the only way for us not to feel awkward around each other is when we could hardly hear each other over the music and the buzz, I rather this be it."

Marian was laughing at me somewhere. "Sucker!" as she would say, "Getting too old to have fun, old man!?"

Yeah, I was an old man, so I just left, that's another thing Marian taught me. That you stink up faster than anything when you said something stupid, and the best way to deal with it would just be "get out of there before somebody else smells it too."

As I walked on the street, alone, I wasn't just blindly walking through the street no more. My vision was back, as I was no longer just putting up a sound wall around that was pushing everyone away.

The streets were packed with people in costume.

I started to see. A lot of the parties around was closing and the quiet late night street was not so quiet no more. A lot of people were out, dressed in all sort of costumes, there were fairies, zombie policewoman, and zombie nuns. There was even a Queen Amidala from Star Wars, who I watched struggled walking around because of the length of her costume. She should have gone with a different one.

I lit up a cigarette, finally with the freedom to smoke as I crossed the street with this bizarre crowd of people, each heading in different directions. Some were heading home, other were probably just like Maddy, was heading to another party somewhere else.

I watched the traffic, with the cab drivers on the side of the street anxiously waiting to pick up their late fare. With many confusion as this sudden influx of people on these narrow streets meant a lot more unintentional bumping around, some were still drinking, some were smoking just like me. Some were just holding onto each other for direction and balance.

A lot of people were meeting for the first time, as coming out from under the darkness and the make ups back in the clubs finally recognized each other now under the brightness of the street lamps and neon lights and headlights. There must be some humor, as they probably were partying right next to each other back in there and yet, did not notice each other at all.

When you were drunk and just came out of the club, you would be deliriously happy with just about everything. And it was funny to watch hundreds of confused, humorously-dressed people laughing at different time at different corners of the street, in short bursts like an unintended symphony, with the signs and the neon-lights, this was almost like a well-choreographed musical. And I was a single man, smoking a cigarette, as I pass them by.

FLYNN DAY

I woke up in my smoke-filled room, having long given up my daily regime, starting with rising early. The hell with it. There was no point in doing any of that. I have been waking up late. I have stopped going to the gym. I have stopped playing basketball. Writing? The words were not coming, as Hemingway would say. Except unlike his cowardice with a shotgun, his toe, and his wall splashed with his brain matter, I was not going to just kill myself.

If anything, something else would have to kill me.

I thought as I lit up another cigarette.

Unfortunately it was also that time of the year, one that I'm just not that excited about. But Rach said we should do something about it. So I went along with it. It was my birthday after all.

Yes, my birthday.

Happy birthday to myself.

I rarely spend my birthday by myself. I usually spend it with the alcoholic, overeating Spaniard who never had to sleep, whose birthday is the same as me, in the combination of overeating, over-drinking, bad dancing with the music to match, and a boatload of hangovers. That Spaniard as you already know, is Flynn, who is born on the same day and the same year as myself.

I never figured out how we could be so joined in the hip, except maybe the fact that our very existence invalidated every astronomy

Hence we always called this day "Flynn Day", in part to satisfy the Spaniard's ego, but also because he was the one who set the traditions on how we spend this day. Normally exclusively only with members of the family, we would go to Dan Ryan's to get fed on all the best reuben sandwich and polenta fries you could have in Taipei. Then one round, maybe more than one round of drinking and toasting each other with single mole whiskey on the rocks, before we light up the cigars Flynn provided for us as we walked across SYS Memorial Hall in the middle of the night, heading to our usual booth in the club that came stocked with chilled bottles of champagne and Grey Goose Vodka and stay there 'til the morning.

It's not going to be like that this year.

I haven't spoken with Flynn since our big fight at his Tamsui mansion. We have decided to go on our separate ways since that afternoon. Whatever, I have not even thought about that or my birthday or anything since then, as I have been serving as a volunteer for elderly care at the hospital, smoked joint for the first time, showed my true color on Dance Dance Revolution in front of hundreds of fashion designers and models, being knocked to the floor full of blood on a basketball court. Then I had to watch my parents move back to their small apartment, knowing full well what was coming next once my father had his strength back...

In short, I have not thought too much about my birthday or the fight I had with Flynn or anything like that. And yet, in spite of my more than a decade of experience at dealing with hangovers now, the headache resulted from this night's debauchery proved to be more than I could handle.

It was all Rach's fault. It's not that she didn't try to give me a good birthday party, it was just she's really bad at this whole thing about organizing parties and stuff of that nature.

First the restaurant. In spite of her best effort at research, which included reading online reviews (Yelp was still not big here, so a number of reviews from individual food bloggers online, she said), reading the comment section on the restaurant's Facebook page, and the recommendations from her colleagues, in spite of all that I really, did not, like this restaurant:

It was a fancy Italian place that makes everything organic and had no menu, served only what the chef was making that night. I had no problem with restaurant serving no menu, except the majority of restaurants that do that here in Taipei don't do it right. And this place with its pretentious decor that looked like it came straight out of a Pottery Barn's catalog only confirmed my fear.

A no menu restaurant is a private dinner house. Usually to run a place like this, the person would have to come with 10, 20 years under their belt in a real landmark establishment, and was not interested at opening up a proper, demanding restaurant, who is someone looking for a little pride of setting up their own place before retirement. It is not for people who had no experience working at Michelin star restaurants but instead had money and thought that could buy them everything, such as experienced staffers, expensive ingredients, and even overpaying chefs with sound resume but lacked the appropriate years of experience to really run a kitchen on their own.

What they don't realize is that this is like a perfectly trained and kept body with all the right parts without a heart. And thus the menu they serve being soulless as it is invisible is perfectly understandable. There's nothing in there that wows you, as a reflection of the owner's inexperience. And it's reflected everywhere, from how they handle customers to how they run the whole service. Money and a passion for food is no excuse to disrespect an industry of professionals who took years to perfect their work to open and operate a place under their own names.

Sorry, the rant there went a bit longer than I expected, as I cut my under seasoned, over garnished scallop zucchini salad over a glass of over-priced white wine that showed up two course too early. Well, Mark picked the bottle. Maybe that's more of his responsibility.

Isn't it lovely to spend your birthday with a new couple when you're single? Mark always make a horrible party guest, as he never understood the guest part; to him, whenever he was invited to something meant it was another opportunity for him to take over with his endless commentaries. He was a bit of a showoff when he gets too comfortable like that.

For example tonight he kept talking about how good the food was, how all the dishes were made with exceptionally fresh ingredient in the "simplest of style that reminds us what good food really should taste like" (God that's such a cliché to say about a dish). How about the fact that a lot of these dishes had ingredients that did not complement one another? Taiwanese sergestid shrimp angel hair pasta? Nice in theory, beautiful in presentation, awful to eat.

But I did my part as the guest of honor and just let him talk. I even did my guest of honor thing by saying "thanks for coming tonight" to every one of those friends that Rach and Mark brought to celebrate my birthday. I could say that a lot since a lot of them seemed to have quite the busy schedule, as people came and went. Most of them were Mark's friends really, heir or heiress to the business, money manager, lawyer, that type of people.

And to conclude the meal section of the evening, we had my birthday cake that tasted like Styrofoam, Styrofoam for crying out loud. I was not even sure what the flavor of that cake was. But Rach looked so happy when she told me that this came from one of the best and most popular bakeries here in Taiwan that again she exhausted her research on, with online ordered queued up for months; so I smiled and took a huge chunk that she had personally cut for me, and ate the whole thing, pretended I loved it as much as the restaurant she picked for me, as the guest of honor that I was should.

That wasn't the only lie I told that night. I also neglected to mention that I was single again. I couldn't do it. I couldn't dampened these people's mood to celebrate a stranger's birthday. If other people wanted to throw a party for you, it's the least you could do to be happy about it, no matter how much it took to fake it: it's only love, and I loved Rach for throwing me this party.

We were supposed to hit the club tonight, except when we met up with Dorian, apparently we couldn't get in.

"I can't get us in." He said.

This was Marquee, one of the busiest night clubs here in Taipei which we frequented.

"Why can't you get us in?" Rach asked, "I thought you know the guy?"

"Someone… booked the whole place for tonight." Dorian replied as if there was something that he didn't want us to know. "Actually the guy said we could all go in, except him." Dorian said while he pointed at me.

"Who the hell would book the entire club…."

And then I got it, even before Dorian made it obvious with his follow up. Rage took over as the sight of being slighted by someone who was supposed to be my brother, simply because I told him the truth that his precious girlfriend was a piece of work, who undoubtedly was in there throwing his dough around to entertain her friends or everyone she could think of to show off her rich, good looking foreign boyfriend. She might even propose to him in there. At least my girl (yes I'm calling Rach a girl for the purpose of this paragraph) invited her friends to celebrate my birthday, not using it as an opportunity to show off to her friends and rub their faces in it.

"Let's go." I declared then and there.

"Let me go talk to him." Rach interjected, seeing the redness that warming up my cheeks.

"No, let's go. I don't need his goddamn permission to go to a club. To go to any club." I said, and as if it wasn't enough I added, "Fuck him, and fuck this fucking day."

But as it turned out, it was impossible to find another club to get into that night. It was as if this whole town that rarely ever had anything happening had all of the sudden decided to get busy that night. We were in the middle of the club district and there was not a single club that had room for us.

Everywhere we went it was booked for some event, or just so happened to be full when we got there; maybe they felt the vibe we were giving off, that we might spoil the business for them that night.

"We literally have been walking for almost an hour." Rach said. "I say here's what we do, let's get out of this snobbish district and go have some real fun! Who needs these snobbish crap, with the glitters, the shots and the lasers and the girls when we have each other?"

Even by Rach's standard, she seemed really over-excited, to a point as if she was compensating for something.

"I have to go." Mark declared suddenly, apparently he wasn't on the phone anymore. "I have to have breakfast with my parents tomorrow."

"Ok." I replied.

"Sorry I didn't get to meet your girlfriend tonight. Maybe next time? This was fun. great dinner!" He really liked that restaurant. Once he said that though, he sort of stayed there as if he wasn't leaving anymore.

'What?" Rach asked her quote, quote not her boyfriend.

"Shall we go?" Mark asked, clearly oblivious to his quote, unquote not his girlfriend's declaration earlier about keep going tonight. "I thought I could drive you home?"

'No need, we're just gonna go somewhere else." She said, with Dorian and I standing on each side of her shoulders.

'But… it's quite late." He said like he was a first grader on a school night, "It might not be safe."

"Well you trust A-Zed and Dorian don't you?"

Rach's more than blunt question I guess took Mark by surprise, and put him in a bit of a conundrum on how answer it with his usual diplomatic choice of words.

"They will protect me, so don't you worry."

"Alright," Mark could only say, "happy birthday A-Zed."

"Thanks for coming." I said.

"God he's such a prep-school boy." Once Mark

disappeared at the intersection down the road in the middle of the dark Taiwanese night, Rach said as if she was nibbling in my ear.

'Not bad enough for you?" I replied, noting the sarcastic undertone of her choice of using the words "prep-school boy".

"Not even close." She said as if she was gonna kiss me. It would have been quite interesting, had Dorian not butt in,

"So you guys are gonna hit some other club?" He asked.

"Yes, we're gonna go across town to those clubs college kids go to near Tai Power Building." She said.

"OK then I'm gonna go." Dorian said, "I'm actually supposed to meet someone tonight, and I'm now… really late."

"Ok!" Rach answered for me, before she smiled somewhat viciously at Dorian and added, "But if I find out, and I will find out, that you went partying with Flynn, I will track you down, and I will kill you. You got that?"

"Yes." Dorian said, having been reduced by fear into an obedient schoolboy, before leaving at a direction opposite from where we were heading.

"So it's just the two of us?" She said, "Where's Maddy now? You wanna call her?"

"I rather we do that after we're actually inside a club."

"Alright! Let's go have some fun!" She said as she wrapped my left arm with her right, "Let mama show you a good time."

"Take me to the mama then, bro!" I replied, knowing that answer would be on her nerves.

"Shut up!" She slapped me as she said, but she was laughing when she said it.

Once it became the two of us the night became easier. Not as much anxiety about the places we were going to. Not as much anxiety doubting if we were entertained or entertaining. Not as much anxiety about adding another year to my age. We were once again just two people out to have fun for the night.

We ended up at a dance club near Tai Power Building -the worst I might add, as all of them were in that location- and we just danced and drank in that low-ceiling underground space with blasting music and filled with smoke that definitely was more than just regular tobacco.

I actually forgot about Maddy while we were in there. I forgot about a lot of things. I forgot about Flynn Day. I forgot about my parents. I forgot about family. I forgot about it all and little by little, Rach and I ended up at a nearby park, drunk and laughing somewhat uncontrollably, as we held onto each other for balance while we walked.

"What the hell was that song they were playing in there?" Rach said, making a comment about the music we suffered when we were sweating in the dance floor. "What's wrong with these college kids now? They can't dance. They don't know their music, and they can't even have a proper conversation."

"You're telling me? I'm dating one." I said, quite wasted myself, "To that big, blonde head of hers, James Brown is a type of doughnut."

"That's so sad!" It really wasn't, but then the way Rach said it, dragging the end of every word and shaking her small head, it sounded REALLY, REALLY SAD.

"Do you remember that first night we met, when we slept together?" She said, "I was drunk off my ass, and you took me to your apartment, and let's face it you could have done anything to me, I wouldn't mind. But no, you helped me cleaned up a bit, loosen my shirt and skirt, rubbed my face with a hot towel, then just let me sleep in your bed."

"My only bed." I said, "I slept on the couch. I warned you about doing shots with Flynn that night."

"Yeah, you know for an asshole, he's really good at some stuff." She said as if with some romantic sentiment of reminiscence about a good time past.

"He's good at A LOT of stuff." I said, "Drinking, guitar, basketball, driving, a lot of stuff."

"Yeah but he's still an asshole." She said.

"A big asshole." I added.

I was feeling a bit uneasy. Normally when I felt this over my limit and hammered I would smoke a cigarette, maybe more than one.

"Just do it!" She said, sensing already what I was craving.

"I don't even know if I have one."

"Stop pretending, I saw it in your shirt pocket." She said, her finger on my swollen pocket as she spoke.

I took one cigarette out of that pocket, put it on my mouth and lit it up. We were at the stage now where verbal communication was unnecessary for these things.

"All I know is, A-Zed?" She then changed her angle, as she focused on me. "You're not doing well. You haven't been. I could tell. You've been looking upset for a long time. Are you still writing your blog?"

"Yes." I replied, "I take it that means you haven't read it?"

"Nope, don't have the time." She said, "You should have went with twitter. Honestly some of the things I read up there make me laugh my ass off."

"Yeah maybe." I agreed, "Maybe I should have."

"Fuck twitter though." She suddenly said after that, as if what she said before was an unfinished point, rather than just one isolated thought in the middle of a conversation. "Fuck the market. Fuck the banks. Fuck everything. You should really do just what you want to do, and don't fucking care if nobody else is paying attention. That's how the world works now anyways. That's probably how it always had worked. Nobody cares until you've made something. So instead of trying to convince people to care about what you're doing, should just do the fucking thing first.

"I'm drunk now. And a little high. And that cake really tasted like Styrofoam."

She was licking her lips as if tasting the cake again,

"Man how did you eat that?"

And before I stopped laughing and give her the answer, she added,

"How could I have bought that?"

"Very valid questions to be pursuing when you're high and drunk." I said.

"You wanna nap like those couples?" Rach said with her animated hand gestures, "You know the ones I'm talking about? They cuddle on the park benches, acting like no one was around and just rest their heads on each other."

"Yeah I know."

"You wanna do that? 'Cause I could use a quick nap."

"Why the hell not." I said, as we sat down on the bench, and I leaned one way so she could lean on me first.

"Oh!" I suddenly exclaimed as she put her weight on me, "I forgot just how heavy you are."

"Shut up, Godfather." She said.

Even with that horrible Styrofoam cake she bought for me still stuck somewhere in my throat as she snored on my shoulder, all I could thought about at this point was,

I love you Rach.

I was single. And when you are a single man living in Asia and needed to have some single man fun, there was only one place to go. Only one place.

ESCAPE TO HK

If you travel as much as I do it would do you some good to have an easy-to-carry, hard-to-lose piece of clothing to keep with you at all time. It would help you along the way a lot. What I have for this is a happy shirt.

What's a happy shirt? Let me explain.

First of all, a happy shirt has to be something that has some sentimental values that would remind you of a happier time, every time when you put it on. It doesn't technically even have to be a shirt. It can be a butterfly necklace you bought at a flea market, or the wallet you paid with your first paycheck.

In my case, it's this brown shirt with Mexican ornaments on its shoulders that I've had since I was fourteen. My Happy Shirt works because it's the best fitting shirt I've ever had in my life. Even to this day, after it has been in my closet for this long, it still fits like the first day I put it on back in the store. Every time I put it on it was like a warm, sweet embrace.

This morning, wearing my happy shirt, taking my passport and my overnight bag, I flew to Hong Kong and intent to stay there for at least two nights.

Hong Kong is the best city to go when you are a single man just want to have some fun. The pace of the city is so fast, you never felt alone.

If you felt it, you can get the best cocktail money could buy to drown it out.

If you felt bored, you can go shop at the best stores money can get you to wash the boredom out.

If you need to clear your head, you can sit on the tallest building overlooking the best view money can buy.

When you have money to spend, this city is the best. And money is the best remedy to make you forget how alone you are in this world.

I went with my routine once I checked into the hotel I booked; nowhere fancy, just really conveniently located with a subway station but a few steps away from the lobby. I went out to Tsim Sha Tsui to get my favorite milk tea at my favorite tea house, still wearing my happy shirt of course.

The minute I was lining up in there, ushered by the cashier muttering Cantonese at me first when they first saw me, then spoke to me in English when I picked up the menu (They must have seen something in the way I picked it that made me looked like a gweilo to them), then gave me the change almost without counting, and it was the right amount every time. That sip of that milky, cool, taste of heavy-baked black tea leaves was felt on my tongue, inside my mouth, I felt right at home.

Hong Kong has a different kind of humidity from Taipei. It was a harbor city and therefore the heat and the sweat even at a higher temperature never felt quite as overwhelming as in Taipei. This was a city so alive it wakes you up in your special place. And when I'm here almost every memory was heart-warming, whether they happened here, or I happened to be thinking about them here, it always happened to be something good.

After the milk tea, I went around the area like I was a tourist out on holiday. This was a tourist district and I liked to pretend to be a tourist sometimes. I loved walking around the city. You give up the better air, better environment, bigger living space to live in the city to live on its life, and there's no better way to feel it than walking on the streets. You feel every beat of its heart, you catch your every breath with its soul and you warm as it warms, you cool as it cools.

My very first date with Marian was a walk around New York. I don't know if I was wearing my happy shirt that, though I wore it a lot that year. I had just moved to the city and my wardrobe was very small, I had to make it count. But I do know when I was definitely wearing it, that night we kissed for the first time. She was wearing a white T-shirt and a pair of blacks jeans, I was wearing my happy shirt. Those are the kind of detail I remember, and would come back to me as quickly as I put this shirt on.

I remember when I called Flynn, who was in LA at the time, and told him about Marian for the first time, how happy he was. He was even happier after I sent him a picture of her (yes we do that. We're guys).

He immediately called me back and told me she's a keeper, how much she reminded him of Lindsay Lohan (This was the pre- car crash, pre-alcohol and arrest Lindsay Lohan we were talking about) and how I should invite her over to visit Flynn together in the summer. How he was learning his way around what he thought was the best State in the US (God how tasteless a thought, even from him) and how he would plan a road trip for us.

When I first bought this shirt, I was still in high school. My high school was not that much different from a lot its distant relatives, in spite of that charm of mystery that it seemed to give out to a lot of families in Taipei, who pushed hard to have their children into this school. We studied very little, partied very hard, formed little groups and we all thought we were gonna be something bigger than we would all actually turn out to be.

Flynn was something of a hero back then. Sure, he didn't like anybody there, since he thought they were all a bunch of snobbish wusses who couldn't do anything without their mommy and daddy's money. But that didn't stop him from becoming one of the most sought-after person, certainly the most well-known feared.

He was always a great athlete, and smart at learning

anything when he put his mind to it. But unlike most people in that criteria, who were generally overachievers that had passion for higher places, he cared very little for grades and extra credit and letter of recommendation and other stuff that were important for that step up that seemed so much easier for him than for many, many others.

Some people saw the obvious and thought it was because since he was already from the higher up, being the heir to a family behind a powerful international conglomerate, like many in his position he simply lacked the motivation. That's only half of it, as we've all seen, those of us close to Flynn, those killer eyes he would flash out whenever the occasion called for it. I believe his lack of motivation come from the fact that it was too easy for him; and so he never want it for himself. He would only go for it if others could convince him to. His underachieving nature is therefore simple: that he cared little for his competition, as he refused to perform.

Flynn only did something because he had a passion for it. You can only understand this not by studying him like in a lab, as most teachers did, but by engaging him like you would to a person. If you did back in those days, then you would have caught him once, at the end of the day alone, sitting on a couch, and playing his guitar.

He would always notice you were there even if he looked like he was fully immersed in the song he was playing, which back in those days was most likely Red Hot Chili Peppers' "Otherside". And once he noticed you a couple of times, he would raise his head and smile at you, and as if answering a question he knew you were wondering about him, he would say,

"I'm here in this school to learn what they don't fucking teach me."

And he lived by it too.

He didn't believe in higher places. Or I should say that he did, but he'd always believed it was more about the mentality than the prestige: one was more about how you look at yourself, the other is how others view you.

As I shopped, I did not see any wine or spirit that I would like to take back with me (they are so much more reasonably priced here than they are in Taiwan). I felt terribly alone, and I know I just said I never felt alone when I'm in Hong Kong. But as you could probably figure out by now, I lied; which was probably why I made the extra effort for my date of the evening.

"Got time for a movie?" I asked her over the phone.

"Let's do dinner, we can talk more." She said to me from the other end.

"Don't you mean a supper?" I corrected her, partly just to annoy her.

"Shush!" I did my job. "You're paying for saying that!"

"My treat, my choice of food." I negotiated.

We met for dinner, without surprise I took her to a French restaurant on the IFC. Of course, I can't continue this story without giving her a name: let's call her Lisa.

Lisa's look is what you would call a "southern beauty" by Chinese Standard. She's slightly shorter than average, small in stature, with very cute shoulders like that of a teenage girl. She had pearly white skin and a pair of small, pouty lips perfect for a dipping smile- a smile well-known in the psyche of Chinese fantasies as one that had both the feminine shyness and the mysterious allure that was so exclusively female.

But those lips were not the most striking feature on Lisa; that would be her hair. Her dark chestnut hair that luster so much it even shimmers in the dark.

"Don't you miss it?"

She asked me as we sat in our table by the window side, where out through it you could see Victoria Harbor and through it, the pacific ocean.

"What, the States?" I asked her for confirmation.

"Yes." She replied.

"Some nights I do. Other nights such as this, not as much."

"This is a pretty authentic place, by the looks of it." She laughed, "Even though it is still horrible that you bring

259

someone from New York on your rare visit to Hong Kong to a French restaurant for dinner."

"How is this horrible? You haven't even tasted the food yet." I replied, "We both appreciate good, authentic food wherever we go to. And this place has got the best French food outside of Beijing. Mark my words."

'You don't expect the two of us finish a full six course dinner, did you? You're CRAZY!" She protested.

"Ok fine, let's do salads and cocktails." I said, knowing that was probably what she wanted the most.

'Now you're speaking my language."

"God you're so from New York." I teased her for the salad and cocktail.

"You could be too, if you ever decide to move back." She said teasingly.

"You know, I'm thinking about it, actually." I played along.

"Oh lucky me. You're finally thinking about it. Please do so I don't have fly here as often no more." She said, "I see you have your happy shirt on?"

"Yes?"

"What's the occasion?"

"I dunno." I said with a smile, "Seeing you I guess."

"You're a writer alright. So full of lies." She teased me.

"That and I am an ABC, like you." I said.

"Yes we are a two-faced specie." She said, knowing what I always said about this subject. "How's your blog? I actually read some of it."

"So somebody is! Yes!" I said, "Do you like it?"

"Some of it. Any plans?" She said as she was cutting the lettuce on her plate with her knife.

"Well I was thinking maybe publishing it later next year or something."

"So you're finally working on your new book? And there I thought my prayers went unanswered." Lisa suddenly had the twinkle of her eyes the minute she hear me mention "publishing it".

"Like you would ever waste your prayers on me." I said

with a crooked smile. "Don't you think it's a little un-Christian-like to pray for non-believers?"

"Actually that's the very definition of core Christian virtues." She corrected me quickly.

"Sure, good Christian Girl."

"Whatever." She said, "What about title? Any thoughts?"

"I was thinking maybe 'Generation Bored'?" I replied rather slyly. "That seems very fitting for a story about these well-to-do, never-do-well group of people that I'm writing about."

"No!" She was quick to shoot it down.

"And why not?" We've danced this dance before, as you can see from the speed of our response to each other.

"It's such a sad title! Who would want to read something with that title?" She said.

'So what would the good Christian girl suggest?" I asked.

"I wouldn't know." She said, "Just not that one. Too sad."

"Ok." I said, "Let me think about it more then."

"Yey!" She cheered, "A new book from you next year! Yey! Can't wait!"

When we got out after the dinner and a couple of martinis in the slightly cold, humid winter night, traffic hours had long passed. There were plenty of empty taxis waiting on the street for us.

I grabbed a taxi that was there, and opened its door for Lisa. After she got in, I followed her in and sat next to her, before I shut the door behind me. The taxi drove on the now quiet road, under the cover of the night as we went on our way, back to her hotel.

When the clock on the dresser hit 3:35AM, I was naked, with but a bed sheet on my body and Lisa's hair casually tickling my left cheek. It lustered in the dark as it carried some of her warmth with its thorny touch on me.

"Do you wanna smoke?" She asked me, being versed into my bedside habits.

"No. Not at all." I replied. "I'm guessing room service's closed."

"It's ok, I'm not hungry." then she inquired, "Are you?"

"Depends on what we're talking about." I replied, "If it's for sex, I'm hungry for a quick bite."

Now she wouldn't stop laughing. I laughed too. All of a sudden we were like two little kids giggling in the park. I felt the vibration from her laugh in the bed we shared and it got me to laughed even more.

"You're terrible!" She said, still giggling, "We don't have the time."

"Doesn't mean we shouldn't try!" I said, grabbing her and pulling her over to my side.

"Ah!" She screamed, and still laughed. "No! No way!"

"Fine!" I relaxed my hand on her arm as I said, "I thought you would at least humor me, being your prized commodity."

"You're not that valuable." She replied.

"How far am I?"

"As far as your next book." She replied coyly.

"Speaking like a true bloodsucking agent of mine." I said.

"I've waited you say that the whole night." She said, still giggling, "I maybe a bloodsucking agent, but I am still your bloodsucking agent."

"Whatever keeps you sleep at night." I said, "So how's the boyfriend?"

"Just fine, why?" Her "why" was filled with sarcastic delays.

"I dunno," But I did, "maybe I just wanna hear some more stories of the fabulous beau name Beau."

"Oh when are you gonna let that go?" She was so cute when she was annoyed. "Stop making fun of Beau's name!"

"That would be never." I replied.

"Oh my gosh you're so annoying!"

She filled her cheeks up with air like a balloon, to show me the typical "I am mad" look that was so popular with Asian girls. She blew it out and made this comeback to me, "FINE!"

That's the worst of Lisa when she's mad, saying the word "FINE" to you as if it was all in capital letters. She's so polite even when she's annoyed, you normally wouldn't know. This was probably why she could put up with me all these years.

"Is that really your worst comeback, Ms. Manhattan?" I asked rhetorically.

"WHATEVER." She said, "You're from New York too!"

"I'm from many places." I replied cleverly.

"Always with something clever to say." And just like that, she read my mind with her comment. As a reward I gave her a kiss.

Perhaps moved by our little kiss, I suddenly felt compelled to finish the subject we briefly touched on over our salad and cocktails. "Would me moving back to New York make things awkward for the two of you? Were you serious about wanting me to move back? Or were you just teasing me?"

"You're not serious." She said, still smiling.

"What if I am?" But I wasn't smiling when I said that.

"You're not serious." This time, she stopped smiling. "What's wrong?"

"Nothing." I said, now I was smiling again.

"No, not nothing. Something's wrong. What is it?"

"I just feel... exhausted. There, I finally found the word to say what I have been feeling this whole time since the summer." I said, "I feel empty and unwanted. Like I'm not doing any good to anyone and I just want to get away."

"So you think New York is the answer?"

What she said stopped me a little bit. And just when I was about fall deep into my thoughts again, she pulled me back:

"Don't get me wrong A-Zed. I want you to move back to New York, but you have to want to be there first. It has nothing to do with Beau, me, or anybody. I want you to be happy wherever you are. And I'm saying it as your two-faced, bloodsucking ABC agent."

"It's not that." I said somewhat wistfully. "I loved New York. I loved the history of it. I loved its life. I loved those late night bagels and pizzas. I loved living weeks on Chinese takeouts. I absolutely loved it.

"I never love Taipei the way I loved New York, of all the cities I've lived in I feel the least connected with Taipei. It's so slow, so warm so nice, so unworldly, it's not me. I'm only there because I lived there, and I'm only doing that here because my family here… you know who I mean by 'MY Family'."

"Of course." She confirmed.

"Most people don't get to choose their family. But in this case, I have chosen my family over my life. I could write anywhere, instead I'm in Taipei and not for the history, the climate, and the cocktails at nights. I'm only here for them." I said, "But that's changed. Now I feel they don't really need me. I feel like I'm actually causing more damage than I am repairing. So I feel like I should move away from them. I'm not doing any good."

"This is about that Flynn character, isn't it?" She asked me, as someone who had read my blog. I saw that warmth coming up on her face again. That warmth that was both a reassurance, and a question. "You can't let the problem you two have become a problem between you and your family. And moving away is certainly not the solution. Most importantly though," She put an emphasis on the word "important", "I don't think you realize how important you are to your family. You talked a lot about how Flynn being there in Taipei helped glued you guys together, but none of it would have happened without you being every step of the way." She then felt the need to add "I've seen your food. Not many people could cook like you, and the power of good, meaningful meal is often overlooked."

"Maybe you're right." Lied back into my side of the bed, I said as I faced the ceiling.

"No, YOU were right." She said, "You were right to come back. You have built something here, and it's more meaning than you are willing to give credit to."

"Yeah maybe." I said, taking a long breath as I did. "I just have this overwhelming feeling that… I have failed my job, and every time I see my parents I just get reminded what failure looks like. I may not have the career they want me to have, but do I want this as a career? Sometimes late at night I am not even sure what I am doing."

"You stayed in the graveyard too long." She said, her double meaning of the word graveyard, both referring to my writing hour and as a metaphor was not lost on me, "You should get out to the living more. Don't overlook the little changes you're making every day. There's something there and you need to discover it for yourself."

"You know who you really sound like right now?" She knew who I was talking about, but I still had to say it.

"Oh shut up Godfather." She said with a smile.

"You know if you didn't know me so well," I said with a smile, "we might have never slept together."

"Cheeky!" She said.

"I'm cheeky, and you like me like that." I said as I arched my arm and lied on my side now, facing her, "Shall we proceed to the quick bite? When's your flight?"

"Cheeky!" She said again, blushing uncontrollably. "Why did I sleep with you in the first place, A-Zed?"

"Relationship is complicated." I said, making a spin now thinking about it, not sure how much of it was true, "sometimes you might feel deep connection with someone you're just not meant to be together with, or settle down, or whatever good Christian girls say these days."

"It's not that." She said not, responding to my use of the title "good Christian Girl", "I just think we have a good thing going. We're companions, maybe, in the oldest definition of the word, meaning…"

"Good friends." I said for her.

"Right. You're just so full of wisdoms sometimes, always so thoughtful that people forget, I guess because they got used to you." I guess she wanted to finish what she was saying, "What you have is this layer after layer of wisdoms that other people would just get used to taking from you and forget… well, that you're a person too. A person who needs to feel wanted at times."

"I'm a person too? Is that what you think of me?" I said with a smile, "I should say that about myself sometimes."

She smiled again, this time so warm and so filled with her Lisa charm that it compelled you to want to kiss her again. And indeed we did, one more time for the night.

"I love you. Not just you, but for everything you did moving back here. You came back and built a family. And I love how you call them that, Godfather."

"We're just kids pretending to be adults." I said, then it suddenly hit me, "Hey you know what? Maybe that's the title? 'The Comeback Kids', how's that?"

"There's a Western ring to it. Almost sounds like a Sam Peckinpah movie." She commented, "I like it."

"Ok." I said, "That settles it then." I said kissing her again, the last kiss we had for the night. "I knew you were good for something."

"Cheeky!" She shot back with another smile.

In the morning, as we both got dressed, she'd cleared up the room and had everything in that single suitcase she took with her. Still in the same blue suit, we went downstairs. I hailed a taxi, and we hugged.

"Take care of yourself," She said, "before you take care of your family, whichever one you want to. Taking care of someone is your choice, not theirs. Disregard what other people might say, including what your Taiwanese self is saying. We know we have a choice, because we are ABCs."

"How can I live without you?" I asked her.

"You already are." She said, "See you next year."

I turned around and got in the taxi. As it took me to my next destination, my mind was occupied not by any of those thoughts that bothered me before no more, only by how lovely Lisa was, and how much I was looking forward to next year.

Somewhere in my mind, I could hear Marian giggling again, at how miserable I was making myself.

I went out shopping again. I decided to do that before my usual drink at Lan Kwai Fong tonight. But with nothing that caught my eyes, I decided to go back to the hotel, freshen up a bit before I head out for my dinner and nightcap.

The one bar I always go every time I was in Hong Kong was this place called "The Blue Whale". It was a bar located at a crooked elbow of that steep, hilly road in the Lan Kwai Fong area. The bar itself was quite narrow and small, which was ironic considering its name. Most people here would just come in, get their drink, and walk out and have it in the open. In spite of that, it was a very popular joint.

To most of these people who came here, they recognize the quality of their cocktail. It was truly exquisite, their special being a concussion named the "Wailing Whale", so named because of the small drops of liquor inside the blue-colored drink. It is a variation of the Royal Blue Cocktail, but with more layers and packed with a slow punch. Two of these, it will knock your socks off.

It was my third, or fourth Wailing Whale of the night, and because of the slow punch I haven't quite felt the full hit yet, only slightly buzzed. I held a cigarette in my left hand, and my drink in my right, staring right into the road down the crooked hill, all the joints on the two sides of the road, all the boisterous crowd and drink and lights, without focusing on any particular thing...

"Yo!"

I felt a violent push in my back that I stumbled a bit, almost spilled my drink.

"Flynn?"

As I turned around, I saw that familiarly tall and powerful man was right behind me this whole time.

"You bet your bitch ass it's me!" He said, as undaunted as always.

"What the hell are you doing here?" I was not amused, least of all by the fact that I almost spilled my cocktail.

There was a shadow of anger that emerged on his face full of smile briefly when he heard me said that, it disappeared as quickly as it was shown until again with a big smile he said to me,

"Oh nothing! I was a little tired of Taipei, so I came here for some fresh air."

His fresh air consisted of a Montecristo No. 2, known as the "Torpedo" to most cigar aficionado.

"What are you doing here?" He asked me, "Where is your

girlfriend?" He turned around and looked into the bar as he spoke, as if looking for her.

"She's not here." I replied somewhat coolly.

"Broke up hm?" Flynn could get quite tactless sometimes, which was really annoying when you were unlike most people, mad at him.

"Yeah." But I replied quickly, to a point where before I actually said it, the break up never really hit me the way it did until now. That's the Flynn effect for you, he makes you tell the truth, especially the kind of truth that hurts.

"Where is Gina?" I asked humorlessly.

"She's not here either." He replied, "I didn't bring her."

I guess he felt obliged to confirm her whereabout to me.

"I see you have your shirt on." He said, pointing at my happy shirt with his cigar. "Do you remember the first time you put it on?" Flynn said, I guess he was quite in the mood tonight, "You picked it up back in high school with that one girl you had a huge crush on, what's her name? Jenna?"

"Jean-Louise." I replied.

"Jean-Louise! Right!" He shook his head, "Geez she's not even French."

"Quebecian." I added.

"Whatever, she's a fake American." He said, "Man those were the days. We spent the weekends at my Tamsui house, smoking cigar and drink my dad's brandy to the last drop when my parents weren't around while listening to Red Hot Chili Peppers at the loudest volume!"

As he spoke, his memory came back like they were my memory, as they mostly were, since there was so much we have shared together, in my mind. It was like a movie, a documentary with his voice as the voiceover that narrate every frame.

"Fuck man, when we all left that year, I thought for sure I was not gonna fucking see all of this again. I thought I was leaving for the last time.

"And I drank up all the brandy that night and I fucking cried man, by myself on that balcony. Seventeen years I've been in Asia, I was practically fucking Asian. Of course I can't fucking speak Mandarin or anything, but fuck man, I was leaving home. I was leaving the only place I grew up from. I cried man, like a little bitch that I was."

He would not admit to this, ever. But he was little teared up now talking about that story too.

"I would have never believed for a second that we would be coming back here after that, never. I never thought we would be drinking here, then fly to Beijing for a rave party, sleep, then fly back to Taipei the next night."

"Yeah until that summer." I said, referring how we spent our first summer after that in Beijing.

"Yeah, but that was different."

Then he stopped speaking for a minute, as if he had suddenly been reminded of something, perhaps some memories of those days. I could probably guess what it was. I knew Angel must be in there somewhere. He must be thinking about all those flights he was taking across the Pacific every three months or so. He must be remembering those long nights fighting jet-lags and homework deadlines, while still remarkably happy with exhilarating joy at all the possibilities that were alive, and only alive, when you were still young.

"We're getting old fast." He said, as if he heard what I was thinking about him. "The bottom of the shit is, I never thought back then I'd be back here drinking the Wailing Whale on this crooked road, and smoking a Torpedo again."

To be honest, I was actually quite moved by what he was saying, but I was still very mad at him. It was very hard for me not to be. But nevertheless I kept my peace and my poker face. What he said next though, really took me by surprise.

"I'm sorry A-Zed," Flynn said, "I've been a fucking jerk and I know it. I've let this break up with Angel hurt not only me, but every fucking one in our little family. I'm sorry. I was so... what's the word?"

"Involved."

"...Involved with my own shit, that I forgot all about you guys. Worst of all I forgot all about you." He then took a slightly longer smoke, before exhaling it into this long white trail of smoke, before he continued,

"We built this family together, but I couldn't have done it without you all these years cleaning the mess I created. And I feel so ashamed that I never knew how fucking awful your family is, and I call myself your brother. I didn't know what a fucking asshole your dad is. I really didn't know, and I used to kinda like him."

"Well it's not your fault, he always used to buy you guys alcohol when we were teenagers." I said, "I mean come on, who wouldn't want that cool guy as a dad right?"

"He's an asshole, that's what I came here to say." Flynn corrected me, "No fresh air, no bullshit, that's why I am here. You're nothing like your dad. I would know, I'm never friends with assholes, certainly not brothers with them." He paused then added with emphasis, "You're not an asshole."

Flynn always say things in ways as if you just had to trust him, as if you should just take his words for it. There was no questioning to the legitimacy of his logic, or to the strength of the conclusion he made. But this time at least, he had a point.

"Please come back to Taipei with me. Don't move out of here. Not without a parting party at least." He concluded his case with that. Now he was waiting anxiously for my reaction.

Just as I was moved by his showing up here and telling me all that, I suddenly realized something.

"Wait how did you know about my dad? Or the fact that I am in Hong Kong?" I said, "I didn't tell anybody about that. Not Rach, Pete and certainly not Dorian."

That's when he cracked open his big smile, "You didn't think you can write a blog without me knowing about it, did you?"

"Oh You son of a bitch." I said suddenly.

"You're the son of a bitch." He said, "First of all your mom obviously is not a bitch, just to be clear. Second of all, you are a son of a bitch for not telling me about this, and for thinking I wouldn't find out about it. And worst of all, write it so fucking much that I had to read it. You know I don't read, I…"

"You do." I finished his sentence just to annoy him.

"Hey don't finish my sentence. This is an emotional moment."

"Right." I teased him with my words, but I agreed with him in some weird, unspoken way. We really knew each other for too long to have anything come between us, in spite of all of our difference.

"So what do you say? Fly back to Taipei tonight? Or maybe we can go inland tomorrow? There's gotta be a party or a rave we can go to in Guangzhou." He said with a big smile.

"Fuck no, I'm going home tomorrow. I need my sleep.'

"I forgot you're a little bitch who needs his beauty sleep."

"Fuck you Flynn."

As a final note before we move on from here though, I just want to say, now do you see the point of wearing the happy shirt? It really does work. Take my word for it.

SQUID SEASON

Winter has come. Here, we call winter squid season.
As you probably guessed, this is because of Flynn.

Flynn was always a little annoyed by how popular Thanksgiving turkey was all across the world as the main winter dish (even here on this subtropical island, Thanksgiving turkey is still lucrative business). Therefore, he arbitrarily declared his main winter course in Taiwan shall be squids.

Fortunately, winter in Taiwan was a good time to eat squid. Taiwan, being an island, is abundant in good seafood sources, and the squids here are fat and delicious.

In most night markets, there are yakitori or BBQ stands that sold all sort of meat and vegetables, including whole squids, that's been marinated with soy sauce and rice wine and grilled over charcoal.

Every year around this season when we hang out, more often than not, we would end up at one of those yakitori grills in Tamsui, where we would be having beer, a very unhealthy drink choice, over these very unhealthy food.

We often would be there until we drank ourselves silly into the wee hours of the day. Most of the time, it only ends with the rising of the sun.

Even so, every squid season was different from the last.

This is how it went this year.

Once we were back in Taipei Flynn took me to a basketball court to play some hoops. He made a comment about how intense I have become with the game, of course not without joking about how "it wasn't enough to stop him".

So, after a few games where I was brutally slaughtered by the guy who with his outside shot and his dunking that was literally fouling me on every shot, was the most dominant street basketball play I ever knew, we sat down courtside and began a conversation.

"Let's have a party." Flynn said, from the sound of it he had this idea for a while. "Get everybody to come, it'll be fun. We'll start this new thing called Sake Day."

"I'm intrigued." I really was.

"We'll have it once a year, like the second Saturday of every November or something... we'll go to Dozo, book their skybox booth, and drink sake all night over yakiniku and sushi. Fuck yeah."

This was the type of thing that Flynn was good at, and the moment that you would miss him the most, when he set up new activities for you as a group and give it meaning, when he's most like a leader.

"Second Saturday... that's this weekend." I said, being the more organized of the two.

"Yeah, set it up." He said. "Guest list, same rule: each member of the family gets to bring one guest. So that's ten people, and the guests that attend would earn the chance of joining future family functions."

"Ok that would mean you and Gina and Rach and..."

"Yeah I know, Mark the bastard. You hash it out alright? Make sure everybody is coming? I'll do the rest." He said it more like an order than a request.

Yeah, leave the hard job to me.

I have to really work it to get Rach onboard this time. She's not gonna like this arrangement at all.

"I don't like this at all." She said to me at Haagen-Daaz during her lunch hour the next day.

"He abandon all of us and now he expect us to all go to his party just like that? he hasn't even apologized to us."

"You have to go." I said.

"What? Are you gonna make me if I don't? I have a boyfriend now." She was joking when she said that, in spite of how it may sound like a threat just in words.

"I hate to break this to you Rach, but your boyfriend is no match to Flynn and let alone me." I said, "Flynn's done a lot of things for us over the years to at least give him a chance to make it up to us this time."

She knew what I mean. Rach was as clear-headed as she was hot-headed, the kind of perplexing combination that was just so her,

"You're right." She agreed, "Mark can't even beat a caterpillar in a fist fight."

"No he can't."

"Fine I'll go." She said, "But only for you."

"Of course for me." I said, "Who else would this be for?"

"You know Flynn might be the charming bad boy," She suddenly cracked a smile as she said, "but you were always the persuasive one."

"That's why we're a family." I said.

"I'll wear my leather skirt too." She added as a final point.

"Now we are really talking."

That was the hardest part, now we just had to wait for the day to arrive: Sake Day.

When it finally came the night of the party, I went alone. As it turned out, I was the only person who showed up alone.

Dorian brought Tanya. Pete brought this student of his, who seriously wore too much make up and fit the description of a western "preyer" too well, one of what they call "Western Dining Chicks" here in Taiwan. Those eyeliner she wore, and her insistence on speaking English even it clearly wasn't an easy language for her. Rach brought Mark, as well as her black leather skirt that ends just above her knees, and her favorite red top.

I wondered how Mark put up with her choice of fashion, that man so conservative he used the same barber that cut his dad's and his granddad's hair perhaps since the dawn of time. But he sure didn't make a scene about it when they got in. And neither did Flynn and Gina, to the disappointment of most of the other of us who were there.

We were seated according to the seating scheme that Flynn has kept for us since the first party we had together. When we were kids, I made the mistake of explaining to Flynn Chinese table manners, including the rules where the host sits at the center of the table, the host seat, and then the guests are organized around him in accordance of their relations to him.

And Flynn loved it. Flynn, as you know, was a man who has never hidden his favoritism to all the people he knew, and I just gave him the perfect excuse of paying respect to local customs.

Thus, the seating arrangement has been the same since earliest of parties, with I always sit on Flynn's right and on his left would be his current girlfriend. Tonight: Gina. To Gina's left was Dorian, and across from him was his art gallery girlfriend Tanya. Then next to Tanya was Pete, next to Pete was Pete's student/girlfriend, then next to her was Rach, and next to her sitting with his back to the entrance, traditionally the position of the least important person in the group, was Mark. As to the seat on my immediate right? It was empty.

"What happened to that girlfriend of yours? Maddy?" Mark asked me when he saw that nobody else was going to join us.

"Umm… we're sort of… taking a break." I answered honestly.

We could have just left it there, except when after a few more rounds of drinks and food, he went to the men's room downstairs with me. And once it was just the two of us there, he said:

"Geez you flip them through like you're flipping through pages in a book, hm?" He said, using that old Chinese analogy for playboys.

"It's not like that." I was going to explain except Mark seemed to have made up his mind about it.

"Haha you foreign kids, all playas." He said it like a man complimenting another on his golf swing, except it rubbed me the wrong way. He didn't even notice my displeasure of course, as he would typically be when he was talking,

"Don't worry, I'll introduce you someone next time. Someone good and more reliable than these foreign girls."

Maybe he was a little tipsy, I thought to myself. And yet, the fact that he knew not to make this kind of comment in front of the others, made me questioned just that little bit about him. But again, it was just a feeling. And the rest of the night went so well I nearly forgot about this.

The skybox booth was the only room in the entire restaurant with a complete view of the entire restaurant. It was inside this glass room on the second floor with its own exclusive staircase to enter. It was the best and most sought-after booth in this entire restaurant.

Dozo is famous for being a high-class Japanese restaurant built with the vision of being a "super-size izakaya"; one that would have the traditional menu of a Japanese izakaya, but compliment it with the entertaining environment of a western bar and grill. It hosts live Taiko performance every weekend, with service staff specially-selected to dress and look like fashion models, serving more than fifty kinds of sake and plum wine, and a complete food menu that had dishes such as fried oysters and yakitori, steamed lobster and crabs and sushi and California rolls.

It was famous for having a long runway in the middle of the restaurant where every coming guest and the waitress leading them to their booth must walk through. Added to the experience of making every paying customer feel like a star: a high profile music producer or someone of the fashion world, as they were pampered like one. You only get to go to a place like this in Taipei. It was the ultimate Taipei experience.

And it was a Flynn party, where you would never run out of

food and drinks. Whenever plates and cups on the table become empty, they would be replaced with different but equally luxurious dishes. Needless to say the party went very well. Regardless of how they felt before, people would always become happy at the sight of good food.

"Hey you know Jamie Chung right?" Pete asked me; his face red after a couple cups of the warm sake he just had.

"You mean that new girl who's naked in like every movie?" I guess I was a little tipsy too.

"I was going to say my girlfriend here looks a little bit like her." Pete, pointing at his student/girlfriend, and stared at me, "You're a horrible person."

Flynn suddenly rose up and with his sake cup high above his head, and shouted,

"Drum roll now!"

Then as if per his order, out of the booth down on the runway, the Taiko drums rolled and performance began. The beating of the drums, as well as vocal chanting in between were so organized, the sound it creates so penetrating, we felt the gravitations on the second floor. It was impressive even to a frequent visitor, not to mention its effect to someone who might have been there for the first time.

"How does he do that?" Pete's student/girlfriend asked him, through the booming sound of the performance.

That's why he's the legend."

"Hey! Hey! Hey! Over here!" Somehow in spite of the drums, Flynn's booming voice still made his presence felt on all of us. We turned around and all of our eyes were now on him, who stood there still with his cup full of sake raised,

"To my best friend." He said, "To the one guy who stuck with me all these years, through all my failures and other craps. Someone who had been my real family, my real brother, who had humored me on all my childish shit over the years. Someone who never really, had his own birthday until today. A-Zed."

I stood up. I looked to the tall, towering man that still seemed like a boy sometimes, who was sometimes irritating, most of the times charming, or both. I looked at him as I held my cup of sake in my hand.

"Happy Birthday A-Zed. Happy Sake Day." He said then drank the cup full of sake.

I, as well as the others, under the drumming of the night, all raised our sake cup and did the same. The warmth of the sake felt exceptionally heartwarming that night.

And that's when they served the grilled squids, the dish of the winter in accordance with Flynn rule, one for the each of us. It was moment like this when you truly appreciate the day when this bossy, petulant, handsy Spaniard came into your life. To me it was really a lifetime ago, even though I was sure to everyone there that night, it felt the same.

The party went on for a long time; I think we were the last to leave the place that night. When we left, Mark was discussing something with Flynn and I pulled Rach aside, asked her as I thought it was appropriate,

"Aren't you glad that you came?"

"Yeah, I love it how Flynn stole my thunder and gave you a birthday party of your life." She said, half-jokingly and half-saddened, a moment when Rach was most like a girl to my eyes.

"You gave me the birthday party of my life." I said then and there, and only to her. "You did. I will remember it forever."

"Thank you, Godfather." She slapped me and we laughed, knowing exactly what each other was not saying with words.

Every squid season was different. But every one of them was as memorable as this one. This year it was not only about a new tradition, but it was also about how we were a family again. And that's what's important.

Happy Sake Day.

CHRISTMAS

Now it was Christmas. In spite of their differences in culture and lifestyle, Christmas is surprisingly similar in most Asian cities; whether you live in Taipei, Hong Kong, Shanghai or Seoul, it's the same Christmas you see:

Huge Christmas trees in every commercial district, Christmas carols on endless loops inside the malls, and long shopping lines at every store. It was almost more Christmassy here, with "Merry Christmas" being the more popular greeting than "Happy Holidays", the religious meaning being lost with translation while the festivity remains.

I never had much luck with Christmas. Nothing good ever happens to me during this season, since the very first one that I could remember.

I was maybe three, four years old, and my mother almost lost me on one of those nights leading up to Christmas Eve when she took me out shopping on the busy winter street of Taipei.

It wasn't her fault, of course; my father could have been there to watch over me, if only the two of them did not argue just before we went out. I was too young to know or even remember what the argument was about. Probably the usual really, money or infidelity, one of those.

Now that I'm older, I think my mother probably took me out that night to get off some steam, which is why she did not pay attention to me as she usually would. And that's how I ended up on a corner of the cold winter street of Taipei, when the cartoons playing on TV in one of the stores caught my child's eyes, when by the time I turned around my mother wasn't with me no more.

I cried maybe only for a short time before my mother came back and found me, but it felt forever. When we went home that night, all my father did was tease my mother for how careless she was and made jokes about how "she" almost lost "his" precious son. I guess he was just trying to cheer us up in his crude ways, afraid that we might both hang under the shadow of my short disappearance for too long.

Since then I never had a good Christmas season. It seemed like each year my Christmas present was just how bad could that year's holiday turn out to be.

Still it is a holiday that celebrated family and redemption, and we had both of those this year. Perhaps that's why I arranged to meet my mother later, to give her the Christmas presents I bought for her. I wasn't stupid enough to meet her at the apartment though, where my father would most likely be around. Instead I had her agreed to meet at a coffeehouse not far away.

It was already the last Sunday before Christmas. This year I stuck to my regime and paced myself with a shopping schedule that spreads out for days so I won't make the mistake of buying too many things too quickly. I was also back on my regime on other things again: rising early and working out and writing. Now almost done with the first year of the blog, I was also working on my next two books at the same time, and I wasn't doing that in the graveyard no more.

I planned this to be my last shopping day, wrap things up before my coffee date this afternoon. From how this season has gone, this should be a happy season. Still I was uneasy about it, as if something was waiting to happen. That said, Christmas is not without good memories for me though.

Every year at this time, one thing I always thought about is my first American Christmas: as an American growing up in Taiwan, I had never had what could be an authentic American Christmas until my first year in New York.

That was an exciting Christmas, my first time spending it without my parents, who were busy with their own things and for the first time in my life did not come around to spend Christmas with me (which turned out to be a good tradition, I might add).

So while I have planned to spend it by myself, in the week leading up to Christmas, while I was with Marian in this hotel in the theatre district, she asked me,

"So what are you doing for Christmas?"

I should first explain we weren't in the hotel for the dining or the sleeping. Not exactly.

When she asked me that question, we were in the men's room at the back corner of an empty conference room of the hotel, where we locked ourselves up in one of the stalls and just to give you an idea to what we were doing in there, in case you haven't quite got it yourself, I had my hands on her waist, holding onto her so she could balance herself, as she had one of her foot on the ground, while the other on the toilet stall behind me, with her panties hanging right on that leg's ankle.

Marian had this thing about doing it at public places. To her credit though, she was very good at it. She always seemed to know just the right places to do it: remote corners of otherwise busy places, places that people are likely to have overlooked. We almost did it once at the Madison Square Garden during a Knicks Game, but that's a story for another day.

As you can imagine, I was very confused when she asked that question, and quite busy as well, so it's understandable I did not answer her right the way.

"I said what are you doing for Christmas? Any plans?" She asked me again seeing that I was not answering.

"Are you seriously asking me that now?" I said.

"Yes!"

"I need a minute to process all this information."

"What, can't think without your brother?"

"Sure."

"Really? You're not gonna argue on this for your sex?" She looked surprised and disappointed at the same time.

"No I mean sure, I have no plans." I clarified, which relieved her somewhat.

"Do you want to spend it with me then? We'll go visit my folks up state together."

"What?"

"Is this what to my proposal now, or are you answering me with a question?"

"Sure."

"Good. Can we switch a little? The way now it's kinda hurting my neck." She said. And the way her head was in the air without back support confirmed it.

"Sure. Maybe you want to turn around?" I suggested.

She quickly pushed her upper body towards me as she held onto me. Then she moved her one foot behind me down so now both her feet were on the floor, as she turned around, before she put her hands on the stall and face me with her back. This was all done in one motion. She was very nimble and flexible, to say the least. She was a natural at this, not just experienced.

"Oh you're so definitely not a virgin."

"I'm not anymore." I replied.

But maybe I was a natural too?

So you're probably thinking from what you've read about Marian that she must have grown up with a wacky, hippie family that eat organic food and talk about the importance of knowing your body and free your spirit when you're supposed to be reading Snow White.

To be honest I thought so too, which might explain my surprise when I turned up with Marian in her Ford pickup at a very normal suburban neighborhood. The kind you see in the movies: a white house with a front porch that had a wooden swing chair on it, a lawn filled with snow, a cleared driveway up to the garage, with a basketball hoop on top of the garage door.

It looked so normally suburban, it made it stranger when Marian warned me as we pulled up in front of the house,

"Ok if they start acting weird, don't tell them anything."

"Ok." I replied. I was a little scared at the prospect of seeing a tofukey at the center of the table.

As we were getting out of Marian's car, her dad came out the door and welcomed us. A fair-haired, middle aged man, whose slightly wrinkled cheeks burst with smile as he waved at us.

"Hi!" I said, smiling and did not know what else to do. I needed Marian to rescue me but she was busy with her car and her overnight bags. I would have helped her, but the whole time of our relationship she never liked me helping her with her bags for some odd American girl reason.

"Hello! I hope my daughter has not scared you off." The man said to me as he pushed his right hand to me, "Come right in. A-Zed, is it?"

"Yes. Merry Christmas, Mr..." I was saying as I shook his hand.

"Oh please drop the mister." He asked me, "Happy Holidays to you too. Call me Todd." And then he pretty much took me in smoothly with my hand still in his.

Marian was definitely his daughter, I thought.

"Sure, Todd, nice to meet you." I could only agree with him

"And it's very nice to finally meet you too, A-Zed. My daughter told us all about you." He said, still smiling.

"Stop talking about me like that, dad. I'm right here. And," Finally catching up to us, Marian quickly angled herself smartly as she entered so she broke me from the gripping right hand of her dad's,

"Don't weird him out." She warned her dad, before going straight into the kitchen to greet her mother.

That was bizarre for me, even today as I thought about it. Not the way I was welcomed into the house, just a Christmas where the whole family met together that did not start with an argument.

That was bizarre for me. Very bizarre.

Sure, I'm sure Marian's seemingly Holiday Season Perfect parents must fight sometimes. And I'm sure her sister, who was back from her freshman year in some Liberal Arts College upstate, was secretly not as nice as she was with me that night.

And I'm sure the dinner wasn't the most traditional of all American Christmas dinner recipe, there had to be changes that people would make over the years. That's what makes things authentic, by making the changes they themselves made into a tradition to be passed on. But to me, it was still the perfect Christmas.

We were two months or so into our relationship right about then, Marian and I. And I was madly in love with her. Marian was just the coolest girl ever, especially when you're barely 18 years old and didn't know your way around the city. She always had these new ideas. She always wanted to try her new ideas. She never settle for what was around. She was always on the lookout for an adventure.

And in the middle of that memorable dinner, Marian whispered in my ear in that she had a present for me that she would like to give me in private.

I might be barely 18 back then, but even with my limited smarts I cracked that code. So when she took me to her room, and closed the door behind us, the room she grew up in, later that night, I could barely hold my excitement.

The room's window overlooked the snow of the street outside. And before we went in, I could tell she was actually holding something in her hands, away from me so I could not see. And once she closed the door, she took it out. It was this little box, no bigger than a cigarette packet, wrapped with red wrapping paper.

"This is for you." She said to me as she pushed the box into my hands.

"What's in here?" I asked while I felt its weight bit with my left hand, "It feels pretty light."

"Open it." She said.

"Ok." I stripped away the red wrappings, and slowly opened the box.

Inside the box there was a piece of card wrapped under a nice clean white cloth. I took the card out, it was only slightly larger than your average business cards, and asked again

"What's this?"

"You have to read it." She seemed quite insistent to make her point this way.

"An A-ff-e-e, Da-v-e-d. What's an Affeedaved?" I read the title, a word in capital letters underlined that I had never seen before. She couldn't stop giggling for a while when she heard my rendition of that word.

And when the giggling finally stopped she said,

"It's an affidavit, you silly!"

Honestly, that was still gibberish to me back then. I had no idea what that word was.

"I guess we still have to work on your American." She said. "Just read the card. It'll make my explaining the whole thing better."

"FINE." I feigned agreement with my "FINE" in capital letters (maybe that's where Lisa got it from?) and still with no idea what the word "affidavit" meant, I read what was on the card out loud,

"I, Marian M., do swear or affirm, to the best of my knowledge and understanding, do fully intend for the benefit for both parties involved, when a period of one year is reached to our relationship, on the date of ..." I'm a little iffy about the exact date on that card now, "I Marian M., would leave you, A-Zed, for the best preservation of both parties involved. On this set date, we shall go on our separate ways. What the hell is this!?"

Even with my English back then, I could half-guess what the card said. As you could imagine now, I was extremely angry at the time. Not at the message but with myself, having just stupidly read that out loud. When I get angry I had this habit of just start pacing back and forth in whatever space was allowed, so I did just that. And even though I tried hard not to pay attention, I could see the weariness on Marian's face as she began to speak to me, as softly as she usually was,

"A-Zed, A-Zed," She called my name and tried to calm the three year old that I was acting like. "Would you please just calm down and listen to me?"

With my 18 years old pride and my 3 years old attitude, of course I was not gonna listen to her. So instead I began the first part of my angry outburst as,

"I can't believe this, are you leaving..."

Then She did the unthinkable. She jumped right in front of me and blocked my pacing.

I told you she was nimble.

With her blocking my way, in her always calm and charming voice, she said,

"Now before you say anything that might spoil the night, just hear me out.

"I love you A-Zed. I don't want to hurt you. I don't want you to see me as anything other than the girlfriend I am to you now.

"I want this entire relationship we have together to be something that we would look back ten, twenty years from now as the best time in our lives. That's what I want. I don't care much for results like marriages or family, or the real life together, or any of that happily ever after fairy tale. I know that cannot be real. Nobody can be that in love after living together for that long. Nobody.

"I want our time together to be nothing short of laughs and love. And what we have now is how I want to keep it, for both of us. I'm not an easy girl to live with, and with time you'll find out. And I don't want you to find out because I love you and I will always love you.

"You must take my word for it. We must agree to separate before the love fades, or not only will we watch our love end, but we would have done it together and have to live with those memories, memories of imperfection."

"I really like you. I like how you have this ambition of

writing the wrong with this world." (Yes, I told her I wanted to run for President. And please, I was 18)

"And You like me for my free-spirit. And how we fit perfectly together now." (She was not wrong with that)

"But a year from now? five years from now? We will graduate, and I would want to travel the world for an indefinite time while you would probably want to set up a law practice somewhere in this state and start building your campaign to run for mayor." (Ah, childhood fancies)

"And sooner or later we would hit a point where nothing would work." She paused a little, a trait for when she's about to deliver the finish line. Something I'd picked up from her and use quite frequently now.

"What then? Do we stay together and fantasize that at some distant future we would feel the same way we feel about each other now? Or would we split up and perhaps regret for all the time wasted chasing a dream that would never come true?"

Perhaps she was just very convincing with her words. Perhaps she was already tired of me, and so she painted this beautiful, picturesque excuse just so she could get rid of me. Perhaps the reason why this speech was so convincing was because I felt the same way at the time.

But of all the things I could have said to refute her points, back then I only sighed and replied to her very long speech in the few minutes we had together alone with,

"This is the worst Christmas ever."

Before running downstairs, leaving the little box and card behind like a little girl I was.

Now thinking back, that Christmas at sub-zero temperature at her parents' place, really wasn't the worst Christmas. It was perhaps the best. It was perhaps the one most like Christmas, where I actually spent it like I was part of a family tradition.

After I finished my shopping, I was now sitting inside this German Bakery Cafe in Tianmu for my date. She was late, so I ordered a cappuccino and just waited. It was mostly expats around me here on this last Sunday afternoon, here for their weekend smoked salmon brunch.

You can only have so many Christmases in your life, just like you could only stomach so many fights in your life. The limitless nature of our mind and imagination must not cloud us from the reality that there are limits to life itself; two worlds as opposite as that do coexist in both the Mongolian steppes and the Gobi desert.

Every Christmas therefore, deserves to be perfect. At the very least, they deserve your full effort to make the best with them. Even what you thought was the worst Christmas, might turn out to be the best, or the most memorable.

After I ran down and spend the remains of the night on night caps with Marian's family, I was a lot more quiet. I tried eggnog for the first time in my life, and I absolutely hated it. This coming from a Taiwanese kid grew up eating tangyuan in jiuniang egg soup, a dish that tasted quite similar to eggnog which traditionally, we ate in the winters, too.

I probably just hated it because of what immediately happened before. Or I really hated that taste. Either way I haven't had eggnog since.

Later, while I slept on the couch by myself, in my T-shirt and my jeans as I was stupid enough not to bring pajamas, (which I did not have anyways, I lived in a dorm) I heard footsteps coming down the stairs.

I thought maybe someone was catching some late night cravings so I did not move myself, did not want to disturb their privacy and catch them doing what might embarrass them or made it awkward, but to my surprise, those footsteps were coming straight to me.

I was never any good at pretending to be asleep. When I was a child, my mother often come back late at nights. During those hours she would come into my room to check on me, and I would always tried to look asleep, didn't want her to think that I stayed awake just to wait for her. Didn't want her to worry.

But then she would stroke my hair, and for some reason I

would always wake up when she did that and start talking to her, completely forgetting what I was trying to do before.

Those footsteps stopped right next to my head. I had my eyes shut. I controlled my breath so it sounded regular, like I was actually sound asleep and oblivious to my surroundings.

And then, something familiar happened.

It started as something very light, almost undetectable. Two soft fingers, small and nimble, were stroking my hair along on the right side, on the back of my head and neck.

"Are you up?" Without opening my eyes, I knew that was Marian. speaking to me as she stroke my hair.

I sat up, opened my eyes. In front of me was my small stature girlfriend with dark brown hair, wearing her spotty pajama, standing there and looking at me.

"Hey." She said.

"Hi."

"Did I wake you?"

"I was... I wasn't..." I was very confused as it was very late, but I quickly cleared my head. "I mean, I thought you were your sister or something, coming down for that last piece of pumpkin pie, so I was pretending to be asleep or it might be awkward."

"How very thoughtful of you." She said, "Listen, about what I proposed to you back in my room with that really, really silly card..."

"It's ok." I interrupted her. "Really, it is."

"I just don't want you to think I want to break up with you or anything. That's not my intention."

"I know. Listen, I want to say something." I did not give her a chance to deny me that. "Look I thought about it. I think I know what you mean. And... let me just say this: Marian, you're a life changer. I would have never tried any of the stuff we did together if it wasn't for you. Not even one of them. I'm just not wired that way. And... if this one year thing is something you think we really should do, then I am willing to do it."

I knew my words touched that unpredictable mind of hers

in some way. And she said to me, almost immediately,

"You just might actually be a virgin."

"Well, get this from this VIRGIN," I said, "I was thinking of doing that thing we were gonna do up in your room."

"What thing?" She teased me.

"You know what thing."

"Well actually, I was thinking more about in my car." She said thoughtfully.

"In this weather?" It was freezing. I was confused why we would leave the heating and the fireplace for that.

"It's in the garage." She said, "We could do it like in Titanic? You know that scene where they went into the car and all the steam came on the window?"

"Ok." I said, "I'll make it titanic."

"You're funny."

And so that night we went into the garage, as we tried another round of something exotic. Something different. Something with an expiration date.

And now several years later, my cappuccino and my apfelstrudel, I sat there, came face-to-face with Maddy on this Sunday afternoon, the last one before Christmas.

Maddy had just opened my gift for her and thanked me. She was happy to see me, said so herself. And she loved the gift, which was a green scarf. Not the expensive stuff, just something practical. She put it on right the way.

It got awkward for a bit after that, as suddenly we weren't sure what to say anymore. Or rather that we both knew what we were supposed to talk about, we were just not sure how to start it. Eventually though, Maddy decided to break the silence.

"I thought about what you said, back on Halloween." She seemed quite concerned with her words. "I dunno… how this would go. I dunno… if we should pursue this. I think… should is a strange word to say about something like this. I wish I was more thoughtful that night, or just with you over the time. I mean I knew since we first met… I was just… never sure about us… and everything."

I tried not to look too harsh as I soften my eyes by not looking directly into her as she spoke. Sometimes it's what you're not doing with words that counts in these situations.

Guess who taught me that?

"But I thought about this." She summoned her courage and said, "I think, I want to try this relationship with you. That is, if you're still interested."

I did not answer right the way. I did not want to tell her how "try a relationship" doesn't really sound that positive in English, in spite of how it may sound in German. Since those years ago as the kid who only knew words as an expression that it would not be the right reaction. So instead, I smiled at her as I put my hand on those bigs hands of hers, and rubbed them softly. She blushed, before we kissed across the table.

After the coffee date I went to visit Flynn at Tamsui.

As I got there, Flynn was cooking some squids on his skillet that had been marinated in rice wine and soy sauce, while his surround sound system was playing through his entire mansion a very familiar song: Red Hot Chili Peppers' "Otherside".

"I have the fucking munchies." Flynn said to me as he saw me, "And you weren't around."

He really created a mess around this kitchen: dirty dishes and open sauce bottles everywhere. I poured myself a glass of XO brandy on the table, before I sat on the barstool facing him at the kitchen table.

I had a sip of brandy, before I broke the news to him:

"Maddy and I are back together."

"Yeah? That's good news my boy." Flynn said as he put the now hot sizzling squids, with mouth-watering smell of cooked soy sauce onto the big ceramic plate on the table. Next to it he casually put two forks down, one for me and one for himself. "Sounds like we should have a party."

"Sure." I replied, I felt the warmth coming up from my stomach with the brandy.

"By the way," Flynn seemed to have remembered something, "I had my people in Beijing cleaned up the apartment. It will be ready for our next visit." Then he slapped my back as the physical guy I knew him to be, "So you won't have to stay in some cheap hotel that smells like diaper the next time you're there."

"Cool." I said, "Yeah we should plan our next trip there. Maybe when the smog clears up."

"Yeah. The whole place will be dust free." He said, "I even have them throw that dead money tree out. Here's a picture of your balcony now."

He then push his phone towards me, showing the picture of that once dusty balcony with a dead bonsai in the middle now all cleared up with the clutters and was spotless.

"You know," Feeling the emotions that were coming, I decided to change the subject, "This song you're playing? 'Otherside'? It's a song about addiction and suicide."

"Is it?" You could tell Flynn began to listen to it more closely once he heard me say that. He puts down the bottle of brandy, and began to tap the beat of the song accurately as he listened to it.

"Yeah I read about it sometime ago. The chorus line of 'how long will I slide, I don't believe it's bad' is a reference to the guy's drug addiction. And 'slitting my throat, that's all I ever', is talking about ending the addiction with suicide." I said, "That's why it's the chorus. It's on repeat cycle because every time he takes it he knew it was going back on it, and the only way to stop the slippery slope is to kill himself. At least that's what I think it means every I play it in the background during my graveyard shift."

"You know," He said, "now that you've mentioned it, it is a fucking weird song to be listening to in the middle of the night."

"Yeah it's your fault." I said, "I used to listen to it all the time because of you. You forced Red Hot Chili Peppers onto all of us, really."

"What could I fucking say? They're the fucking classic." He answered, "You can't blame me for introducing you to good music."

"You've made it pretty good." I complimented the squid as I tasted it. "I'm gonna need you give me a ride later."

"Yeah? Where to?"

"I need to go see my parents and drop something off for them."

"Yeah no problem. Just tell me when."

Flynn said, when suddenly he jumped to a different subject wistfully, in a completely different demeanor, as something out the window seemed to caught his eye again like back in Beijing when we were supposed to be there one last time. It's something which always took you by surprise if you didn't know his ways well:

"If this isn't the end of an era, I mean, I fucking hate thinking about questions like this. But I can't fucking help it. But if this wasn't the end, then what is? You know? When will this all end?"

I almost thought about it first before I answer his sudden need for deep meaningful, soul searching. But like I said, I "almost" thought about it first,

"Don't use big words like era too often, Godfather." I said with a smile, "It'll give you a headache or something."

"Oh fuck you Godfather!" Flynn said as he got up, "I'm gonna go get some wine to go with this. You Fucking ok with that, Mr. Big Words?"

"Sure." I was giggling as I said.

While I sat there alone, watched him off as he made some noise in the cellar looking for just the right bottle, I leaned towards the table and looked out the window. I looked down the crooked mountain road, and into the ocean.

Was this the end of an era? Of course not. At best, this is only the beginning. I really didn't know how much longer this little family of ours would last. But I knew this, as long as one of us is here, Flynn, Rach Dorian and Pete and I, then all of us would be here. And that's where the story will be, too. Because this story is about us. This is our story.

The story of The Comeback Kids.

ABOUT THE AUTHOR

H.J. Luke studied political science in UCSD, before working as a consultant in L.A. and Beijing. He currently resides in Taipei, Taiwan, and still travels often for work.
H.J. Luke is available for selective reading and lectures. To inquire about a possible appearance, please contact his representatives at rroalm@gmail.com